Praise for *All the Time in the World*

"For decades, Mr. Doctorow has been a first-rate artist in the short form. . . . As the assessments of [Doctorow's] long career commence, it is clear that he has been, like his characters, a man apart from his contemporaries. The stories of *All the Time in the World* do not seem to belong to any school or style but to emanate from his own solitary visions."   —*The Wall Street Journal*

"Stories [that] hum with resonance and vitality . . . distinctive, sharply focused, glistening with crisp language . . . Wherever they take place, these memorable stories reflect a novelist's intimate understanding of human frailty and penchant for delusion. . . . Savor *All the Time in the World* for its elegance, its intuition and for Doctorow's understanding of the complexity of the human drama."
—*The Miami Herald*

"The best of [these stories] have [an unquantifiable] effect, resonating as they do with the mysterious rhythms at the heart of ordinary life. . . . Read these fine stories and you may find yourself with that same inexplicable feeling, something articulated only by our best artists, writers such as Doctorow who show us that we read to lose ourselves as much as to find."
—ALAN CHEUSE, *The Dallas Morning News*

"Wonderful descriptions . . . gorgeous sentences . . . seem to fall effortlessly from Doctorow's fingertips. . . . Doctorow's stories generally come back to the melancholy reality of imminent doom—yet

they are rarely dreary and can be, in fact, quite funny. His characters, trapped as they are, manage to make a ragged music by rattling their chains."
—*Chicago Tribune*

"[*All the Time in the World*] gives us a sense of breadth, of movement, of the scope of Doctorow's career. . . . The six older stories . . . trace, with grace and acuity, the tension between longing and obligation, between who we are and who we mean to be. . . . 'Wakefield' [is] the best of the new pieces and one of the finest stories Doctorow has composed."
—*Los Angeles Times*

"As prolific as he is protean, E. L. Doctorow regularly serves up new observations on peculiarly American characters. . . . Doctorow seems telepathic in his ability to channel . . . men and women from a wide range of eras, landscapes, ethnicities. This virtuosity is one reason he's such a revered writer. . . . As ever, Doctorow has captured the mood of our time and rendered it in compelling fiction."
—*The Philadelphia Inquirer*

"Once you immerse yourself in these stories, you'll wish you had all the time in the world. . . . All these stories work on another level, revealing news about the world, yes, but also revealing the mysteries that lie at the heart of human behavior. In the title story . . . the narrator notices the beauty in the everyday with a sharpness that makes every page a revelation. . . . 'I feel,' he says, 'as if I've risen from one element to another.' Read these fine stories, and you may find that you'll have that same feeling."
—NPR, *All Things Considered*

"Virtuoso Doctorow is revered for his grandly dimensional novels, but he is also a superlative and transfixing short-story writer. The incandescent new stories and forever stunning vintage tales . . . that Doctorow selected for this powerhouse collection portray psychological outliers on the edge of either liberation or an abyss. Doctorow is rightfully treasured for his social acuity and fluency in urban life, but he is also a penetrating observer of nature and our concealed primal selves. . . . Doctorow's complex and masterful tales of the strangeness, pain, and beauty of life are wise and resplendent." —*Booklist*

"*All the Time in the World* serves as a handy index to the great man's themes. . . . His writing has always had an almost European sense of world-historical sobriety, conveying something fatalistic and weighty and dark-toned. . . . Doctorow passes the same gift along to the reader, with the same careful density and emotional heft."
—*The Washington Post*

"First rate . . . Never as simple as they seem on the surface, [Doctorow's] stories are full of paradox and good humor with a sometimes caustic underbelly; they're absurd in a funny sort of way. He reveals the quirks of our society in the kind of stories others can only aspire to write." —*Star Tribune*

"Doctorow prefaces the new collection by saying he doesn't expect readers to see the 'light' that guided his selection and sequencing of the stories, but it shines vividly and creates a distinctive, sometimes disturbing constellation." —*The Oregonian*

"[With] its soulful writing and vagrant characters . . . *All the Time in the World* feels, more often than not, like a haunting collection of ghost stories." —*Richmond Times-Dispatch*

"The mystery, tension and shock Doctorow is known for are all here in this collection. If you're a fan you will not be disappointed in the new, and happy to be reacquainted with the old." —*USA Today*

"[A] delightfully idiosyncratic collection . . . Here, Doctorow trains his discerning eye on characters facing fraught predicaments of both historical and contemporary life. . . . These pieces are classic Doctorow." —*Time Out New York*

ALSO BY E. L. DOCTOROW

All the Time in the World

NEW and SELECTED STORIES

—

RANDOM HOUSE TRADE PAPERBACKS | NEW YORK

E. L. DOCTOROW

—

All the Time in the World

2012 Random House Trade Paperback Edition

Copyright © 2011 by E. L. Doctorow

All rights reserved.

Published in the United States by Random House Trade Paperbacks, an imprint of The Random House Publishing Group, a division of Random House, Inc., New York.

RANDOM HOUSE TRADE PAPERBACKS and colophon are trademarks of Random House, Inc. RANDOM HOUSE READER'S CIRCLE & Design is a registered trademark of Random House, Inc.

Originally published in hardcover in the United States by Random House, an imprint of The Random House Publishing Group, a division of Random House, Inc., in 2011.

Original publication information for the stories that appear in this work can be found on page 279.

LIBRARY OF CONGRESS CATALOGING-IN-PUBLICATION DATA
Doctorow, E. L.
All the time in the world: new and selected stories / E. L. Doctorow.
p.   cm.
ISBN 978-0-8129-8203-9
eBook ISBN 978-0-679-60462-4
I. Title.
PS3554.O3A79 2011   813'.54—dc22   2010042500

Printed in the United States of America

www.randomhousereaderscircle.com

246897531

Book design by Barbara M. Bachman

Donald Doctorow

PREFACE

—

As I've assembled the stories for this volume, I see that there is no Winesburg, Ohio, here to be mined for its humanity. These are wide-ranging pieces, they are set all over America from New York City to suburbia, to the South and Midwest and far West. One takes place in Europe and one in no place that can finally be recognized. I am not sure that stories collected in a volume have to have a common mark, or tracer, to relate them to one another. But if these pieces are not unified by their geography and if they move about in time as they do from the late nineteenth century to a moment in the future, and if they are voiced as testimonies, or are given to authorial omniscience, or more deviously sounded in what is known as the indirect free style, what may unify them is the thematic segregation of their protagonists. The scale of a story causes it to home in on people who, for one reason or another, are distinct from their surroundings—people in some sort of contest with the prevailing world.

These stories have been written over the course of many years. I find each of them having its own particular light, though I don't expect that light to be visible to the reader. I may only be projecting my state of mind at the time of their composition or attributing to them the light of wherever I happened to be when I set them down. But I have banded the stories in packets of similar mental light—a principle of order no more arbitrary than any other.

E. L. Doctorow
November 2010

CONTENTS

—

All the Time in the World

WAKEFIELD

—

PEOPLE WILL SAY THAT I LEFT MY WIFE AND I SUPPOSE, AS A FACTUAL matter, I did, but where was the intentionality? I had no thought of deserting her. It was a series of odd circumstances that put me in the garage attic with all the junk furniture and the raccoon droppings—which is how I began to leave her, all unknowing, of course—whereas I could have walked in the door as I had done every evening after work in the fourteen years and two children of our marriage. Diana would think of her last sight of me, that same morning, when she pulled up to the station and slammed on the brakes, and I got out of the car and, before closing the door, leaned in with a cryptic smile to say good-bye—she would think that I had left her from that moment. In fact, I was ready to let bygones be bygones and, in another fact, I came home the very same evening with every expectation of entering the house that I, we, had bought for the raising of our children. And, to be absolutely honest, I remember I was feeling that kind of blood stir you get in anticipation of sex, because marital arguments had that effect on me.

Of course, the deep change of heart can come over anyone, and I don't see why, like everything else, it wouldn't be in character. After having lived dutifully by the rules, couldn't a man shaken out of his routine and distracted by a noise in his backyard veer away from one door and into another as the first step in the transformation of his life? And look what I was transformed into—hardly something to satisfy a judgment of normal male perfidy.

I will say here that at this moment I love Diana more truthfully than ever in our lives together, including the day of our wedding, when she was so incredibly beautiful in white lace with the sun coming down through the stained glass and setting a rainbow choker on her throat.

On the particular evening I speak of—this thing with the 5:38, when the last car, where I happened to be sitting, did not move off with the rest of the train? Even given the sorry state of the rail-roads in this country, tell me when that has happened. Every seat taken, and we sat there in the sudden dark and turned to one an-other for an explanation, as the rest of the train disappeared into the tunnel. It was the bare, fluorescent-lit concrete platform out-side that added to the suggestion of imprisonment. Someone laughed, but in a moment several passengers were up and banging on the doors and windows until a man in a uniform came down the ramp and peered in at us with his hands cupped at his temples.

And then when I do get home, an hour and a half later, I am nearly blinded by the headlights of all the SUVs and taxis waiting at the station: under an unnaturally black sky is this lateral plane of illumination, because, as it turns out, we have a power outage in town.

Well, it was an entirely unrelated mishap. I knew that, but when you're tired after a long day and trying to get home there's a kind of Doppler effect in the mind, and you think that these dis-connects are the trajectory of a collapsing civilization.

I set out on my walk home. Once the procession of commuter pickups with their flaring headlights had passed, everything was silent and dark—the groomed shops on the main street, the court-house, the gas stations trimmed with hedges, the Gothic prep school behind the lake. Then I was out of the town center and walking the winding residential streets. My neighborhood was an old section of town, the houses large, mostly Victorian, with dormers and wraparound porches and separate garages that had once been stables. Each house was set off on a knoll or well back from the street, with stands of lean trees dividing the properties—just the sort of old establishment solidity that suited me. But now the entire neighborhood seemed to brim with an exaggerated presence. I was conscious of the arbitrariness of place. Why here rather than somewhere else? A very unsettling, disoriented feeling.

A flickering candle or the bobbing beam of a flashlight in each window made me think of homes as supplying families with the means of living furtive lives. There was no moon, and under the low cloud cover a brisk unseasonable wind ruffled the old Norwegian maples that lined the street and dropped a fine rain of spring buds on my shoulders and in my hair. I felt this shower as a kind of derision.

All right, with thoughts like these any man would hurry to his home and hearth. I quickened my pace and would surely have turned up the path and mounted the steps to my porch had I not looked through the driveway gate and seen what I thought was a moving shadow near the garage. So I turned in that direction, my footsteps loud enough on the gravel to scare away whatever it was I had seen, for I supposed it was some animal.

We lived with animal life. I don't mean just dogs and cats. Deer and rabbits regularly dined on the garden flowers, we had Canada geese, here and there a skunk, the occasional red fox—this time it turned out to be a raccoon. A large one. I have never liked this animal, with its prehensile paws. More than the ape, it has always seemed to me a relative. I lifted my litigation bag as if to throw it and the creature ran behind the garage.

I went after it; I didn't want it on my property. At the foot of the outdoor stairs leading to the garage attic, it reared, hissing and showing its teeth and waving its forelegs at me. Raccoons are susceptible to rabies and this one looked mad, its eyes glowing, and saliva, like liquid glue, hanging from both sides of its jaw. I picked up a rock and that was enough—the creature ran off into the stand of bamboo that bordered the backyard of our neighbor, Dr. Sondervan, who was a psychiatrist, and a known authority on Down syndrome and other genetic misfortunes.

And then, of course, upstairs in the attic space over the garage, where we stored every imaginable thing, three raccoon cubs were in residence, and so that was what all the fuss was about. I didn't know how this raccoon family had gotten in there. I saw their eyes first, their several eyes. They whimpered and jumped about on the piled furniture, little ball-like humps in the darkness, until I finally managed to shoo them out the door and down the steps to where their mother would presumably reclaim them.

I turned on my cell phone to get at least some small light.

The attic was jammed with rolled-up rugs and bric-a-brac and boxes of college papers, my wife's inherited hope chest, old stereo equipment, a broken-down bureau, discarded board games, her late father's golf clubs, folded-up cribs, and so on. We were a family rich in history, though still young. I felt ridiculously righteous, as if I had fought a battle and reclaimed my kingdom from invaders. But then melancholy took over; there was enough of the past stuffed in here to sadden me, as relics of the past, including photographs, always sadden me.

Everything was thick with dust. A bull's-eye window at the front did not open and the windows on either side were stuck tight, as if fastened by the cobwebs that clung to their frames. The place badly needed airing. I exerted myself and moved things around and was able then to open the door fully. I stood at the top of the stairs to breathe the fresh air, which is when I noticed candlelight coming through the stand of bamboo between our property and the property behind ours, that same Dr. Sondervan's house. He boarded a number of young patients there. It was part of his experimental approach, not without controversy in his profession, to train them for domestic chores and simple tasks that required their interaction with normal people. I had stood up for Sondervan when some of the neighbors fought his petition to run his little sanatorium, though I have to say that in private it made Diana nervous, as the mother of two young girls, that mentally deficient persons were living next door. Of course, there had never been a bit of trouble.

I was tired from a long day, that was part of it, but, more likely suffering from some scattered mental state of my own, I groped around till I found the rocking chair with the torn seat that I had always meant to recane, and, in that total darkness and with the light of the candles slow to fade in my mind, I sat down and, though meaning only to rest a moment, fell asleep. And when I woke it was from the light coming through the dusty windows. I'd slept the night through.

WHAT HAD BROUGHT on our latest argument was what I claimed was Diana's flirtation with someone's houseguest at a backyard cocktail party the previous weekend.

I was not flirting, she said.

You were hitting on the guy.

Only in your peculiar imagination, Wakefield.

That's what she did when we argued—she used the last name. I wasn't Howard, I was Wakefield. It was one of her feminist adaptations of the locker-room style that I detested.

You made a suggestive remark, I said, and you clicked glasses with him.

It was not a suggestive remark, Diana said. It was a retort to something he'd said that was really stupid, if you want to know.

Everyone laughed but you. I apologize for feeling good on occasion, Wakefield. I'll try not to feel that way ever again.

This is not the first time you've made a suggestive remark with your husband standing right there. And then denied all knowledge of it.

Leave me alone, please. God knows you've muzzled me to the point where I've lost all confidence in myself. I don't relate to people anymore. I'm too busy wondering if I'm saying the right thing.

You were relating to him, all right.

Do you think with the kind of relationship I've had with you I'd be inclined to start another with someone else? I just want to get through each day—that is all I think about, getting through each day.

That was probably true. On the train to the city, I had to admit to myself that I'd started the argument willfully, in a contrary spirit and with some sense of its eroticism. I did not really believe what I had accused her of. I was the one who came on to people. I had attributed to her my own wandering eye. That is the basis of jealousy, is it not? A feeling that your congenital insincerity is a universal? It did annoy me, seeing her talking to another man with a glass of white wine in her hand, and her innocent friendliness, which any man could mistake for a come-on, not just me. The fellow himself was not terribly prepossessing. But it bothered me that she was talking to him almost as if I were not standing there beside her.

Diana was naturally graceful and looked younger than she was. She still moved like the dancer she had been in college, her feet pointed slightly outward, her head high, her walk more a glide than something taken step by step. Even after carrying twins, she was as petite and slender as she had been when I met her.

And now in the first light of the new day I was totally bewildered by the situation I had created for myself. I can't claim that I was thinking rationally. But I actually felt that it would be a mistake to walk into my house and explain the sequence of events that had led me to spend the night in the garage attic. Diana would have been up till all hours, pacing the floor and worrying what had happened to me. My appearance, and her sense of relief, would enrage her. Either she would think that I had been with another woman or, if she did believe my story, it would strike her as so weird as to be a kind of benchmark in our married life. After all, we had had that argument the previous day. She would perceive what I told myself could not possibly be true—that something had happened predictive of a failed marriage. And the twins, budding adolescents, who generally thought of me as someone they were unfortunate to live in the same house with, an embarrassment in front of their friends, an oddity who knew nothing about their music—their alienation would be hissingly expressive. I thought of mother and daughters as the opposing team. The home team. I concluded that for now I would rather not go through the scene I had just imagined. Maybe later, I thought, just not now. I had yet to realize my talent for dereliction.

WHEN I CAME DOWN the garage stairs and relieved myself in the stand of bamboo, the cool air of the dawn welcomed me with a soft breeze. The raccoons were nowhere to be seen. My back was stiff and I felt the first pangs of hunger, but, in fact, I had to admit that I was not at that moment unhappy. What is there about a family that is so sacrosanct, I thought, that one should have to live in it for one's whole life, however unrealized one's life was?

From the shadow of the garage, I beheld the backyard, with its Norwegian maples, the tilted white birches, the ancient apple tree whose branches touched the windows of the family room, and for the first time, it seemed, I understood the green glory of this acreage as something indifferent to human life and quite apart from the Victorian manse set upon it. The sun was not yet up and the grass was draped with a wavy net of mist, punctured here and there with glistening drops of dew. White apple blossoms had begun to appear in the old tree, and I read the pale light in the sky as the shy illumination of a world to which I had yet to be introduced.

At this point, I suppose, I could have safely unlocked the back door and scuttled about in the kitchen, confident that everyone in the house was still asleep. Instead, I raised the lid of the garbage bin and found in one of the cans my complete dinner of the night before, slammed upside down atop a plastic bag and held in a circle of perfect integrity, as if still on the plate—a grilled veal chop, half a baked potato, peel-side up, and a small mound of oiled green salad—so that I could imagine the expression on Diana's face as she had come out here, still angry from our morning argument, and rid herself of the meal gone cold that she had stupidly cooked for that husband of hers.

I wondered now at what hour had she lost patience. That would be a measure of whatever slack she granted me. Another woman might have refrigerated the dinner, but I lived in Diana's judgment; it shone upon me as in a prison cell where the light is never turned off. I lacked interest in her work. Or I was snide and condescending toward her mother. Or I wasted beautiful fall weekends watching dumb football games on television. Or I wouldn't agree to have the bedrooms painted. And if she was such a feminist why did my opening a door for her or helping her on with her coat matter so much?

All I had to do was stand outside my home in the chill of the early morning in order to see things in their totality: Diana felt that she had married the wrong man. Of course, I didn't imagine I was the easiest person to get along with. But even she would have to admit that I was never boring. And, whatever problems we had, sex, the crucial center of our lives, wasn't one of them. Was I under an illusion to think that that was the basis of a sound marriage?

Given these thoughts, I could not bring myself to walk in the door and announce that I was home. I made my breakfast of the congealed veal chop and the potato as I sat out of sight behind the garage.

I HAD MET DIANA when she was dating my best friend, Dirk Morrison, whom I had known since middle school. Because she was going with him, I looked at her more closely than I might have otherwise. I registered her as pretty, of course, very attractive, with a lovely smile, light brown hair pulled back in a ponytail, and what the merest glance could affirm was a fine body, but somehow it was Dirk's interest in her, which was clearly of the most intense kind, that made me consider Diana as a potentially serious relationship for myself. At first, Diana wouldn't go out with me. But when I told her I had gotten permission from Dirk to ask her out she relented, obviously from feelings of hurt and bitterness. Of course, I had lied. When eventually she and Dirk realized my perfidy, things became bitter all around, and in the ensuing competition, many months in duration, the poor girl was torn between us and, all told, we made the unhappiest ménage you could imagine. We were all children, the three of us, what—barely out of Harvard Law, in my case? And Dirk with an entry-level Wall Street job? And Diana working for a PhD in art history? Young, self-styled Upper East Siders. There were times when Diana wouldn't see me, or wouldn't see Dirk, or wouldn't see either of us. Of course, in retrospect, it's clear that all this was quite the normal thing, when, adrift in their hormonic tides, people in their twenties are about to land on one shore or another.

I didn't know if, before I broke into their relationship, Diana had been sleeping with Dirk. I knew now that she was sleeping with neither of us. One day, in a stroke of genius, I told Dirk that I had spent the previous night with her. When he confronted her, she denied it, of course, and, showing his lack of insight and understanding of the quality of the person he was dealing with, he didn't believe her. That was his fatal error, which he compounded by trying to press himself on her. Diana was not a virgin—nobody was by our age—but, as I was later to learn, neither did she have much experience, though that quality of sexy innocence I have mentioned could easily have passed for it. At any rate, you didn't try to force yourself on this woman if you ever expected to see her again. His second mistake, Dirk, before he disappeared from our lives altogether, was to punch me out. He was the heavier of us, though I was the taller. And he landed a couple of good ones before someone pulled him off me. That was the first and last time I've ever actually been hit, though I've been threatened a few times since. But my black eye brought out a tender resolution of Diana's feelings for me. Perhaps she understood that all my tactical cunning was a measure of my devotion, and, as her cool lips brushed my bruised cheek, I could not imagine myself ever having been happier.

After we had been married for a year and some of the energy had gone out of the relationship, I did wonder if my passion might have been pumped up by the competition for her. Would I have been all that crazy about her had she not been my best friend's girl? But then she became pregnant and a whole new array of feelings entered into our marriage and, as her belly swelled, she became more radiant than ever. I had always liked to draw—I drew seriously as late as my freshman year at Harvard—and my knowledge of art had been one of the things that attracted her to me. Now she allowed me to draw her as she posed naked, with her small breasts fruited out and her belly gloriously ripened, as she lay back on some pillows with her hands behind her head and turned on one hip with her legs slightly pulled up but pressed together for modesty, like Goya's *Maja*.

I SPENT THAT FIRST DAY watching through the bull's-eye window for the sequence of events that would occur when it became clear that I had gone missing. First, Diana would get the twins off to school. Then, the minute the bus had turned the corner, she would call my office and satisfy herself that I had been seen off by my secretary at the usual time the night before. She would ask to be notified when I showed up for work, her voice not only under control but doggedly cheerful, as if she were calling about a minor family matter. I reasoned that only after a call or two to whichever of our friends she thought might know something would the panic set in. She would look at the clock, and, around eleven, steel herself and call the police.

I was wrong by half an hour. The squad car came up the driveway at eleven thirty, by my watch. She met the patrolmen at the back door. Our town police are well paid and polite and they are not very different from the rest of us in their distant relationship to crime. But I knew that they would take down a description, ask for a photo, and so on, in order to put out a missing-persons bulletin. Yet, when they were back in their car, I saw through the windshield that the cops were smiling: where else were missing husbands to be found but in St. Bart's, drinking piña coladas with their chiquitas?

All that was wanting now was Diana's mother, and by noon she was up from the city in her white Escalade—the widow Babs, who had opposed the marriage and was likely now to say so. Babs was what Diana, God help us, might be thirty years hence—

high-heeled, ceramicized, liposucted, devaricosed, her golden
fall of hair as shiny and hard as peanut brittle.

IN THE DAYS FOLLOWING, cars pulled up at the house at all
hours as friends and colleagues came to show their support and to
console Diana, as if I had died. These wretches, hardly able to re-
strain themselves in their excitement, were making victims of my
wife and children. And how many of the husbands would hit on
her the first chance they got? I thought about bursting in the
door—Wakefield arisen—just to see the expression on their faces.

Then the house grew quiet again. There weren't many lights
on. Occasionally, I'd see someone for a moment in a window without being able to tell who it was. One morning after the school bus
had stopped to pick up the twins, the garage doors below me
rolled up and Diana got in her car and went back to her curator's
job at the county art museum. I was hungry, having lived off scraps
in our garbage and neighbors' garbage, and also fairly rank at this
point, so I slipped into the house and availed myself of its ameni-
ties. I ate crackers and nuts from the pantry. I was careful when
showering to rinse out my towel, put it in the dryer, and return it,
properly folded, to the linen closet. I stole some socks and briefs
on the theory that there were drawers full and a few missing would
not be noticed. I thought about taking a fresh shirt and another
pair of shoes but decided that that would be risky.

At this stage, I still worried about money. What would I do
after I had spent the slender amount of cash in my wallet? If I
wanted to disappear completely, I could no longer use my credit
cards. I could predate a check and cash it at the downtown branch
of our local bank, but when the month's statement came Diana
would see it and think that my abandonment of my family had
been premeditated, which, of course, it had not.

Early one evening, at that time of day when the apple blossoms release their lovely scent, Diana came out to stand in the backyard. I watched her from my garage atelier. She took a blossom from its branch and put it to her cheek. Then she looked around, as if she had heard something. She turned this way and that, her glance actually passing over the garage. She stood there as if listening, her head slightly tilted, and I had the feeling that she almost knew where I was, that she had sensed my presence. I held my breath. A moment later, she turned and went back inside, and the door closed and I heard the lock click. That loud click was definitive. It sounded in my mind like my release into another world.

I felt the stubble on my chin. Who was this fellow? I had not even thought about what I had left behind in my law office—the cases, the clients, the partnership. I became almost giddy. There would be no more getting on the train. Below me in the garage was my beloved silver BMW 325 convertible. Of what use was it to me? I felt uncharacteristically defiant, as if I were about to roar and pound my chest. I did not need the friends and acquaintances accumulated over the years. I no longer required a change of shirt or a smooth, shaven face. I would not live with credit cards, cell phones. I would live how I might on what I could find or create for myself. If this were a simple abandonment of wife and children, I would have written Diana a note, telling her to find a good lawyer, taken my car out of the garage, and been on my way to Manhattan. I would have checked in to a hotel and walked to work the next morning. Anyone could do that, anyone could run away; he could go as far as he could go and still be the same person. There was nothing to that. This was different. This strange suburb was an environment in which I would have to sustain myself, like a person lost in a jungle, like a castaway on an island. I would not run from it—I would make it my own. That was the game, if it was a game. That was the challenge. I had left not only my home; I had left the system. This life in the glittering eye of the prehensile raccoon was what I wanted, and never had I felt so absolutely secure, as if the several phantom images of myself had resolved into the final form of who I was—clearly and firmly the Howard Wakefield I was meant to be.

For all my exuberance, I did not fail to understand that I might have left my wife but I would still be able to keep an eye on her.

OF NECESSITY, I WAS NOW a nocturnal creature. I slept in the garage attic by day and went out at night. I was alert and sensitive to the weather and the amount of moonlight. I moved from yard to yard, never trusting sidewalks or streets. I learned much about people in the neighborhood, what they ate, when they went to sleep. As spring turned to summer and people left on vacation, more of the houses were empty and there were fewer opportunities for trash-can forage. But then there were fewer dogs to bark at me as I passed under the trees, and, where the dog was big, so was the dog door, and I could crawl in and avail myself of the canned and packaged foods in kitchen pantries. I never took anything but food. I felt an equivalence, but not seriously, to the Native American buffalo hunter who slew the creature for his meat and fur and thanked his risen soul afterward. I really had no illusions about the morality of what I was doing.

My clothes began to show wear and tear. I was growing a beard and my hair was longer. As August approached, I realized that if Diana wanted to do what we had done for many years she would rent the house we liked on the Cape and take the girls there for the month. In my garage den, I took pains to restore the disarray. I planned to sleep out of doors until they came up there for the life jackets, the pontoon float tube, the swim fins, the fishing rods, and whatever other summer junk I had bought so obediently. With a keen sense of dispossession, I wandered out of the neighborhood to find someplace to sleep, and discovered that I had barely begun to use the resources available to me when I came upon an undeveloped piece of land as wild as I could wish. It took me a moment to recognize, in the dim light of a half-moon, that I was in the town's designated Nature Preserve, a place where elementary-school children were taken to get an idea of what an unpaved universe looked like. I had brought my own children here. My law firm had represented the wealthy widow who had deeded this land to the town with the provision that it be kept forever as it was. Now its true wildness loomed before me. The ground was soft and swampy, fallen tree branches lay over the paths, I heard the obsessive self-hypnotizing cicadas, the gulp of the bullfrogs, and knew with an animal sense only lately developed in me that there were some four-footed creatures about. I found a small pond at the bottom end of these woods. It must have been kept fresh by an underground stream, because the water was cold and clear. I stripped and bathed myself and put my clothes back on over my wet body. I slept that night in the crotched trunk of a dead old maple tree. I can't say that I slept well; moths brushed my face and there was a constant stirring of unknown life around me. I was really quite uncomfortable but I resolved to see it through until such nights as this were normal for me.

Yet when Diana and the girls had gone on their vacation and I was able to reclaim my pallet in the garage attic, I felt despicably lonely.

WITH MY NEW DEATH'S-DOOR LOOK, I decided that I had at least an even-money chance to go about unrecognized. I was lean and long-bearded and with a shock of hair that fell down the sides of my face. As my hair grew out, I saw how barbering it in the old days had hidden its increasing grayness. My beard was even farther along. I took myself in my tatters to the business district and availed myself of the town's social services. In the public library, which, not incidentally, had a well-kept men's room, I read the daily papers as if informing myself of life on another planet. I thought it was more my image to read the papers than to sit at one of the library computers.

If the weather was good, I liked to take up residence on a bench at the mall. I did not beg; had I begged, the security people would have shooed me off. I sat with my legs crossed and head up, and projected attitude. My regal mien proposed to passersby that I was a delusionary eccentric. Children would come up to me at the urging of their mothers and put coins or dollar bills in my hands. In this way, I was able occasionally to enjoy a hot meal at Burger King or a coffee at Starbucks. Pretending to be mute, I pointed to what I wanted.

I regarded these expeditions to the town center as daring escapades. I needed to prove to myself that I could take risks. While I carried no I.D., there was always the possibility that someone, even Diana herself, if back early from her vacation, might come by and recognize me. I almost wished that she would.

But after a while the novelty of these trips wore off and I reclaimed my residential solitude. I embraced my dereliction as a religious discipline; it was as if I were a monk sworn to an order devoted to affirming God's original world.

Squirrels traveled along the telephone wires, their tails rippling like signal pulses. Raccoons lifted the lids off the garbage pails left at the curb for the morning pickup. If I had preceded them at a pail, they knew immediately that there was nothing there for them. A skunk each night made its rounds like a watchman, taking the same route past the garage and through the stand of bamboo and diagonally across Dr. Sondervan's backyard, and disappearing down his driveway. At the preserve pond, my occasional swim was observed by a slick, slime-covered rat-tailed muskrat. His dark eyes glowed in the moonlight. Only when I had climbed out of the pond did he dive into it, silently, with no apparent disturbance of the water. Most mornings, invader crows arrived, twenty or thirty of them at a time coming out of the sky and cawing away. It was as if loudspeakers were strung in the trees. Sometimes the crows would go quiet and send out reconnaissance, one or two of them circling and landing in the street to examine a candy wrapper or the dregs of a garbage can that the sanitation men had emptied incompletely. A dead squirrel was occasion for a feast, a great black mass of fluttering feathers and bobbing heads stripping the carcass down to its bones. Altogether they were a kind of crow state, and if there were any dissidents I could not find them. I did dislike it that they drove away the smaller birds—a pair of cardinals, for example, who nested in the backyard, and didn't have the range of these ravenous black birds who would be off as quickly as they had come, in powerful flight to the next block or the next town.

There were house cats always on the prowl, of course, and dogs barking late at night in one house or another, but I did not see them as legitimate. They were sheltered; they lived at the behest of human beings.

One night in early autumn, with the swampy ground of the Nature Preserve papered with fallen leaves, I was hunkered down to examine a dead snake about a foot in length whose color I thought might in life have been green, when, as I stood, I felt something brush the top of my head. As I looked up I saw the wings of a ghostly pale owl fold into his body as he disappeared into a tree. The feathery touch of the owl wing on my scalp left me shivering.

These creatures and I either were food to one another or were not. That was all there was to it. I was presumptive from my lone-liness, an unrequited lover as incidental to all of them as they had once been to me.

DIANA WAS ALWAYS comfortable in her body and was careless about covering herself in front of our girls. She didn't mind being seen in the nude, and when I suggested that it might not be the best thing for them she replied that, on the contrary, it was in-structive for them to see how naturally accepting and unself-conscious a woman could be about her physical being. Well, then, how about a man, if they were to see me walking around in the al-together? I said. And Diana said, Really, Howard, Mr. Prude in the nude? Not a chance.

In our bedroom, Diana seemed not to care if the blinds were open when she was dressing or undressing. I was always the one to close them. Who are you trying to attract? I would say to her, and she'd say, That very good-looking fellow out there in the apple tree. But she seemed as oblivious of her effect nude in a bedroom window as she was when attracting men at cocktail parties. All this behavior was ambiguous and kept me wondering.

And now, though I was not up in the apple tree, I had found various salients in our half acre that allowed me to see a good deal of her at night, when she went to bed. It was always alone, I was satisfied to see. She would sometimes come right up to the window and stare into the darkness while brushing her hair. In those mo-ments, with the light behind her, I would see her lovely shape only in silhouette. Then she would turn and walk back into the room. A long-waisted girl with narrow shoulders and firm buttocks.

Oddly enough, seeing my wife in the nude usually got me thinking of her financial situation. I did this to assure myself that she would not find it necessary to sell the house and move elsewhere. Her salary at the museum was just adequate, and we had a mortgage, prep-school tuition for the twins—all the usual presiding expenses. On the other hand, I had set up a savings account in her name and had added to it regularly. My investments were in a revocable trust of which she as well as I was a trustee. And I had paid down a considerable part of the mortgage with my last year's partner's bonus. She might have to cut back on her clothes purchases and all the little luxuries she enjoyed, she would have to give up her hope of redoing the bathrooms in marble, but that was hardly to suggest her impoverishment. I was the impoverished one.

My spying was not restricted to her bedtime. Now in the autumn it grew dark earlier every day. I liked to know what was going on. I would hunker down in the garden foliage under the windows and listen to the conversation. There she would be in the dining room, helping the twins with their homework. Or they would all three be putting together their dinner. Never once did I hear my name mentioned. Arguments I could hear from the very edge of the property, one of the twins, screeching and stamping her foot. A door would slam. Sometimes Diana came out on the back porch and lit a cigarette, standing there holding her elbow, the hand with the cigarette pointing at the sky. That was news—she had quit the habit years before. Sometimes she was out for the evening and all I could see were the flickering colored lights of the TV in the family room. I didn't like it that she left the twins alone. I kept watch at the bull's-eye window in my attic until I saw her car come up the drive.

On Halloween, the street was busy with parents escorting their cutely costumed children from one porch to another. Diana always prepared for the onslaught by buying tons of candy. All the lights were on in my house. I heard laughter. And here passing under the window of my garage attic were a few of Dr. Sondervan's patients.

They had come through the bamboo, ambling down the drive, these larger children, carrying shopping bags for the treasures to be collected from somewhat uneasy neighbors receiving them at the front door.

EVERY TWO WEEKS, the town residents put out for trash their hard, nonorganic items: old TVs, broken chairs, boxes of paperbacks, end tables, busted lamps, toys their children had outgrown, and so on. I had come away previously with a usable, only slightly torn and sperm-stained futon from this resource, as well as an old portable radio that looked as if it might work if I could find some batteries for it. I did miss music as I missed nothing else.

On this night I went looking for some shoes. Mine had worn away. They were falling apart. It was a damp night; it had rained in the afternoon and slick wet leaves were pressed to the streets. Timing was crucial: By one in the morning, anything that was going to be thrown out was on the sidewalk. By two, anything that was usable was gone. On these nights, people from the south end of town cruised around in their old pickups or in cars that tilted to one side, and they'd pull up and, with their motors running, hop out to judge items, grabbing each thing for examination, to see if it met their exacting standards.

Some winding blocks away from my home base, I spotted in the light of a streetlamp a promising trove—an unusually large pile of curbed junk that could have passed for an installation in a Chelsea gallery. It bespoke someone's desperation to move—stacks of chairs, open cartons of toys and stuffed animals, board games, a sofa, a brass headboard, skis, a desk with a lamp still clamped to it, and, underneath everything, layers of men's and women's clothing going damp in the dew. I was busy putting things aside and digging under the suits and dresses, and didn't hear the truck approach or the men get out, a pair of them, who were suddenly there beside me, two guys in sleeveless T-shirts to show off their muscular arms. They were talking to each other in some foreign language and it was as if I weren't there, because, as they worked their way through the trove, lifting away the furniture to put in their truck, the cartons of toys, the skis and everything else, they got around rather quickly to the pile of clothes under which I had just found three or four shoe boxes and they pushed me aside to get at these things. Just a minute, I thought, having found a pair of white-and-tan wingtips, not my style at all, but they seemed in the moonlight to be right out of a store window and close to my size. I kicked off the sole-flapping holey pair I was wearing. At this point, I had no reason to think that these scavenger men were anything but boors. Now it appeared that a woman was with them, who was wider and heavier in the arms than they were, and, as I stood there, she decided that my pair of shoes, too, should be theirs. No, I said. Mine, mine! The shoe box was wet and, with each of us pulling, it came apart and the shoes dropped to the ground. I grabbed them before she could. Mine! I shouted and slapped them together, sole against sole, in her face. She shrieked and a moment later I was running down the street with the two men chasing me and shouting curses, or what I assumed were curses, great hoarse expletives that echoed through the trees and set dogs barking in the dark houses.

I found myself running well, a shoe stuck paddle-like over each hand. I heard heavy panting behind me, then a cry as one of the men slipped on the wet leaves in the street and went down. As I ran, I visualized the blunt faces of these people and decided that they were a mother and two sons. I supposed they made a business out of their collectibles. This was to be admired—entry-level work into the American dream. But I'd had them first—the shoes, I mean—and by the law of salvage they were mine.

Mine! I had said like a child. Mine, mine! These were the first words I had spoken in all the months of my dereliction. And as I uttered them I almost thought it was someone else speaking.

I had an advantage in knowing the neighborhood, and gained on my pursuit by cutting across yards and up driveways and through garden gates, punishing my tender wet feet every step of the way. I heard a rhythmic wheeze and realized that it was coming from my aching chest. I didn't dare look behind me. I heard their truck somewhere on an adjoining street and imagined the mother, that sturdy peasant of a woman, behind the wheel, peering over her headlights for a sight of me. I was nearing my atelier now, coming up the back way through my neighbor Sondervan's yard. I reasoned that I did not want these people to know where I lived. Retribution could be theirs at any time they chose if they saw me climb the stairs to the garage attic. My solution was not entirely logical: as I approached the stand of bamboo, I veered off, and ducked down the three stone steps to the basement door of Sondervan's house.

The door was unlocked. I slipped inside and slid down against the wall and attempted to catch my breath. At the end of a short hallway was another door, indicated to me now by the light that came on behind it. The door opened and I had to raise my arms against the light. I must have made an odd picture, sitting there with each hand in a wingtip shoe, as if that were how shoes were worn, because whoever was standing there began to laugh.

In this way, I became a familiar of two of the unfortunates who lived in the basement dormitory under the care of Dr. Sondervan.

ONE WAS A DOWN-SYNDROMER by the name of Herbert. Emily, his pal, was the other—I don't know what she was, but she couldn't keep from smiling, out of unceasing happiness or a neurological glitch, but either way it was eerily unnatural. This bucktoothed girl with very thin hair, I couldn't tell her age—she might have been anything from fourteen to nineteen. She and Herbert, who was smaller in his proportions than he should have been, with a round head, slanted eyes, and a nose that looked as if he'd had a boxing career, seemed distinct from the four other patients down there, who were aloof, who took me in with a glance that first night and couldn't care less after that—teenagers, apparently, three male, one female, physically normal-looking, compared with Herbert and Emily, but living in their own minds, with not much concern for what went on around them. I assumed that they were a variety of autistics, though of course I knew nothing about autism, except what I had read in magazines or seen on television.

But Herbert and Emily loved me from the moment they saw me sitting there with the shoes on my hands, as if they had found someone mentally less fortunate even than they, who may not have known much but did know that shoes were more properly worn on the feet. They didn't ask what had brought me to their door, but welcomed me as one might a stray cat. From that first moment, they were solicitous and protective, instructing me to repeat their names after them to make sure I understood, and then asking my name. Howard, I said, my name is Howard.

They brought me a glass of water and Emily, giggling all the while, brushed the sweated thatch of hair from my forehead. Howard is a fine name, she said. Don't you love the autumn, Howard? I love the falling leaves, don't you?

They took the shoes from my hands and fitted them on my wet feet, Herbert, with his mouth open as befit his concentration, tying the laces, and Emily looking on as if it were a surgical procedure. Neatly done, Herbert, very fine indeed, she said. As soon as I judged it safe to go, they insisted on following me to my garage and watched as I climbed the stairs to make sure that I did not fall.

So now two of Dr. Sondervan's mental defectives knew about

me. It would be a costly pair of shoes if they blabbed about Howard, the nice man who lived next door over the garage. There was
not only the doctor but his staff, the three or four women who ran
the household, to whom they might say something. I looked
around the attic, my de facto home. The only sensible thing to do
was to leave. But how could I? While I struggled with this, I maintained a watch by day and didn't make my nightly forage until well
past their lights-out.

A couple of mornings later, I saw Herbert and Emily and the
others in the backyard. They were sitting on the ground, and there
was Sondervan addressing them, like students in a class. The doctor was a tall but stooped man in his seventies, with a gray goatee
and black horn-rim glasses. I had never seen him without a jacket
and tie, and in deference to the season he had added a short-
sleeved sweater that served as a vest. I couldn't hear what he was
saying, though I could hear his voice; a thin, high elderly man's
voice, it was, but self-assured and with an almost smugly assumed
authority. At one point, Herbert grabbed a handful of fallen leaves
and tossed them up so that they rained down on Emily's head. She,
of course, laughed, thus interrupting the lecture. The doctor
glared. How normal this all was. Had Herbert and Emily revealed
my whereabouts, wouldn't I by now have heard from someone—
from Sondervan himself, or from Diana, or from the police, or
from all of them, my little world crashing down on my head? I understood that for whatever reason, perhaps a dissident impulse
that they might not even understand, the retarded children, if they
were children, had decided to make me their secret.

IT WAS ODD—on the occasions when they could visit me safely, I
enjoyed their company. I found my own mind comfortable with
the reduced wattage that conversation with them required. They

did see things, notice things. Their predominant emotion was wonder. Everything in the attic was examined, as if they were visiting a museum. Herbert opened and shut the brass snaps of my litigation bag over and over. Emily, digging in Diana's hope chest, came up with an antique silver hand mirror in which to study herself. Perhaps, not having spoken with another human being for some months, I was overly responsive, but I was happy to explain how a life jacket worked, and why the game of golf required many clubs, or how spiderwebs were made, or why I, yet another exhibit, lived here in this attic. I gave them the expurgated version of that: I told them that I was a wanderer, a hermit by choice, and that this attic was one stop on my life's journey. Then I had to assure them that I had no intention of moving on for quite some time.

I worried that they would be found missing back at their place, but somehow they knew when they could get away safely. And they brought me things, little gifts of food and bottled water, knowing without my having to explain that I was a person in need. They would bring me a piece of cake and solemnly watch me eat it. Herbert, with his dark almond eyes in that globular head, had the most intense stare. He would hold himself at the shoulders and watch how my jaw moved. And Emily, of course, chattered on, as if she had to speak for both of them. Isn't that good, Howard? Do you like cake? What is your favorite? I like chocolate cake the best, though strawberry is good, too.

They may have been heartbreaking—and they were, casting me into the realm of remorseless normality—but in fact Herbert and Emily were there when I needed them. Sharply honed as my survival skills had become, some residual upper-middle-class indifference to the weather had left me unprepared for winter. What was thrown into the neighborhood garbage pails after Thanksgiving had fed me nicely for several days, but I was chilled as I foraged, and within a week the wind was whistling through the siding

of my attic hideout. I had no heat up here. Winter, with its assort-
ment of effects, was a threat to my lifestyle.

I cursed the homeowner I had been for neglecting the upkeep
of this place. I rummaged about in all the junk I lived with and,
finding some antique curtains in Diana's inherited hope chest, I
laid them atop the old coat that I used for a blanket and, pulling
down over my ears the watch cap that I had found on the street, I
snaked down under these pathetic coverings on my salvaged futon
and tried to keep my teeth from chattering.

How could I stay abreast of what was going on in my house if,
when the snow came, my every footstep in the yard would leave a
trail of incrimination and such clear proof of a prowler on the
grounds as to get Diana on the phone to the town police?

I was tempted during one dry cold spell to let myself in the back
door of my house and keep warm beside my basement furnace,
safely spending a few hours down there between midnight and
dawn. But I would not surrender to my former self. Whatever I
did I would do as I had done. Which meant also that going into a
shelter for the homeless—there had to be one somewhere in town,
probably at the south end, where lived immigrants, undocumented aliens, and the working poor—that, too, was out of the
question. And never mind principles: even the homeless have
names, histories, and inquisitive social workers. If I played dumb,
went mute, how could I not end up committed somewhere? Better
to freeze to death. As I understood it, it wasn't half bad—you simply grew warm and fell asleep.

Another option, one not prohibited by any vows I had taken,
was to find shelter in Dr. Sondervan's house. While it is true that I
did more than once sneak into the basement dorm to use the bathroom, and on occasion I even risked a shower with Herbert and
Emily guarding the door, and while another time, late at night,

they led me into the dark kitchen, whose antiseptic smell was an offense to my nostrils, and whose ticking clock suggested discipline verging on tyranny, so that it was almost as a courtesy to them that I accepted an apple and a chicken leg, I could not reasonably expect in this odd doctor's sanatorium to go unnoticed as an overnight guest.

And so, as I pondered and worried and accomplished nothing, the winter blew in with a wild snow that scoured the streets and roared through my meager shelter like the vengeful God of the Old Testament.

Of course, I was not trapped; I just felt as if I were. I thought what a brilliant evolutionary expedient was hibernation, and if bears and hedgehogs and bats had managed to work it into their repertoire why hadn't we?

Actually, as the snow was blown against the siding of the garage it stuck there, sealing off the cracks, and my atelier became a bit cozier, though not in time to keep me from falling ill. I thought I had caught cold when I awoke with eyes watering and a sore throat. But when I tried to get up I felt too weak to stand. I could actually feel the virus humming happily through me. There comes a moment when you have to admit that you're sick. How could I have expected otherwise, as undernourished and poorly prepared for the winter as I was?

I had never in my life felt so bad. I must have been running a high fever, because I was out of it half the time. I have an image of two alarmed young retards standing in the doorway looking down at me. Perhaps I gave them a pathetic wave of my pale, bony hand. And then one of them must have come back that night or another, because I woke up in the small hours with a hot-water bottle under my feet. And—this is the most phantasmic impression of all—once I awakened to find Emily in my bed, clothed, with her arms and legs wrapped around me as if to provide warmth. At the same time, though, she was pressing her pelvis rhythmically against my hip and cooing something and kissing my bearded cheeks.

AFTER SEVERAL DAYS, I found myself still alive. I got up from my poor pallet and did not collapse. I was a bit weak but steady on my feet and clearheaded. If one can feel physically chastened, as if having been scrubbed down to another skin, that's what I felt. I studied myself in the antique silver hand mirror: what a thin, gaunt fellow I had become, though with eyes bright with intelligence. I decided that I had passed through some crisis that was more a test of spirit than a lousy virus. I felt good. Tall and lean and limber. There was a stale sandwich and a glass of frozen milk beside my bed. The jars that served as my urinals were empty and aligned in a gleaming row. Sun came through the bull's-eye window and cast an oblong rainbowed image of itself on the attic floor.

Wrapping my coat around me, I went outside into the cold pure air of the winter morning, careful not to slip on the icy steps. The bamboo copse was encased in clear ice. I looked for my friends, for some sign of them, but there was not even one track in the snow covering Sondervan's backyard. I saw no smoke from the chimney, no lights at the back basement door that had always burned there, day and night. So they were gone, the whole crew of them, patients, staff. Do you take a houseful of mentally problematic people for a Christmas vacation? Or had the neighbors finally gotten a court to rule against Sondervan's little sanatorium? And the doctor? Had he fled to his practice in the city? I didn't know.

They had been like little elves tending to my illness, Herbert and Emily, there but not there.

I spent that day getting used to the fact that I was alone again in the fullness of my hermitage. It was not a bad feeling. The childishness of the two of them had migrated somewhat to me, and, while I felt bad for them, their home, such as it was, taken from them, it was a relief to be back in my own mind, undistracted, uninvolved. That night I was once again out on my rounds, and the takings were good. I put together a fine dinner and for drink I melted snow in my mouth.

WHEN THE WEATHER SOFTENED, leaving only patches of snow on the ground, I resumed my nighttime surveillance of my home. I found some subtle changes. Diana had done something with her hair, cut it shorter. I was not sure it was right for her. There was a jauntiness in her step. The twins appeared to have grown an inch or two since the last time I had looked in the window. Quite the young ladies. No more fighting, no door slams. Mother and daughters seemed very together, even happy. The undecorated fir tree in the dining room told me that Christmas had not yet arrived.

Why did all of this come to me as a presentiment? I was uneasy as I climbed back to my atelier. I found myself thinking of the law. I knew that, having disappeared and not been found after diligent inquiry, I would be declared an absentee and Diana, as my spouse, would become temporary administrator of my property. Had she not seen to that, I was sure that one of my partners would have seen to it for her. What I could not remember was how much time would have to elapse before I was declared legally dead and the provisions of my will would come into play. Was it a year, two years, five years? And why was I thinking about this? "Spouse"? "Diligent inquiry"? Why was I thinking with these words, these legal terms? I had expunged the law from my mind, I had wiped the slate clean, so what was the matter with me?

I did something then out of a gleeful-seeming desperation that

I still don't understand. A couple of times a year, an old Italian man who had a knife-and-tool-sharpening business in his van would come to the back door and ask if anything needed to be sharpened. He had his van outfitted with a gas-powered grinding wheel. Diana would give him kitchen knives, poultry shears, scissors, even if they didn't need sharpening, just because she knew he needed work. I think it was the Old World quality of this gentle peddler that appealed to her. So there I was, looking out the window and watching him come up the driveway and stand at the door while Diana went into the kitchen to find something for him.

A moment later, I was standing behind him with a big grin; I was this tall, long-haired homeless soul with a gray beard down to his chest, who, for all Diana knew, as she returned with a handful of knives, was the old Italian's assistant. I wanted to look into her eyes, I wanted to see if there was any recognition there. I didn't know what I would do if she recognized me; I didn't even know if I wanted her to recognize me. She didn't. The knives were handed over, the door closed, and the old Italian, after frowning at me and muttering something in his own language, went back to his van.

And, back in my atelier, I thought of the green-eyed glance of my wife, the intelligence it took in, the judgment it registered, all in that instant of nonrecognition. While I, her lawful husband, stood there grinning like an idiot. I decided that it was good that she hadn't recognized me—it would have been disastrous if she had. My devilish impulse had pulled off a good joke. But my disappointment was like one of those knives, after sharpening, in my chest.

A DAY OR TWO LATER, in the late afternoon, as the setting sun reddened the sky over the big trees, I heard a car pulling into the driveway. A door slammed, and by the time I got to the attic window whoever it was had disappeared around the front of the house. I had never seen this car before. It was a top-of-the-line sedan, a sleek black Mercedes. Long after the sun had set and all the lights were on in my house, I could see that the car was still there. I kept going back to the window and the car kept being there. Whoever it was, he was staying to dinner. For, of course, I knew it was a he.

The moon was out, and so it was somewhat risky for me to go around to the dining room and look in the window. The shades were drawn—what was she trying to hide?—but not completely; there was an inch or two of light above the windowsill. When I bent my legs and peered in, I could see his back, and the back of his head, and, across the table from him, my smiling radiant wife lifting her wineglass as if in acknowledgment of something he had said. I heard the girls' voices; the whole family was there, having themselves a grand time with this guest, this special guest, whoever he was.

I lurked about through dinner; they took their damn time, all of them, and then there was coffee and dessert, which Diana liked to serve in the living room. I ran around to that window and again saw his back. He was a well-tailored fellow with a good head of salt-and-pepper hair. He was not particularly tall but sturdy, strong-looking. It was no one I knew, not anyone from my firm, not one of our friends come to hit on Diana. Was it someone she had met? I was determined to keep watch and to satisfy myself that he did not stay past dinner. But surely that was not in the cards, not with the twins in the house. Nevertheless, I lingered at the window, even though the night was cold and getting colder. And then he did leave; they were handing him his coat and I turned and ran around the back of the house and took a position at the corner, where I could see the driveway. I was looking at the front of his car, and when he got in and the cabin of the car lit up, I had a clear view of his face, and it was my former best friend, Dirk Morrison, the man from whom I had stolen Diana, a lifetime ago.

THE NEXT DAYS were busy ones. I washed as best I could with melted snow and dried myself with one of Dr. Sondervan's towels, a gift from Herbert and Emily. I took my wallet out of the top drawer of the old broken-down bureau. In it was all the cash I had come home with that night of the raccoon, my credit cards, Social Security card, driver's license. I dug around for my checkbook, house and car keys—all the impedimenta of citizenry. I then contrived to get myself to town, cutting through the Sondervan backyard to the next block and thence to the business district.

My first stop was the Goodwill store, where I replaced my tattered rags with a clean and minimally decent brown suit, unironed shirt, overcoat, wool socks, and a pair of brogues that were no better fitting than my wingtips but more appropriate to the season. The ladies at the Goodwill were shocked when I walked in, but my courteous demeanor and the clear effort I was making to better myself left them smiling approvingly as I left. And don't forget to get yourself a nice haircut, dear, one of them said.

That was exactly my intention. I walked into a unisex place on the theory that my shoulder-length hair would not alarm them as it would a traditional old-time barber. Still, there was resistance— Can't come in here without an appointment, the hairdresser-in-chief sniffed—at which point I laid two crisp hundred-dollar bills on the cashier's table and an empty chair materialized. A layered cut and not too short, I said.

I watched in the big mirror as, snip by snip, I traveled back in time. With each falling hank of hair, more and more of the disastrous lineaments of my previous self emerged, until, big naked ears and all, staring back at me was the missing link to Howard Wakefield. Yet a shave was still required for the transmogrification, and this took another fifty dollars, shaves not being in the repertoire of this crew of artistes. Somehow they came up with shears and a straight razor and several of the staff gathered around to agree on a strategy. I didn't want to see. I lay back in the chair and prepared to have my throat cut. I didn't care. I was disappointed in myself and how easily I was acclimating to the old life. It was as if I had never left.

Finally, I was sat up to see the result, and it was me, all right, looking pale and somewhat skinnier, the eyes perhaps too importunate, a new loose fold of flesh under the chin, Howard Wakefield redux, a man of the system.

That was enough for one day.

That night, in my unaccustomed togs, I slipped around to the house to see if anything special was going on. Another visitor, perhaps, a justice of the peace to accompany Dirk Morrison? But all was quiet. No strange cars in the driveway, and my wife at her dressing table, not quite naked in her negligible concession to winter. She had something on the stereo, her favorite composer, Schubert, whom she had touted to me when we were dating. It was one of the Impromptus, played by Dinu Lipatti, and it brought back the old days, before such music was no longer ours. I felt as if an artery had been opened, and ran back to my attic.

The next morning, the garage doors opened beneath me and I watched as Diana, with the girls in tow, backed the SUV down the driveway. Of course. Christmas shopping. They would head for the mall. They would lunch there as well. I waited a few minutes, took out my car keys, went downstairs, and turned on the engine of my BMW. It started right up.

I had heard about Dirk over the years that he had made himself a fortune. And why not, as he was a hedge-fund manager who was quoted on the business pages.

Remarkable how I still knew how to drive, and how I remembered all the shortcuts to the highway to New York. An hour later, the city rose up before my eyes, and in a moment, it seemed, I was in it, in all the noisy raucous chaos of souls flowing through the city's canyons, each of them with an imperial intention. They were underground, too, rumbling along in the subways. They were stacked above my head, too, forty, fifty stories of them. It was stunning. I was in shock and barely able to negotiate the entrance to a garage.

Had I actually worked in this city most of my adult life? Would I have to again?

My Madison Avenue haberdashery was still where it had always been and my man was there standing in the suit department as if he'd been waiting for me. I had had myself barbered and had clothed myself in a reasonably presentable outfit at the Goodwill before coming here, just so that I could get through the door. He looked at me and shook his head. He beckoned. Come with me, he said.

And that is how that evening, after parking the BMW in front of the next house, and taking the trouble to reclaim my litigation bag from the attic, I stood at my front door in my black cashmere coat and pin-striped suit with a Turnbull & Asser spread-collar shirt and a sober Armani silk tie, American-flag suspenders, and Cole Haan black English calfskin shoes, and I turned the key in the lock.

Every light in the house was on. I could hear them in the dining room; they were decorating the Christmas tree.

Hello? I shouted. I'm home!

EDGEMONT DRIVE

—

WHAT KIND OF CAR WAS IT?

I don't know. An old car. What difference does it make?

A man sits in his car three days running in front of the house, you should be able to describe it.

An American car.

There you go.

A squarish car with a long hood. Long and floaty-looking.

A Ford?

Maybe.

Well, definitely not a Cadillac.

No. It looked tinny. An old car. Faded red. There were big round rust spots on the fender and the door. And it was filled with his things. It looked like everything he owned was in there with him.

Well, what do you want me to do? You want me to stay home from work?

No. It's nothing.

If it's nothing, why did you bring it up?

I shouldn't have.

Did he look at you?

Please.

Did he?

When I turned around, he started the engine and drove off.

What do you mean? So before you turned around—

I felt his eyes. I was weeding.

You were bending over?

Here we go again.

You know this creep pulls up in front of our house every morning and you go out to the garden and bend over?

Okay, end of conversation. I have things to do.

Maybe I can park at the curb and watch you weeding. The two of us. That's something, anyway. Seeing you in your shorts bending over.

I can't ever talk to you about anything.

It was a Ford Falcon. You said it was squared off, hard edges, a flattened look. A Falcon. They built them in the sixties. Three-speed manual shift on the column. Only ninety horses.

Okay, that's wonderful. You know all about cars.

Listen, Miss Garden Lady, to know a man's car is to know him. It is not useless knowledge.

Fine.

Guy is some immigrant up from Tijuana.

What are you talking about?

Who else would drive a forty-year-old heap? Looking for work. Looking for something he can steal. Looking for something from the lady with the white legs who bends over in her garden.

You're out of your mind. You've got this know-it-all attitude—

I'll take the morning off tomorrow.

Immigrants don't have long gray hair and roll the window down so I can see his pink face and pale eyes.

Oh, ho! Now we're getting somewhere.

YOU DON'T MOVE OUT of here I'm writing down your license plate. The cops will I.D. you and see if it's someone they know . . .

You're calling the police?

Yes.

Why?

Why not, if you don't move? Go park somewhere else. I'm giving you a break.

What is my offense?

Don't play dumb. In the first place, I don't like some junk heap in front of my house.

I'm sorry. It's the only car I have.

Right, I can see that no one would drive this thing if he didn't have to. And all this bag and baggage. You sell things out of the trunk?

No. These are my things. I wouldn't want to let anything go.

Because nobody in this neighborhood needs anything from the back of a car.

Well, I'm sorry we've gotten off to the wrong start.

Yes, we have. I'm not too friendly when some pervert decides to stalk my wife.

Oh, I'm afraid you're under a misconception.

Am I?

Yes. I didn't want to disturb anyone, but I should have realized that parking in front of your house would attract notice.

You got that right.

If I'm stalking anything, it's the house.

What?

I used to live here. For three days, I've been trying to work up the courage to knock on your door and introduce myself.

AH, I SEE THE KITCHEN is quite different. Everything built-in and tucked away. Our sink was freestanding, white porcelain with piano legs. Over here was a cabinet where my mother kept the staples. A shelf swung out with a canister for sifting flour. That impressed me.

I'd probably have kept it. This is their renovation—the people who lived here before us. I have my own ideas for changing things around.

You must have bought the house from the people I sold it to. You've been here how long?

Let's see. I count by the children's ages. We moved in just after my eldest was born. That would be twelve years.

And how many children have you?

Three. All boys. I've sometimes wished for a daughter.

They're all in school?

Yes.

I have a daughter. An adult daughter.

Would you like some tea?

Yes, thank you. Very kind of you. Women are more gently disposed, as a rule. I hope your husband won't be too put out.

Not at all.

To speak truly, it's unsettling to be here. It's something like double vision. The neighborhood is much as it was. But the trees are older and taller. The homes—well, they're still here, mostly, though they don't have the proud, well-to-do look they once had.

It's a settled neighborhood.

Yes. But you know? Time is heartbreaking.

Yes.

My parents divorced when I was a boy. I lived with my mother. She would die in the master bedroom.

Oh.

I'm sorry, I sometimes speak tactlessly. After Mother died, I married and brought my wife here to live. I've never stayed anywhere else for any length of time. And certainly never owned property again. So this is the house—please don't misunderstand me—this is the house I've continued to live in. I mean mentally. I ranged all through these rooms from childhood on. Until they reflected who I was, as a mirror would. I don't mean merely that its furnishings displayed our family's personality, our tastes. I don't mean that. It was as if the walls, the stairs, the rooms, the dimensions, the layout were as much me as I was. Is this coherent? Wherever I looked, I saw me. I saw me in some way measured out. Do you experience that?

I'm not sure. Your wife—

Oh, that didn't last long. She resented the suburbs. She felt cut off from everything. I'd go off to work and she'd be left here. We hadn't many friends in the neighborhood.

Yes, people here stick to themselves. The boys have school friends, but we hardly know anyone.

This tea helps. Because this is a dizzying experience for me. It's as if I were squared off, dimensionalized in these rooms, as if I were the space contained by these walls, the passageways, the fixed routes of going to and fro, from one room to another, and everything lit predictably by the times of day and the different seasons. It is all and indistinguishably . . . me.

I think if you live in one place long enough—

When people speak of a haunted house, they mean ghosts flitting about in it, but that's not it at all. When a house is haunted—what I'm trying to explain—it is the feeling you get that it looks like you, that your soul has become architecture, and the house in all its materials has taken you over with a power akin to haunting. As if you, in fact, are the ghost. And as I look at you, a kind, lovely young woman, part of me says not that I don't belong here, which is the truth, but that you don't belong here. I'm sorry, that's quite a terrible thing to say. It merely means—

It means life is heartbreaking.

—

HE CAME BACK? He was here again?

Yes. It seemed so sad, his just sitting out there, so I invited him in.

You what!

I mean, it wasn't what you thought, was it? So why not?

Right. Why wouldn't you invite him in, since I told him if he came around again I'd call the cops?

You should have invited him in yourself when he told you he'd lived in this house.

Why is that a credential? Everyone has lived somewhere or other. Would you want to relive your glorious past? I shouldn't think so. And this is not the first time.

Don't start in, please.

Husband says white, wife says black. The way it works. So the world will know what she thinks of her husband.

Why is it always about you! We're not the same person. I have my own mind.

Do you, now!

Hey, you guys, we got an argument brewing?

Close your door, son. This doesn't concern you.

Every time another man comes into this house you go berserk. A plumber, someone to measure for the window blinds, the man who reads the gas meter.

Ah, but is your man a man? Awfully fruity-looking to me. Wears his white hair in a ponytail. And those tiny little hands. What does the well-known fag-hag have to say?

He's a PhD and a poet.

Jesus, I should have known.

He gave up his teaching job to travel the country. His book is on the dining-room table. He signed it for us.

A wandering minstrel in his Ford Falcon.

Why are you so horrible!

ARGUING IS INSTEAD OF SEX.

It has been a while.

This is better.

Yes.

I don't know why I get so upset.

You're just a normally defective man.

So we're all like this? Thank you.

Yes. It's an imperfect gender.

I'm sorry I said what I said.

I'm thinking now, with all three of them in school all day, I should get a job.

Doing what?

Or maybe go for a graduate degree of some kind. Make myself useful.

What brings this on?

Times change. They need me less and less. They have their friends, their practices. I carpool. They come home and stay in their rooms with their games. You work late. I'm alone in this house a lot.

We should go to the theater more. A night in town. Or you like opera. I'll do opera as long as it isn't Richard fucking Wagner.

That's not what I'm saying.

You chose the suburbs, you know. I work to pay off the mortgage. The three tuitions. The two car payments.

I'm not blaming you. Could we turn on the light a moment?

What's the matter?

There's no moon. In the dark, it feels like a tomb.

—

THIS IS VERY EMBARRASSING.

What were you doing there at three in the morning?

Sleeping. That's all. I wasn't bothering anyone.

Yeah, well, the cops are touchy these days. People sleeping in their cars.

It used to be a ball field. I played softball there as a boy.

Well, it's the mall now.

You don't mind that I gave them your name?

Not at all. I like being known as a criminal associate. Why didn't you just check into the local Marriott?

I was trying to save money. The weather is clement. I thought, Why not?

Clement. Yes, it's definitely clement.

Is it the habit of the police to go around impounding cars? Because if they think I'm a drug dealer, or something like that, they will find only books, my computer, luggage, clothes, and camping gear and a few private mementos that mean something only to me. Very unsettling, strangers digging around in my things. If I'd stayed at a hotel, I'd be on my way right now. I'm really sorry to impose on you.

Well, what's a neighbor for.

That's funny. I appreciate humor in this situation.

I'm glad.

But we'd be neighbors only if time had imploded. Actually, if time were to implode we'd be more than neighbors. We'd be living together, the past and the present moving through each other's space.

Like in a rooming house.

If you wish, yes. As in a sort of rooming house.

—

SO HE'S THERE. What—hitting on your wife?

No, that won't happen. It's not what he's about. I'm pretty sure.

So what's the problem?

He comes on like some prissy fusspot poet, doesn't have it together, drives a junk heap, claims to have quit his teaching job but was probably fired. And, with all of that, you know he's a player.

Yeah, I know people like that.

His difficulties work in his favor. He gets what he wants.

So what does he want from you?

I'm not sure. It's weird. The house? Like I've defaulted on the mortgage and he's the banker come to repossess.

So why'd you bring him home? He could sit in a Starbucks while they went through his car.

Well, he called. And I hang up and there she is looking at me. And I'm suddenly into proving something to her. You see what's happening? I can no longer be me, which is to say to the guy, I don't know you. Who the fuck cares if you lived here or didn't live here? They'll give you back your damn car and you can leave. But no, he works it so that I have to prove something to my own wife—that I am capable of a charitable act.

I guess you are.

So, like, he's now some new relative of ours. This touches on the basic fault line in our marriage. She's naïve in principle—she forgives everybody everything. Always excusing people, finding a rationale for the shitty things they do. A clerk shortchanges her, she imagines he's distracted and just made a mistake.

Well, that's a lovely quality.

I know, I know. Her philosophy is if you trust people they will be trustworthy. Drives me crazy.

So they'll give him back his car and he'll go.

No. Not if I know her. She'll drive him to pick it up. The day will have passed, and she'll ask him to stay for dinner. And then she'll insist that he shouldn't be allowed to drive off in the night. And I will look at her and sit there and agree. And she will show him to the guest room. I'll give you odds.

You're a bit overwrought. Have another.

Why the hell not?

WITH AGE, YOU SEE how much of it is invented. Not only what is invisible but what is everywhere visible.

I'm not sure I understand.

Well, you're still quite young.

Thank you. I wish I felt young.

I'm not talking about one's self-image. Or the way life can be too much of the same thing day in and day out. I'm not talking about mere unhappiness.

Am I merely unhappy?

I'm in no position to judge. But let's say melancholy seems to suit the lady.

Oh, dear—that it's that obvious.

But, in any case, whatever our state of mind life seems for most of our lives an intense occupation—keeping busy, competing intellectually, physically, nationally, seeking justice, demanding love, perfecting our institutions. All the fashions of survival. Everything we do to make history, the archive of our inventiveness. As if there were no context.

But there is?

Yes. Some vast—what to call it?—indifference that slowly creeps up on you with age, that becomes more insistent with age. That's what I'm trying to explain. I'm afraid I'm not doing a very good job.

No, really, this is interesting.

I get very voluble on even one glass of sherry.

More?

Thank you. But I'm trying to explain the estrangement that comes over one after some years. For some earlier, for others later, but always inevitably.

And to you, now?

Yes. It's a kind of wearing out, I suppose. As if life had become threadbare, with the light peeking through. The estrangement begins in moments, in little sharp judgments that you instantly put out of your mind. You draw back, though you're fascinated. Because it's the truest feeling a person can have, and so it comes again and again, drifting through your defenses, and finally settles over you like some cold, very cold, light. Maybe I should stop talking about this. It is almost to deny it, talking about it.

No, I appreciate your candor. Does this have something to do with why you've come back here—to see where you used to live?

You're perceptive.

This estrangement is maybe your word for depression.

I understand why you would say that. You see me as the image of some colossal failure—living on the road in a beaten-up car, an obscure poet, a third-rate academic. And maybe I am all those things, but I'm not depressed. This isn't a clinical issue I speak of. It's a clear recognition of reality. Let me explain it this way: it's much like I suppose what a chronic invalid feels, or someone on the verge of dying, where the estrangement is protective, a way of abating the sense of loss, the regret, and the desire to live is no longer important. But subtract those circumstances and there I am, healthy, self-sufficient, maybe not the most impressive fellow in the world but one who's managed to take care of himself quite well and live in freedom doing what he wants to do and without any major regrets. Yet the estrangement is there, the truth has settled upon him, and he feels actually liberated because he's outside now, in the context, where you can't believe in life anymore.

WHY WOULD ANYONE come to New Jersey to die?

Sir?

And the house is nothing special, you'll grant me that. The usual Colonial with white vinyl siding, a one-car garage, the gutters packed with the crap of I don't know how many autumns. Actually, I've been meaning to get to that.

Sir, please. We ask and you answer and we leave. Can you tell us anything more about the deceased?

Well, you see, I knew him mostly as a corpse in the hallway. Ah, you are skeptical. And why not, with my wife weeping away like he was a close relation?

So you're saying—

Hard to believe, isn't it? Not even an old boyfriend of hers, not even that.

You have no heart.

No, it's an interesting experience, a total stranger falling dead in his underwear on the way to the bathroom. And to see him carried out the door in a body bag! Wouldn't miss it for the world. Good for the kids, too, a life experience before going off to school. Their first suicide.

Sir, the man died of an acute myocardial infarction.

Says who?

The EMTs examined him.

Well, they're entitled to their opinion.

It's more than an opinion, sir. They see things like this every day. They didn't even try to resuscitate.

No, he took himself out, for sure, wily fellow that he was. That's why he came here—it was all planned.

Why are you being like this? He came here, it was like—

Like what?

A pilgrimage.

Oh, right. He came here to fuck up our lives is why he came here. Came here like a dog to lift his leg and mark his territory. And where does that leave us? Living in a dead man's house. I thought my home was my castle.

I didn't think you had such homebound loyalties.

Well, folks, we'll be leaving now.

I didn't! Somewhere to stash the wife and kids is as far as it went with me. But, by God, I paid for it with my labor. I've done everything I was supposed to do. Gave you a house, a safe if dull neighborhood, three children, a reasonably comfortable life. To make you happy! And have you ever been? What but your dissatisfactions could have led you to invite this walking death wish into your home!

Well, folks, as I said, we'll be leaving now. We may have some more questions after we sort things out.

And what are you going to do about his damn Ford Falcon sitting in my driveway?

We've gone through the car. We've inventoried the contents. Got his I.D. Closest relative.

He said he had a daughter.

Yes, ma'am, we have that.

But the car!

We have no more interest in the car. It becomes part of the deceased's estate. The daughter will decide its disposition. In the meantime, I will ask you to leave it where it is. Safer here than downtown. Keys are in the ignition.

Jesus!

Sir, there are procedures for situations like this. We are following the procedures. The cause of death will be confirmed by the medical examiner, the death certificate filed with the town clerk's office, the body placed in the morgue, pending instructions from the closest relative. That will be the daughter.

Officer, I will want to write her.

Soon as we make contact, ma'am. I see no reason why you can't. We'll be in touch.

Thank you.

And, hey, Officer?

Sir?

Tell her the good news. Daddy has come home.

SO, FINALLY, I AGREE WITH YOU.

Yes?

We can't live here anymore. I pass through the hallway and sidle along the wall as if he were there on the floor, staring. It's eerie. I feel dispossessed. I'm a displaced person.

Not the best time to be selling, babe. And what about the kids' school? Right in the middle of the term.

You're the one who said we couldn't ever get this out of our mind.

I know, I know.

The boys won't come upstairs. The playroom's their dormitory. And it's damp down there.

All right. Okay. Maybe we should think about renting something. Maybe a sublet somewhere till we get squared away. We'll see. You want another?

A half.

I am really sorry. I don't blame you. I speak in the heat of the moment.

No, I suppose I should have known. The way he talked. But it was interesting. His ideas—how unusual to hear philosophical conversation. That someone would reveal himself to that extent. So though I thought he was a depressed person, I was fascinated by the novelty that someone could be talking that way as if it were the most natural thing.

You know, it's really funny . . .

What?

She's just like him, the daughter. A gamer.

Yes, I did think it odd.

I would not call that a close relationship, would you?

Hardly.

Couldn't care less. You know, I found—when Goodwill took away all his stuff—I found that the actual naked car inside was clean. Upholstery's okay. And I looked under the hood. Needs an oil change, and the fan belt looks a bit ragged. Took it around the block and it bounces a bit on the road. Maybe new shocks.

You like that car, don't you?

Well, with a good paint job, maybe some detailing . . . You know, people collect these things, Ford Falcons.

It was his home.

No, dear one. This is his home. That's just a car.

Our car.

Appears to be. We ought to frame her letter. Or bury it in the yard along with the can of ashes.

Oh, but she meant for them to be strewn.

Strewn? Did you say strewn?

Scattered?

Why not sprinkled?

Sown.

Okay, sown. I'll go with sown.

ASSIMILATION

—

W HERE RAMON WORKED WASHING DISHES, THE OWNER CALLED him in one day and said that he was raising him to busboy. Ramon would wear the short red jacket and black trousers. Ramon's hands were cracked and peeling from the hot water, but he was wary of the promotion because the owner was selling it to him like there was a catch. They were all foreigners—the owner, the owner's wife, and the people who came there to eat. Big people with loud voices and bad manners. You are in the waiting pool now, my friend, and on a good night your share could be thirty, forty dollars, under the table.

ON SUNDAY MORNING, Ramon took the bus upstate to see Leon. They talked through the phones. I don't know why he wants to see my certificate, Ramon said.

What certificate?

Of my birth.

He wants to make sure you're an American, Leon said.

So I can?

Why not? Figure they're illegals—maybe not the owner, because he has a business that requires a license—but a lot of them. Born here is a commodity, it has a value, so see what the deal is.

—

WHEN RAMON PRESENTED his birth certificate, they sat down with him in the back after the restaurant was closed for the night—Borislav, the owner, his wife, she of the squinting eyes, and another man, who was fat, like Borislav, but older and with a brief-case in his lap. He was the one who asked the questions. After Ramon gave his answers, they talked among themselves. He heard harsh mouthfuls of words with deep notes—it was not a mellifluous language like the bright bubbling of water over rocks of his language.

And then, with a flourish, the owner placed on the table a photograph. Look, my friend, he said. The photograph was of a girl, a blonde with sunglasses propped in her hair. Her hand gripping the strap of her shoulder bag was closed like a fist. She wore jeans. She wore a blouse revealing the shoulders. Behind her was a narrow street with an array of motorcycles and mopeds parked front wheels to the curb. She was half sitting sideways on a motorcycle seat, her legs straight out and her feet in their sandals planted on the paving stones. She was smiling.

HOW MUCH? LEON SAID.

A thousand. Plus air and hotel expenses.

They are messing with you. This is good for three thousand, minimum.

And then?

Why not? It will pay for filmmaker's school. Isn't that what you want?

I don't know. It's selling yourself. And it's a defilement of sacred matters.

You still have it for Edita?

No, *eso es cuento viejo.*

Then what's the problem? You sell yourself washing dishes, little bro. This is the country of selling yourself. And what sacred matter do you mean, which this scam bears no resemblance to, if you think about it?

WHEN THE PLANE LANDED, Ramon crossed himself. He took the bus to the city. It was already late afternoon and the city was under the heavy dark clouds he had flown through. Packs of motorcycles and mopeds kept pace with the bus and then shot past. Linked streetcars ground around corners and disappeared as if swallowed. It was an old European city of unlighted streets and stone buildings with shuttered windows.

He had the address of the tourist hotel on a piece of paper. There was just time to change into the suit and they were calling from downstairs.

The girl from the picture gave him a quick glance of appraisal and nodded. No smile this time. And her hair was different—pulled tight and bound at the neck. She was dressed for the occasion in a white suit jacket with a matching short skirt and white shoes with heels that made her taller than Ramon. She seemed fearful. A bearded heavyset fellow held her elbow.

They all rode in a taxi to a photographer's studio. The photographer stood Ramon and the girl in an alcove with potted palms on either side of them and a plastic stained-glass window lit from behind by a floodlamp. They faced a lectern. When Ramon's shoulder accidentally brushed hers, the girl jumped as if from an electric shock.

Some sort of city functionary married them. He mumbled and his eyes widened as if he were having trouble focusing. He was drunk. When the photographer's flash went off behind him he lost his place in his book and had to start again. He swayed, and nearly knocked over the lectern. He clearly didn't understand the situation because when he pronounced them man and wife he urged them to kiss. The girl laughed as she turned away and ran to the heavyset fellow and kissed him.

The photographer placed a bouquet of flowers in the girl's arms and posed her with Ramon for the formal wedding picture. And that was that. Ramon was dropped off at the hotel and the next day he flew home.

HE LEARNED THE GIRL'S name when the lawyer with the briefcase put in front of him the petition to bring her to the States: Jelena. It attests that she is your lawful spouse and you are in hardship without her presence beside you, the lawyer said.

Jelena, Ramon said, to hear the sound of it. He had not heard it properly, as uttered by the drunken fool who married them. Jelena.

Yes. This is all here, everything, marriage certificate, copy of birth certificate, passport, and here is the wedding picture. It couldn't hurt for you and bride to smile but okay.

The lawyer slapped a pen down on the table. The John Hancock, he said.

Ramon folded his arms across his chest. The figure was three thousand, he said. I have seen only one thousand.

Don't worry, that is to come.

Ramon nodded. Okay, when it comes, then I will sign.

The lawyer pressed his hand to his forehead. Borislav, he called to the owner. Borislav!

And then for an hour the owner and the lawyer threatened and appealed and threatened again. The owner's wife came over. She said to Ramon, Who are you to have three thousands of dollars!

She turned to her husband. I told you he was no good, the mestizo, I warned you.

Borislav raised his hand. Please, Anya, he said, you are not helping.

Ramon, he said. This is family, the daughter of my late uncle. I have entrusted you. We are trying to give her a life here where there is hope. Jelena is to pay you the remainder from her wages.

You did not tell me that when I agreed, Ramon said.

I promise you. She will work beside you as a waitress. And I am raising you to full-time waiter. You hear me? Wages and tips, wages and tips, equal to all the staff. You will see, so do this.

And while Ramon sat thinking the lawyer said to him, This is a fraud which you have committed, you know that? There is a law— to marry only so that the girl can have a legal residency is to break that law. She is over there, so they cannot touch her. But you! I have just to call them. You know what you get for bringing some- one here by pretending love? Five years, my friend. Five years and monetary penalties of an amount you cannot dream. And all I have to do is tell them.

So tell them, Ramon said. And I will tell them that you wrote the letter for me to sign. And I will tell them that Jelena is of the family of Borislav, the man who employs me. So let's all tell them.

You are not to call me Borislav, the owner muttered. That is for friends and family, not for one who works for my wages.

I CHECKED IT OUT, Leon said through the glass. It's bullshit. The C.I.S. can't keep up with the traffic. The risk is small, Ramon. If they do call you in, you say you love the girl. They know you're lying—but she will back you up, naturally, since it is in her inter- est. But just to have some insurance you should learn a few things about her.

What things?

You know, she watches what TV shows, if she has a birthmark, where it is located. Things.

She brought her boyfriend to the wedding, Ramon said.

Of course.

I didn't like that. It was unnecessary.

In two years, once she has her green card without conditions, she will divorce you and bring him here in turn. And they will marry and be Americans.

Maybe. Maybe the lovers will not be able to wait that long. He will come for a visit and I will kill him.

Yes, of course, Leon said smiling. Listen, Ramon, she is just a dumb Hunky. No class, from the sound of it.

She is still my wife, Ramon said.

I say split the difference with them. Sign the paper and you're good for two years. You wait tables and make some decent money. She gets the card with no strings, and you go on to be a famous movie director.

HE DID KNOW a thing about her, that she had English as a school-girl because she spoke it well enough. And that she wore a navel ring, a silver bar with three teardrop crystals hanging from it. But, of course, everyone knew about her navel because Jelena made sure that they did. She was the one waitress at Borislav's and so her red jacket was cut for the female figure and between it and the short black skirt a flat band of flesh was visible, the teardrops dangling from her navel and sometimes catching the light as she walked with the tray held high and balanced on her palm.

Of course the patrons ogled her and the regulars asked for her tables, but that was all right—her tips went into the pool.

Ramon himself had picked up the waiter's craft quite easily, after all his time busing, and he discovered that his formality and careful, quiet demeanor and efficient service had the effect sometimes of raising the manners and lowering the voices of the boors he served.

Jelena smoked. She would take a drag in the kitchen and leave the cigarette burning in a dish as she went out through the doors, and it would be there smoldering until she came back in for another order and another hit.

She did not match the photograph of the smiling blonde with the sunglasses in her hair. She was, instead, an ordinary working girl with a life of serious plans and no time to pose for a picture, with her long legs in the sun and a European city behind her.

He wanted to learn everything about her, maybe for insurance as Leon advised, but more because he felt he had rights as her legal husband. It was Jelena's habit, when she had a moment, to step into the alley to use her cell phone. He saw her cast in a red glow from Borislav's electric sign. He listened at the slightly opened door, hearing her voice despite the kitchen shouts and the clatter rushing past his ears. She spoke loudly as if to cover the great distance to her boyfriend in Europe. Of course it was her boyfriend, that heavy fellow with the sloping shoulders who had been at the wedding. Who else in Europe would she be calling at night? With the time difference, she had to have awakened him, or maybe he had not yet been to sleep. Perhaps she was making sure that he was not with someone else, because sometimes she seemed about to cry—this could be inferred from the tone of voice, never mind the language.

Jelena lived in Borislav's house, a few blocks from the restaurant. I'll walk you home, Ramon would say at the end of a night's work. Good night, Ramon, Jelena would say, but made no further effort to stop him as he walked beside her. On these occasions, he would ask her about her family, if her parents were alive, what her father did, did she have brothers and sisters, where she went to school. She would not answer.

It is not wise for you to keep things from your husband, Jelena.

Ramon, you are a pestilence, you know that?

Not a pestilence, Jelena, you mean a pest. Nevertheless, the time may come in front of the authorities when I need to know these things, for your sake, not for mine.

And when that time is here I will tell you.

He would wait in the street while she climbed the steps and entered the house and wait some more until the light went on in her room on the top floor. Then he would continue on to his own room, several blocks away. He thought in the moonlight of the things he knew about her: the jewelled navel, the thin face and high cheekbones, the gray eyes that slanted upward at the corners, and her long stride for a girl.

IN THE FALL, Leon was sprung and called Ramon to invite him to a party. It was to be on a Monday night. Borislav's was closed on Mondays, so Ramon could go. He insisted that Jelena go with him. She needs to know about me, he said to Borislav, just as I need to know about her. She will meet my family and have some idea in the event that we are ever questioned by the authorities. Borislav nodded and informed Jelena. She was furious. Don't talk to me of government, Uncle! Why did I come here and risk losing everything if not to have an end to government in my life?

What is the everything you risk losing? Ramon said.

Oh, shut up, you—going to Borislav like a child.

When Monday came, Ramon picked her up in a car supplied by Leon. She was clearly taken aback by this luxury—a town car with a driver in a black suit—but she pretended to be unimpressed, just as he'd expected she would. It was a warm night and she wore her white jacket from the wedding, but with pale olive slacks and a flower-patterned blouse, with an Orthodox cross hanging in her cleavage. Ramon supposed that the cross and the pendant on her navel were in a direct line. She saw him looking and grabbed his tie and pulled him toward her. Listen, Mister Ramon pest, you can wrap Borislav around your finger, but I know what is in that mind of yours and I'm telling you it will never happen, you understand? Never! Is that clear to you, my husband? Never! And she let go and sat back in the car.

Ramon adjusted his tie. He said, I don't like you, either, Jelena, but if you required me to perform the conjugal duties of a husband I would comply, if only to honor our sacred bond.

THE PARTY WAS in Leon's loft and it was filled with glamorous people, sinuous and of high fashion, all of them dancing intensely. A DJ was running the show. Music throbbed up from the floor and colored lights rotated slowly over the dancers, as if examining them. Jelena shook her head and he got her to say something. She said that the lights reminded her of her childhood, when search-lights had moved over the rooftops at night.

Ramon found a place for them among glass tables for two in a far corner of the loft, where on wheeled carts food was set out for the taking: platters of shrimp, sushi, slices of roast beef, a sculpted pyramid of caviar on a salver with points of toast, diced onion, sour cream, capers, and lemon in attendance.

Jelena's eyes widened. She sipped her Coca-Cola. She moved her chair closer to Ramon's. Let me ask you something that I don't understand, she said. This is your brother, a very rich man, I guess, to have all this. I see his place with its paintings and big windows overlooking the river and all his friends of every color, who are what is called beautiful people, yes? But Ramon the brother waits tables in Brooklyn. How is this explained?

Ramon said, I love my brother, but I do not share his life's values.

Saying this, he looked over the crowd and recognized several of Leon's men.

Two had been at the door as he came in. For a moment, he'd seen a question in their eyes, perhaps because of Jelena, but a moment later Leon was there and the brothers hugged and Ramon said, Leon, this is my wife, Jelena.

Leon saw them now and came over. Why aren't you dancing? he said to Ramon.

She chooses not to.

Come, Leon said, and without giving Jelena a choice in the matter he took her by the hand and led her to the dance floor.

Ramon watched them, Leon flushed with exuberance, with freedom, a graceful dancer with creative moves, and Jelena clearly feeling out of her element, seeing around her the young women in all the fashions of planned carelessness and comparing herself badly, a provincial, maybe smart enough in the cafés of eastern Europe, and a star at Borislav's, but here a poor relative. Ramon felt sorry for her.

Leon had kept himself fit in prison. His short-sleeved jersey showed his biceps. His head was shaved and he wore stylish black-rimmed glasses. He was elegant and had a self-assurance that Ramon could imitate only in moments of conscious effort.

When the party went into its loose-limbed, heedless phase, loud with stoned laughter and drunken appreciations, the music pulsing through the acrid atmosphere, Ramon decided that it was time to leave.

Jelena was already out the door when Leon said, Ramon, if you want to, my sense is that it is possible.

Why?

She told me that you never smile.

So how does that mean anything?

It means that she observes you. I told her that she should give you something to smile about.

That is very unlikely.

I told her how smart you are, how you could read at the age of four.

Oh, sure, that will certainly help. She is indebted to me for a thousand dollars. I haven't seen any of it.

Leon laughed and gave Ramon a big hug. Ah, my brother, maybe you are not so smart after all.

AFTER THE NIGHT AT LEON'S, Borislav's restaurant with its dark furniture and thick carpets and red velvet drapes and amateur paintings seemed to Ramon unforgivably tacky. Yet working the same room with Jelena, doing the same thing at the same time, gave him a feeling of being home. And now he regretted bragging to her about what an independent person he was, with his un-compromising values. The truth was that Leon had seen him through four years at City College. And neither did this life he had drifted into have anything to do with values. He had felt rest-less, with only a vague ambition to make films, and gripped with a kind of wanderlust, though he had not wandered farther than Brooklyn. He'd gotten off the El one day when the sun shone in the window. It seemed to him a different light here than you had in Manhattan. He walked around and found sand in the streets and here and there a trace of a trolley track in the worn-out concrete. By and by, he came to the beachfront. The air was fresh, gulls rode the breezes, and Ramon felt unaccustomedly at peace in the wind-buffered sun with the blue seawater in his eyes. This feeling stayed with him as he wandered back into a local business district and saw the sign in Borislav's window: DISHWASH IS WANTED. He liked that locution, suggestive of a foreign tongue, and so he walked in and become a dishwash, only to rise to busboy, waiter, and married man.

THEN CAME THE NIGHT that Borislav closed the restaurant to the public. Tables were pushed together, new linen was laid out, as well as cut-crystal glasses that Ramon had not seen before. A strange man arrived and strode into the kitchen. Jelena looked at Ramon in surprise, though Borislav, as well as his shrew of a wife, in a fancy dress and with her face made up, were clearly expecting this. He is the chef of this evening, Mrs. Borislav said. Ramon saw the chef's imperious glance as he looked over the kitchen and the help, including the cooks. The chef shook his head in disapproval, then turned to Borislav and began giving orders.

The dinner party for which the entire restaurant had been reserved turned out to have just fourteen guests, all men. Apparently they liked a quiet room. Borislav had excused the staff for the evening, except for Ramon and Jelena. When Ramon began his service, with bottles of sparkling water, conversation stopped and a man at the head of the table looked at him. Ramon felt Borislav's hand on his shoulder and heard his somewhat deferential voice saying, in its mouthful language, that the boy was okay because he was just a mestizo who didn't understand a word—which Ramon, of course, understood, because the look he'd got from the head man and the jovially responsive voice of Borislav provided all the understanding necessary.

In the kitchen, Jelena was nervous. Before the guests had arrived she'd gone to the alley with her cell phone and a man standing there had told her to go back inside.

Ramon, you know what they are? she whispered. Do you realize?

She held out her hands and they were shaking. Ramon fingered her wedding ring. When had she got it? He couldn't keep from smiling.

You've been cleared for the evening, Jelena. You are family. Just don't look at them. Keep your eyes down and be your efficient self and everything will be all right.

How do you know to be so calm? Jelena said.

I am familiar with the species.

WHEN THE DINNER of the fourteen was over and the limos had driven off and the doors were closed for the night, Borislav and his wife poured themselves glasses of blackberry brandy and sat down in the back. A while later, the old lawyer was admitted and the three of them chatted softly, as if Ramon might overhear them. Jelena had gone home and Ramon was about to leave when Borislav called him to the table.

You did well, Ramon.

Thank you.

Sit, sit. The counsellor wants to speak with you.

The lawyer said, April fifteenth, as you know, is for paying taxes. As I suspect, your income is the poverty level?

Even counting tips, Ramon said.

You see how ungrateful? Mrs. Borislav said.

The lawyer continued, We assume the Immigration does not want Jelena, your wife, to be a ward of the state—this is their main concern for the green card, and so we are signing on Borislav, who is a man of substance, to be a co-sponsor of her.

Borislav nodded in solemn acknowledgment of his substance.

In that way, the Immigration is assured that Jelena does not apply for Welfare, though her husband is in the poverty class. And the arrangement is affirmed by Jelena living in the Borislav residence.

Okay with me, Ramon said, rising.

One moment. Since as marriage partners you are to file a joint tax return, you and Jelena together, for this is what married people do, we find it necessary that you live with Borislav as well, in his house, and therefore with the same address on the tax return.

Is it not my house also? Anya Borislav said to the lawyer.

Of course, the lawyer said. My apologies.

So let him be grateful to me as well. That we are giving the mestizo everything, including a roof over his head. But I tell you, she said to Ramon, this is not a hotel and I am not a maid. You understand? Your bed you will make yourself, your room you will clean, and your wash you will take to the Laundromat, and your food you will eat elsewhere.

Ramon ignored her. I have conditions, he said to the lawyer.

What conditions?

That the money I am owed is paid to me now.

Jelena has not been paying you? Borislav said.

No, nor have I asked her. She is my wife. Since we are married and filing a joint tax return it is not income if it is passed from one of us to the other. So I will need from you the money I'm owed before I consent to live in your house and suffer the insults of Mrs. Borislav.

At this the woman rose from the table and began to scream and curse in her native tongue. Spittle flew from her lips.

Borislav stood and tried to calm her but she pushed his arm away and screamed at him. Anya, he said, please, please. We know what we are doing!

It was that remark that Ramon remembered later. Borislav and the lawyer had agreed to pay him the money. But what was it, exactly, that they knew they were doing?

BORISLAV'S HOUSE WAS of red brick with a roof of green tile. It stood out in this neighborhood of small two-family homes on small lots. The inside reflected the same taste—probably Mrs. Borislav's—as the restaurant: heavy, dark furniture, thick rugs, lamps with tasselled shades, and toylike things on every surface—things of glass, things of silver, things of ceramic, dancing ladies in swirling skirts, horses pulling sleighs. Only when Ramon had climbed the stairs to the third floor did he find a window that was not heavily curtained. His room was across the hall from Jelena's. It was small with a narrow bed and a chest of drawers, but its window was covered only with a pull shade, and when that was rolled up the seaside morning light streamed in so that he awoke with the sun on his face.

In secret, of course, he was excited to be living so close to Jelena. When it came time to walk home after work, they had the same destination. He opened the door with her key and walked behind her up the stairs and said good night only when they stood at their doors. There was a bathroom, too, that they shared and so he got to know the products she used for her hair, her skin, her eyes. Her potions, creams, sprays, and soaps gave him a behind-the-scenes look at how she took care of herself. With respect, he always put the seat down. And so he felt in this illusion of their intimacy something more like the married state.

What puzzled him was her reaction to this closeness. He had expected her to object to having him as a housemate, and to be even angrier and more remote than before. But she was not. She was formal, perhaps, but no longer offhand in her treatment of him. She regarded him judiciously as he spoke to her. And when it became apparent that Mrs. Borislav regularly checked his room and went through the entire house to see if he had stolen anything, Jelena told him this would be unforgivable if the woman were sane. Anya Borislav, Jelena confided, is not a little crazy. I don't know how Borislav endures her.

One Monday morning, Jelena said, I'm going to the beach. Would you like to come with me? And so there he was applying sunblock to her thin back, while the gulls wheeled about and the little birds with stick legs went running along in the wet sand, just out of reach of the incoming tide. Jelena's bathing suit hardly deserved the name, some bits of cloth and a strap or two. Ramon did not own a suit. He'd removed his shirt and rolled up his trousers. There were very few bathers this workday morning, but the beach was embellished with the refuse of the weekend past—hunks of charred firewood, beer bottles, McDonald's wrappers, plastic bags, balls of aluminum foil, wet newspapers, and the occasional used condom. But they had found a reasonably clean spot where Ramon had only to dispose of a few pieces of broken glass and so here they were in the sun with the hushing waves rolling in and the gulls crying and Jelena's vertebrae easily countable as she bent forward and he rubbed the sunblock over her back.

Afterward, they sat side by side on their towels and watched the waves.

Ramon, would you like to hit me?

No. Of course not. Jelena, what a strange thing to say. Why?

I have been rude to you when you have done something only for my sake. I would deserve it.

No, I understand your mind, Jelena. Nothing is settled for you. You are new in another country. You are loosely attached. My mother, just before she died, told me that she had never really got used to the States, though she'd lived most of her life here. Of course, everyone is different, but it takes time to make yourself American.

Well, if not you then someone will have to hit me. Maybe Alexander. He knows to do it.

Who hits you? Alexander? Is that your boyfriend?

Yes. In a way of speaking. But it is best if you hit me, Ramon.

She turned to him, removed her sunglasses, and he saw that she was crying. Forgive me, she said, I am the worst of people. I don't know anymore what I am doing.

Ramon's heart beat faster. Is Alexander coming here?

He says. But he speaks through Borislav. I am of no importance. Oh, I am so wretched, she said. And she got up and walked to the surf and stood there as, even in his misgiving, he recorded her lovely figure, the long legs, the small, firm haunches, the huddled shoulders as she stood at the water's edge hugging herself.

LEON SAID, RAMON, you should talk to me first. You have made a mistake.

You know those people?

Of course. It is my business to know. When they came into his restaurant Borislav's stature should have risen in your estimation to the level of the totally untrustworthy.

I am in love with Jelena.

It can be felt as love when you want to fuck someone and can't.

We are man and wife. In my love for Jelena, I will fuck her.

You would have been better off still walking her to the door and leaving. Now you are in there with all of them and you are vulnerable.

What can they do?

They will speed things up. And you could be out on your ass with no job and a court appearance. And I am a busy man, Ramon.

I don't need this thing of my brother for our lawyers to divert themselves and the P.D. to smirk at.

I will not touch her.

They don't need you to. You're in the house, the husband, you're right there—what is it your movie people say—on location? You're on location, Ramon! It is a federal law—they made it to punish domestic violence against women. She gets hit and she gets the divorce right now, and the whole thing is done not in two years but in two weeks. And here is this Alexander flying in on her green card to be married.

She would have to bring charges against me. Jelena would not do that.

Oh, please, Ramon. What am I dealing with here? So they give her a couple of black eyes, a broken nose—you think she would like more of the same if she refused to bring charges?

None of this will happen, Leon. So, as I understand it, it's not for Jelena, the daughter of Borislav's late uncle, to make a better life for herself in America?

We're still looking into that. It may be no more than what it seems. There are other ways to have got him in, long before this. So if they've taken these pains, and it is not what it seems, we have something to learn. He hasn't been a faithful boyfriend, we know that. Listen, Ramon, in the meantime just get out of there. Leave your clothes like you're coming back. They'll wait. They need you around to make the strongest case. You've got your cash. Let them look for you if they want to set you up.

THEY TOOK THEIR LUNCH to have on the beach. But it began to rain—a misty rain with the combers rolling in, and everything was gray, the sky, the seawater, and there was no line at the horizon.

They sat on the boardwalk with their bags of sandwiches and

drinks on the bench between them. Jelena had pulled up the hood of her sweater. He could not see her face.

I love you, Jelena.

I know. You are reliable, Ramon. As a husband should be.

You're making fun.

No. I have come to respect you. I find myself thinking about you without meaning to. You are very odd.

I made a decision to love you when Borislav showed me your picture and sent me to marry you.

A decision.

Yes, this was an arranged marriage, and they are the best, when the decision is to love someone you don't know. Those have always been the most sacred, the marriages arranged before there is love and by other people.

The old way, from long ago, yes, and there is a good reason that it was given up.

Well, I know that my mother and father's marriage was arranged by their parents. The two young people sat there in embarrassment while their families negotiated. They had not met before. My mother told me that. And she and my father were together for forty years. And when he died she wept, how she wept. Neither my brother nor I could console her.

Well, Ramon, that may be, but you and I have not sat in embarrassment while our parents negotiated. So where were the parents? It is a written green-card marriage, yours and mine.

But it is still a sacred bond. Whether the marriage is arranged by one's parents or by a drunken idiot, with the bride kissing the wrong man, and all for the wrong reasons—it is the same. Whether through one's family or out of a desire to go to another country, it is the same mysterious thing going on underneath, doing its work in the manner of fate. And once it is done there can have been no other thing.

That is very philosophical, Ramon. Your brother told me you are a graduate from college.

And there is the sea in front of us, Jelena, that you have come over, to be in this country. And so that's the way it is.

Ramon carefully slipped her hood back and touched her cheek and she turned to face him. He leaned forward and kissed her lips.

Here is what we will do now, Jelena. We will find a taxicab and leave. Just the way we are. We will buy what we need in the city. I have money.

Ramon—

It is no longer safe for you here. Or for me. Come. Anyway, it is too cold here in the rain. Take the sandwiches. Aren't you hungry? I am. We will eat on the way.

WHEN LEON CAME in that evening, he found Ramon and Jelena standing at the window looking at the lights of the city. They were holding hands.

Leon coughed to get their attention. They were flustered, as if they'd been caught doing something forbidden.

Leon shook his head and smiled. Is this the lovely Jelena? So it is! Snatched from under their foreign eyes. Ah, my brother, he said, I should have known. I should have known.

Leon went behind the bar and brought out a bottle of champagne. Come, we'll drink to it. He set out the glasses and popped the cork. Let the war begin, he said.

LINER NOTES:

The Songs of
Billy Bathgate

—

—

The Orphans' Home (3:12)

Now the Bronx is a borough of hills and valleys but you don't see this if you live there. What you see is the picture of where you're going and the dusty windows of the stores you pass and the miles of old apartment houses six stories high, and the buses you dodge and the stoops you read the chalk legends on and the parks with no leaves on the trees. Occasionally you notice, where the tar is worn away, the gleam like a bare foot in a holey shoe of an old streetcar track. But you don't notice what a place of rolling hills it is unless you are old and hanging between your shopping bag and your cane; or unless you are an orphan. And I am talking about an orphan of my mind who takes these trips regularly, feeling every hill its height and every valley its depth; and who hopes to find a certain street in the valley of the Third Avenue El. It is a noisy market street crowded with pushcarts and open-front stalls, and it flows like a river through the richest fields of the earth: fruit and vegetable stalls with oranges and apples, grapes, plums and pears, peaches, tomatoes, all banked up in pyramids; and stacks of celery in their crates, corn in its green husks, bushel baskets of potatoes, and huge, misshapen green peppers. Open dairy stores with cheese in nets slung from the ceiling. Clean and hallowed butcher stores with only smoked meat showing, but the good clean rich fresh meat is behind the heavy doors, the white clanking doors in the back, and the butcher wears a wool hat, and a sweater under his white smock. Appetizer stores with smoked fish and kegs of olives and barrels of pickles and trays of nuts and bins of dried fruit, and sawdust on the floor. And stores where live fish swim in tanks until the fishman lifts them out with a hand net, grabs them by the gills, slaps them down on the block, which stuns them, and cuts off their heads—fat steaks of fish wrapped in polished paper from the big roll. And along the curbs peddlers display from their pushcarts pairs of shoes tied by the laces, or billows of ladies' silken underpants, or miniature amphitheaters of spools of sewing thread and packets of needles and pins and buttons and ribbons every color of the rainbow. And the cries of life echo from the stalls, from the street, from the fire escapes above, the cries of survival—merchants of free enterprise plucking their customers from the river that stomps by, slow, eddying, full of shoals, dangerous. A boy has to watch his step in these treacherous shallows— he can be squeezed against fat women with their bundles or stuck on the umbrella battens of spiteful old men. As he smells the life of the people from their homes, and the smells of oranges, cheese, chicken and fish and cheap new shoes, he must keep a practiced lookout for what is behind him and what is in front. Six, seven years on this earth, he is prey of big kids—Negro, Irish, Italian— who swoop, hover, sting, invisible as darning needles; of cops; of the Truant Officer; of Retribution, pulling him back by the ear to the home, to the Hebrew Home for Orphans some hills away, some deep deep valleys faraway, ascents and descents too tilting, too steep, for such small rubber sneakers, for such bunched-up drooping socks. And if he is lucky he has copped an orange or a celery stalk first. Or a plum whose pit remains in his mouth till it is as bare and juiceless as a stone. He may release it when the Scholar gets to him, and beats him on the shoulders, the head, the back, with the book of prayers, the book of wisdom; himself an orphan, a full-grown bearded black-coated orphan by choice, teeming with wrath and merciless pity. Afterwards the Welfare Lady will take the kid and dry his tears and mother him in her fat arms, and the smell of her will not be unpleasant as she cups his head and sits him on her lap and fails to tell him that though he runs away every week in the year, that rich fertile avenue he today discovered, that newfound land he came upon only by good fortune, is the street where they always look and always find him because he always goes there and nowhere else. Why? she may wonder sitting with him in the building of green tile walls and brown ceilings. Why there? Oh Momma Momma because I'm hungry. But some years will pass before, one day in his run over the hills of the Bronx, he goes in another direction and they never find him to bring him back. He is gone to make his way down every harvest street in the world. In the meantime the Scholar and the Welfare Lady bounce his life between them, tough to gentle, gentle to tough, like the old, half-dead volleyball bestowed for games in the school yard. Now three things make up my songs, the words, the music, and the attitude. And of these the least understood is the attitude. I mean in this song some critics think I am talking about Life or America or the Futility of Orgasm or some goddamn thing, but I am not, I am talking about the place where I grew up, The Orphans' Home: *Agon danced a lively tune   Misero played the violin   Such performances are given   To benefit the orphans' home   Children who lack a daddio   Whose mommas left you on the doorstep   Let's have a big hand for Agon   And the violin of Misero   They're here every night but Wednesday   To dance and play a tune or two   When you finally leave these portals   Others will sit in for you*

Short-Order Cook (2:35)

I am asked how I made it. About making it there is no one way, there is no highway that will lead you there. That way you cut, it is like the little band that Moses led, and when they got there the sea closed behind them. Of no use to anyone chasing after. But you won't know that if you listen to people telling you how to make it, telling you to do this or that indispensable thing as if there is a road with paving. The ones who know the directions are the ones who never get there. I have done some hard traveling, is how I made it. Whereas Missy made it in one song. But let me tell you about my ethnic period, when I was early in the game. I didn't go see Woody. I'd gotten all I needed of Woody. I went to stand in the beefy blueblack shadow of John Malcolm, who lived on his farm in east Tennessee. When I got there, old John was cooking up his supper. The sun was going down over the hills, and it was orange and pink in the western sky, and sitting on John's porch, and lying in his yard, playing with his hounds, looking at their boots, drinking water from his pump, were all these fretting guitar pluckers who looked just like me. So I had to laugh at my proud noble dirty lonesome self with his heartfelt wanderings and his pious worships. You knew these kids were waiting for a word from the master. You knew they were hoping he'd take up his guitar and sit on the porch steps and invite them to play along with him. Which he didn't do. He just ate his supper and got in his truck and went to town to shoot some pool. And you knew what they wanted from him because it was what you wanted. But if he sang or didn't sing, listened or didn't listen, it was all the same. It wouldn't do anybody any good, one way or the other. And no matter how dirty your jeans or dusty your boots or filthy and tangled you were in the hair, you couldn't ever be John Malcolm. He, as a matter of fact, was clean-shaven and neatly dressed. And when he left the only music I had heard that day was music I didn't have to leave MacDougal Street to hear. And that was the end of my ethnic period. When you talk about making it you are talking about a generation that comes out like a new season on the earth. You are talking about a teeming nation with a craving for nourishment. My friends, you are talking about the all-night diner where you go for the one who can serve up the emotion. Who can serve it up like a good short-order cook: greasy, and on a dirty plate; but fast, and hot. And that is what this song is about.   *Esso Texaco Gulf and Shell   Mark the highway going to hell   Stop at the diner, I mean to tell   The short-order cook, he feeds you well.*   It shows the challenge to the short-order cook, who never appears in the song except as the waitress calls to him the orders she gets. And each order the waitress calls out is more complicated than the last, and more difficult for him to fill. From something simple like *Draw one through a ring*, which is coffee and a donut, or *Gimmee the earth before Columbus*, which is a waffle; to *Paint the stripes and cut the grass and satellite some succotash*, which is the spaghetti special but instead of the tossed salad lay on a vegetable. Till finally a customer comes into the diner and asks for God, he orders God, and the waitress calls over the counter to the short-order cook: *White on rye and hold the bread! Sorry Mister, the cook is dead.*

Song to the Leaders of the World (3:26)

I stopped singing like other people after I stopped singing other people's songs. I became myself early. And who comes after me will be himself earlier. The RPMs get faster. But when I began to sing my own songs I thought that since they were mine no one else could sing them. And then there came one summer's night to the big Festival, someone no one had ever heard of, and sang my song to the leaders of the world. Now I do that one slow over a fast beat, and I do it looking up from the gutter. I spit it out. But Missy stood with her arms straight at her sides, and looking over everyone's head she sang it a cappella, full of sorrow and stately warning like the purest most harrowing sermon in church history: with that voice.   *Remember the fire that chills the sun   Remember the light that*

turns a man to stone   Remember the one who rang the world like a bell
Remember how his blood ran out and boiled away in Hell.   Everything
Missy ever had was working for her by the end of that song:
straight, pure, uncanny straight pure singing by a pure straight
plainly frocked girl with straight hair so blond it was almost white.
The try of it was the thing—as always with Missy, till her dying
day—a song was a try, not a performance. And that was there in
the song, trying it and making it. And her voice. It was saying I
know who I am, and now you know who I am. And to all those
stunned and dazzled people in the park I was not a major attraction that summer but she had added a dimension to my presence.
And when I walked out on the stage they were ready for me. The
disquiet of her voice, and her mystery, were still in that park, and
so I had to take her, make them forget her, and I moved into a
realm where I had never been before, and in that long big-time
night of work only two things happened, Missy and young Bathgate. I would not learn to resent her feat for a long long time. You
stand in the blinding light and the approval splits your eardrums.
At the end of the evening, with everyone onstage for the farewell,
I found myself taking her hand, and that triggered the biggest roar
of all. And then we milled off and when she got to the side she sat
down on a chair she was shaking so, trying to hold her face with
her shaking hands. She was ice cold and small, smaller than I expected, a thin smaller girl than showed in the lights with her knees
together and the bluewhite skin of her small thin hands holding
that face in its fall of goldwhite hair. And she couldn't stop her frail
shoulders trembling, and I said something to her but she couldn't
look up. I took a stance like a cop, feeling this was the place to
stand and protect this girl, and suddenly Mr. John Malcolm is beside us, he is holding the neck of his guitar in his big beefy blueblack hand, and his old blueblack face with all the lights is sad and

puzzled, and in that deep gentle voice that sings like water when he talks John Malcolm says I got sixty-one years on me and I know where I come from, I come from the fields. What I don't know is where you come from, where is it you kids come from so fast I never even seen you coming.

Even and Odd in the Garden of Adding (5:15)

But for those of you who follow great tales of true love, like my institutional mothers stirring the soup pots while the radio played them their favorite daytime stories, I just want to remind you that's how we met, Missy and me, on a stage, in front of twenty thousand people, and we each heard the other's performance before we ever said hello. There is something we live with, like another sense, or like another dimension added to all our senses, and it is merely the knowledge that if we choose to be somewhere at a certain time then others will choose to be there too. That is power, and it is a strange kick, weird and possessive, it is like an imposition on your being that adumbrates the edges. How to stand in relationship to it was Missy's constant struggle, and so I made it mine too. See, you can choose to be somewhere for free, for instance, because it's worthy and small and shabby and nobody expects you. And doing that reduces your market value, except that since history is riding in you everything you do turns out to be right, even what you do to diminish yourself. So then you are accused of sanctimony—as she often was—and the next time when something worthy small shabby and self-diminishing comes along, the position you take must be just a shade more defined, sharpened, in its responsibility. It is a nerve-shredding bag when history makes you a gift of the world. I live with it by believing you put the song out and move on. I hid this from her because I was engrossed in the touch of her cheek on my fingers like the skin of a flower. And her hair falling to her shoulders, and the down like penciled sunlight on the curve of her back. But I had to talk integrity to her round gray serious clear eyes, because conversation was important. Everything was important—sitting on a park bench, as well as making love, reading a book as well as singing to a stadium of people. The first time she began to realize the profound differences in our natures she called me lazy. It was a march just too damn far away from where I happened to be at the moment. She took her acolytes and went alone without me, thinking perhaps in that long ride just what lazy meant, like if you probe a sore tooth with your tongue the pain will finally occupy the entire world. But I was way ahead of her: once we were in London, having a good time in Soho with our English brothers, and it was down in this Italian cellar-restaurant, and we were drinking red wine and eating fettuccine and receiving all these famous people who we didn't know but had heard of their books or seen their flicks calling us by our familiar names (for it doesn't matter how you get there, you are all in the same club and share the same worldwide unlisted telephone number), and maybe it was the self-satisfied laughter, the inanity that exists at the top of the world, or maybe it was the color of the walls, but she suddenly said to me, Billy I've got to get home. I called a cab, but by home she meant all the way, so we flew to New York, but in New York she meant all the way, so I got us a car and drove through the night to Columbus, Ohio. Now I had never been in that town before but have since played it and it is a state capital where in the restaurants they serve a side dish of fruit salad on lettuce with a topping of mayonnaise. I stopped at seven thirty in the morning at a tract house with a small green lawn in front and a chrome sprinkler lying at rest in the dew. Carrie Mae was waiting in her apron at the open door and the moment she and I looked at each other began our life of enmity as the slim fair girl slipped past us both into the house. Carrie Momma, Missy said from inside, this is *the* Billy Bathgate—he drove me all the way home all night, what energy! Billy, this is Mrs. Carrie Mae Wilson who is like a momma to me. I think he's hungry for breakfast, Carrie Momma. And inside was a small neat house with wall-to-wall bluegreen carpeting and shiny maple furniture, Van Gogh reproductions on the wall, the kind with the computer paint strokes, a gilt mirror with a gilt American eagle set over the fireplace, and on a shiny cobbler's bench next to the Morris chair was a low stack of *National Geographic* magazines. Missy's growing-up home, all you cats. I washed up in the guest bathroom and sat in the cozynook off the kitchen while Carrie Mae angrily whipped up the pancake batter. She kept looking at my lace-up boots, my buckskin jacket. Upstairs a shower ran. Carrie Mae knew I was listening so she began to talk to me and I learned that her anger was not worry, because she knew her baby and her baby could take care of herself, but simple personal displeasure at my appearance and the selfishness of its pretense. She was a wise old Negro lady, and my automatic enemy. She knew before Missy that it could never be. I learned there was a father, that he was a public works engineer who sank water lines and sewage pipes into the ground and was away weeks at a time, and that he was a fine man and good father who loved his daughter and was proud of her. And then Carrie Mae grew still. Because there was singing upstairs and I thought for a moment it was Missy and realized then it was her record player and one of those operatic sopranos was singing something wild, like Richard Strauss, something soaring, some fierce Kraut thing. And then I corrected myself for it was her after all, singing along, matching that chesty record note for note. With a little bit extra amplification of what I would call love for the music. This purely slim chick with breasts of small fruit and a rib cage you could crack with your two hands. She came down a few minutes later and the warm breakfast smells had made me drowsy and my aspirin had worn off and she came in dressed for bed like a barefoot high school girl in her round-collared nightdress, and she sat down to her fresh orange juice and her pancakes and her glass of milk and smiled at me such a fair fine peaceful smile of recognition that I have never forgotten it and never will; it was the lovely smile of no tricks and no secrets, of the profound and gentle courtesy in her tough heart. You see when it was bad for Missy she had someplace she could go anytime, day or night, summer or winter, and she knew someone would be there to serve her a meal and turn back her bed. That was the difference between us right there. Then what happened was we cut a record she and I. The song is not unknown, "The Single-Bullet-Theory Blues," and it was one of the few times we got together in our professional travels and the only time to sing on the same record; and we sang many takes, and tried many ways, and finally stood at the same mike and held hands and closed our eyes and sang, as if closeness would make our voices match. But they didn't. Our voices didn't belong next to each other. So I knew that as a sign. Missy's talking voice was an ordinary girl's talking voice with no suggestion of how large it could sing. But my talking voice becomes my singing voice with just a slight heightening of attitude. And in our different relationships to our performing voices I had read the future. But I remember things about her that don't harden up. That, for instance, I thought for a while her singing voice was accountable to her fear; she was always so scared of being up there, the tremolo in the large, witchy voice was the sound of her fear. But I was wrong. That she was physically delicate and had to rest herself every day, strong in nerve and soul and in the clearness of her mind and determination, but just a slim girl in her bones and with a scarf for her throat on a warm song day of mild breezes. That she saw no contradiction in her practical commonsense decency recipes for the fucked-up world and her private belief in mystical presences, nameless powers who inhabited pebbles and stones, the clouds in the sky, and sometimes the face in her mirror. That she loved to bet I couldn't make her laugh, and always lost. That she was happy for all the money she made but worried that it compromised her. That she enjoyed the way we made it in our own style, cool and concessionless. That she liked big-beat dancing. That people sent her books they had written— which she never read. That, for a while, while I was writing the songs she liked, she revered me. That maybe I am wrong in thinking I was way ahead of her in the knowledge of us, for perhaps what she called lazy was her glimpse down the tunnel of my eyes to the deep seabed of my murky soul where my songs waited like electric fishes. And one other thing is true: after she caught up to me and neither of us had a secret left, and we were done; after she knew there was nothing I would not try and no road I would not go down; I called her once or twice and she came. When I'd had it with all the clanking machinery of being Billy, with everybody and everything lining up on me—not just the managers and accountants, not just the armies of hacks and flacks and makers of sweatshirts who live off you because they live off the idea of success, but the very iron filings of historical fashion loading themselves on my outlines. And when it was this bad she came and went away with me to my hideout and let me persuade her that we were the only two people alive on the earth. And let us find some air to breathe and breathe it. And let us make up the names of grasses we found and bushes and berries. And love each other's face in the different lights of morning and afternoon. And eat crackers and canned fruit and go to bed early. And it was   *Even and Odd in the Garden of Adding   And we ate all the fruit we could find   From apples persimmons peaches and plums   To the sour green watermelon rind   And me*

*and my lady we did what was shady   And we tried to add up for our
kind   But Odds add up Even and Even's in Heaven   And God has
gone out of his mind*

Billy's Dream of a Dead Friend (3:40)

When you take away a man's sensations he will make up his own:
take away his seeing and his hearing and let him smell nothing and
let nothing touch him, he will see and hear and smell and feel what
his mind makes up. And what does that prove but the loneliness we
are born into, that we are born hungry for the world and lonesome
in our hunger, and that the heart floods its banks of loneliness and
runs over the earth, and is soaked away till there is no more blood
of the lonely heart's spring and our river runs dry. And my dream
is of the pale-bled heart of Missy having run its courses and the last
drops of its blood sifting into the sands of that southern beach; and
the wind of my waking hours cleanses and dries the sands, but each
night those darkening stains spread out again, just where they
were before. Because my dream is made of facts and the facts can't
be dreamed away. Nobody over thirty in the whole country believed her the times she spoke out. But I knew that she never
lied—that was not when she lied. She didn't lie when she showed
up on TV in the country where we were at war, she didn't lie when
she mourned for the three murdered men in Mississippi, she didn't
lie at the church in Birmingham or on the Mall in Washington,
D.C. So one day the police come upon her as she's out for a stroll
down this country road with an old Negro lady. And they stop
their car to investigate. And she says, We're going to the beach.
We're looking to find a breath of fresh air. And all the grown-up
liberals said she might be a sanctimonious fake and a phony, but
she is a shrewd genius for that line; imagine saying that to that cop
a good hundred and ten miles from the nearest ocean. The age of

marches was over but a new age is begun and we will have a march to the sea for that old Negro lady. But the truth is she meant what she said, the words themselves, for when she said it that became her intention. And that old Negro lady was Carrie Mae, who sang to her in the cradle all the blues she sang; who grew her up in Columbus, Ohio; and who'd gone back to her home in South Carolina to live before she died. And Missy went down to see Carrie Mae and that was how they were taking a walk down the country road, the old woman in a fine black dress from Saks Fifth Avenue and a sun parasol on her shoulder and forty-five-dollar orthopedic shoes on her feet, arm in arm with Missy in her shirt and jeans and sandals and shades, the two of them out for a stroll on this hot dusty road where the police car is what kicked up the dust. And Missy says in front of the deputies, Momma Carrie how fine it will be when we smell the ocean breeze and can sit down on the cool wet sand and bathe our feet in that cool, absolving, never-ending ocean. And breathe air that has some breath in it. And the old woman, who knows her Missy from birth, from the moment she pushed out of real, soon-to-be-dead Momma, she smiles and says, All right. And pretends with her and believes with her at that moment that that is just what they'll do. For it is a hot day, and the air is bad for breathing, as Carrie Mae knows because she has asthma, a bad, lifelong asthma. And the deputies hear that, and see them smiling at each other, old Carrie Mae and this famous trouble-maker white girl, smiling in their love for each other, and they take offense. And when they radio the sheriff it becomes an infraction and when the AP stringer drives up he puts it on the wire and it becomes a news story, and by the next morning when the women get out of the jailhouse and stand before the judge, a wish to ease an old woman's breathing has become a categorical truth for Missy, for nobody was ever more stubborn with the stubborn soul of a saint. She took a County Cab back to the old woman's redbrick

ranch house and packed a pull-string laundry bag and came back
to town and the two of them walked east out of that town arm in
arm for a summer if they wanted of walking free together wherever they wanted. But it wasn't a march till the next morning when
twenty-five seminarians from Columbia, S.C., stepped out of their
bus and followed along. And it wasn't a demonstration till the kids
begin to pour down from the west and north. And it wasn't a riot
till days later when five thousand of them pushed their way gently
and firmly through the patriots drinking their beers and throwing
the bottles. And one was thrown back. Which is what the police
with their helmets, shades, and carbines had been waiting for. And
because I wasn't there, what I see is myself walking up to Missy
who faces the ocean like Venus about to go back into the sea, and
I gently touch her shoulder and she turns and smiles at me her
lovely smile of recognition and whispers words of a song I write
for her in our minds: *What do you believe, Billy?   Tell me what you
believe, Billy*   And I raise my hand, which is the signal for the car-
bine bullet to slam into her throat, and fell her, and spill her voice
into the sand except for that portion of it that reddens the white
surf and washes back into the blue ocean. And that is my dream-
song of a dead friend. In life her life was whole major chords—
nothing diminished, nothing flatted, nothing minor, nothing
pushed a half tone off center. What kind of music was that? It was
music for the bright and early morning. It sounds all right until
those shadows of night begin to creep around the earth like the big
dark hands of God, like the dark hands of God around your throat,
children. And when you feel those hands is when you sing. When
God is squeezing the breath out of you is the time to sing. So hear
what I'm saying: when she spoke she represented herself truthfully. It was when she sang that she lied. And her lying is what gave
her that voice, that truest purest voice in the whole amazed world,
that uncanny voice stronger and sweeter than Christ's Himself.

Listen: it is so truly perfect it is raw it is so pure. And doesn't she sing sad? And doesn't she sing those Baptist blues hymns bluer and deeper blue than anyone? Well that blue is night blue, the blue of the shadow of God, and that was when Missy lied, because she never allowed that His shadow was in her being.

The Ballad of W. C. Fields (2:20)

And so we come to my most recent song, this ballad of W. C. Fields. I sat down not to write it but to give the urgency in my breast a controlled release through my fingertips, and this song is what happened. It happened so fast I didn't even have time for the music, just the words and the beat. And so it is in the form of a walking song, it walks me through the underworld of the dreaming masses, where this pudgy demon of truth, Mr. W. C. Fields, with his dirty top hat, his run-down elegance of manners, his drunken scrollwork of a personality, presides like the Chief Official over the technology of our souls. And the singer doesn't want this, he doesn't like it, and he begins the song by telling Mr. Fields to go away: *Go way from my window Mr. W. C. Fields   Go way from this beautiful place   Go way from my window Mr. W. C. Fields   You're blocking the view with your ugly face.*   But the clown won't go away, you see, for he is taking the singer by the hand and leading him through the window over the great landscape of the underworld that looks so beautiful from the window of the safe house and showing him what it really is. And he sees the bubbling sulfur pits of intentions, and the slake mountains of ideals, and great plains of gray ash as far as he can see, the ashes of innocence creased by rivers of blood. And every man he sees is blind and running around in circles and no sound from the tapping of his cane to tell him where he's going. And a great pestilential wind suppurates the skin of the people and sears their eyes and their hair, and it is the wind of Mr. W. C. Fields ranting. But the worst thing he sees is an old couple exempt from all the misery, a beautiful fair girl and boy in their youth who have grown old together, an aged couple who have loved each other and lived in each other all their lives, in joy and comfort, and now sit chuckling, immune to their surroundings, chuckling in their awful senility. And when the singer is back behind his window and the view looks fine and good and green again, he understands who Mr. W. C. Fields is, and he says: *Some day we will stop laughing at you, Mr. Fields   At your bulbous nose and the pain of your distress   At your thirst and your drunken pratfalls, Mr. Fields   At your bitter, bumbling, saintliness.*   And Mr. Fields brings forth a bottle and blows the dust from two glasses and rubs them on his dirty elegant sleeve and pours us each a drink and says to me: *Drink it down, drink it all down, my boy   And kick the kids at Christmas   I give you my crooked cue stick, Billy   Cause you know what the game is*

HEIST

—

S—

UNDAY AFTERNOON. A PEDDLER IN A PURPLE CHORISTER'S ROBE selling watches in Battery Park. Fellow with dreadlocks, a sweet smile, sacral presence. Doing well.

Rock doves everywhere aswoop, the grit of the city in their wings. And the glare of the oil-slicked bay, and a warm-throated autumn breeze like a woman blowing in my ears.

At my back, the financial skyline of Lower Manhattan sunlit into an islanded cathedral, a religioplex.

And here's the ferry from Ellis Island. Listing to starboard, her three decks jammed to the rails. Sideswipes bulkhead for contemptuous New York landing. Oof. Pilings groan, crack like gunfire. Man on the promenade breaks into a run. How can I be lonely in this city?

Tourists stampeding down the gangplank. Cameras, camcorders, and stupefied children slung from their shoulders. Sun hats and baseball caps insouciant this morning, now their serious, unfortunate fashion.

Lord, there is something so exhausted about the New York waterfront, as if the smell of the sea were oil, as if boats were buses, as if all Heaven were a garage hung with girlie calendars, the months to come already leafed and fingered in black grease.

But I went back to the peddler in the choir robe and said I liked the look. Told him I'd give him a dollar if he'd let me see the label. The smile dissolves.

You crazy, mon?

I was in my mufti grunge—jeans, leather jacket over plaid shirt over T-shirt. Not even cruciform I.D. to flash at him.

Lifts his tray of watches out of reach: Get away, you got no business wit me. Looking left and right as he says it.

And then later on my walk, at Astor Place, where they lay their goods on plastic shower curtains on the sidewalk: three of the sacristy's purple choir robes neatly folded and stacked between a *Best of the Highwaymen* LP and the autobiography of George Sanders. I picked one and turned back the neck, and there was the label, Churchpew Crafts, and the laundry mark from Mr. Chung. The peddler, a solemn young mestizo with that bowl of black hair they have, wanted ten dollars each. I thought that was reasonable.

They come over from Senegal, or up from the Caribbean, or from Lima, San Salvador, Oaxaca, and find a piece of sidewalk and go to work. The world's poor lapping our shores, like the rising of the global-warmed sea. I remember how, on the way to Machu Picchu, I stopped in the town of Cuzco and watched the dances and listened to the street bands. I was told when I found my camera missing that I could buy it back the next morning in the market street behind the cathedral. Sure enough, next morning there were the women of Cuzco, in their woven ponchos of red and ocher, braids depending from their black derbies, broad Olmec heads smiling shyly. They were fencing the stuff. Merciful heavens, I was pissed. But, surrounded by Anglos ransacking the stalls as if searching for their lost dead, how, my Lord Jesus, could I not accept the justice of the situation?

As I did at Astor Place in the shadow of the great, mansarded, brownstone-voluminous Cooper Union people's college with the birds flying up from the square.

A block east, on St. Mark's, a thrift shop had the altar candlesticks that were heisted along with the robes. Twenty-five dollars the pair. While I was at it, I bought half a dozen used paperback detective novels. To learn the trade.

I'm lying, Lord, I just read the damn things when I'm depressed. The paperback detective never fails me. His rod and his gaff, they comfort me. Sure, a life is lost here and there, but the paperback's world is ordered, circumscribed, dependable in its punishments. More than I can say for Yours.

I know You are on this screen with me. If Thos. Pemberton, DD, is losing his life, he's losing it here, to his watchful God. Not just over my shoulder do I presumptively locate You, or in the Anglican starch of my collar, or in the rectory walls, or in the coolness of the chapel stone that frames the door, but in the blinking cursor . . .

TUESDAY EVE. UP TO Lenox Hill to see my terminal: ambulances backing into the emergency bay with their beepings and blinding strobe lights. They used to have QUIET signs around hospitals. Doctors' cars double-parked, patients strapped on gurneys double-parked on the sidewalk, smart young Upper East Side workforce pouring out of the subway walking past not looking. Looking.

It gets dark earlier now. Lights coming on in the apartment buildings. If only I was rising to a smart one-bedroom. A lithe young woman home from her interesting job, listening for my ring. Uncorking the wine, humming, wearing no underwear.

In the lobby, a stoic crowd primed for visiting hours with bags and bundles and infants squirming in laps. And that profession of the plague of our time, the security guard, in various indolent versions.

My terminal's room door slapped with a RESTRICTED AREA warning. I push in, all smiles.

You got medicine, Father? You gonna make me well? Then get the fuck outta here. The fuck out, I don't need your bullshit.

Enormous eyes all that's left of him. An arm bone aims the remote like a gun, and there in the hanging set the smiling girl spins the big wheel.

My comforting pastoral visit concluded, I pass down the hall, where several neatly dressed black people wait outside a private room. They hold gifts in their arms. I smell non-hospital things. A whiff of fruit pie still hot from the oven. Soups. Simmering roasts. I stand on tiptoe. Who is that? Through the flowers, like a Gauguin, a handsome, light-complected black woman sitting up in bed. Turbaned. Regal. I don't hear the words, but her melodious, deep voice of prayer knows whereof it speaks. The men with their hats in their hands and their heads bowed. The women with white kerchiefs. On the way out I inquire of the floor nurse.

SRO twice a day, she says. We get all of Zion up here. The only good thing, since Sister checked in I don't have to shop for supper. Yesterday I brought home baked pork chops. You wouldn't believe how good they were.

ANOTHER ONE HAVING trouble with my bullshit—the widow code-named Moira. In her new duplex that looks across the river to the Pepsi-Cola sign she's been reading Pagels on early Christianity.

It was all politics, wasn't it? she asks me.

Yes, I sez to her.

And so whoever won, that's why we have what we have now?

Well, with a nod at the Reformation, I suppose, yes.

She lies back on the pillows. So it's all made up, it's an invention?

Yes, I sez, taking her in my arms. And you know for the longest time it actually worked.

Used to try to make her laugh at the dances at Spence. Couldn't then, can't now. A gifted melancholic, Moira. The lost husband an add-on.

But she was one of the few in the old crowd who didn't think I was throwing my life away.

Wavy thick brown hair parted in the middle. Glimmering dark eyes, set a bit too wide. Figure not current, lacking tone, Glory to God in the highest.

From the corner of her full-lipped mouth her tongue emerges and licks away a teardrop.

And then, Jesus, the surprising condolence of her wet salted kiss.

FOR THE SERMON: open with that scene in the hospital, those good and righteous folk praying at the bedside of their minister. The humility of those people, their faith glowing like light around them, put me in such longing . . . to share their innocence.

But then I asked myself: Why must faith rely on innocence? Must it be blind? Why must it come of people's need to believe?

We are all of us so pitiful in our desire to be unburdened, we will embrace Christianity's rule or any other claim of God's authority for that matter. God's authority is a powerful claim and reduces us all, wherever we are in the world, whatever our tradition, to beggarly gratitude.

So where is the truth to be found? Who are the elect blessedly walking the true path to Salvation . . . and who are the misguided others? Can we tell? Do we know? We think we know—of course we think we know. We have our belief. But how do we distinguish our truth from another's falsity, we of the true faith, except by the story we cherish? Our story of God. But, my friends, I ask you: Is God a story? Can we, each of us examining our faith— I mean its pure center, not its comforts, not its habits, not its ritual sacraments—can we believe anymore in the heart of our faith that God is our story of Him? What, for instance, has the industrialized carnage, the continentally engineered terrorist slaughter of the Holocaust done to our story? Do we dare ask? What mortification, what ritual, what practice would have been a commensurate Christian response to the Holocaust? Something to assure us of the truth of our story? Something as earthshaking in its way as Auschwitz and Dachau—a mass exile, perhaps? A lifelong commitment of millions of Christians to wandering, derelict, over the world? A clearing out of the lands and cities a thousand miles in every direction from each and every death camp? I don't know what it would be—but I know I'd recognize it if I saw it. If we go on with our story, blindly, after something like that, is it not merely innocent but also foolish, and possibly a defamation, a profound impiety? To presume to contain God in this unknowing story of ours, to hold Him, circumscribe Him, the author of everything we can conceive and everything we cannot conceive . . . in our story of Him? Of Her? Of whom? What in the name of our faith—what in God's name!—do we think we are talking about!

WEDNESDAY LUNCH.

Well, Father, I hear you delivered yourself of another doozy.

How do you get your information, Charley. My little deacon, maybe, or my Kapellmeister?

Be serious.

No, really, unless you've got the altar bugged. Because, God knows, there's nobody but us chickens. Give me an uptown parish, why don't you, where the subway doesn't shake the rafters. Give me one of God's midtown showplaces of the pious rich and famous, and I'll show you what doozy means.

Now, listen, Pem, he says. This is unseemly. You are doing and saying things that are . . . ecclesiastically worrying.

He frowns at his grilled fish as if wondering what it's doing there. His well-chosen Pinot Grigio shamelessly neglected as he sips ice water.

Tell me what I should be talking about, Charley. My five parishioners are serious people. I mean, is this only a problem for Jewish theology? Mormon? Swedenborgian?

There's a place for doubt. And it's not the altar of St. Timothy's.

Funny you should say that. Doubt is my next week's sermon: the idea is that in our time it is no more likely that a religious person will live a moral life than that an irreligious person will. What do you think?

A tone has crept in, a pride of intellect, something is not right—

And it may be that we guardians of the sacred texts are in spirit less God-fearing than the average secular individual in a modern industrial democracy who has quietly accepted the ethical teachings and installed them in himself and/or herself.

Lays the knife and fork down, composes his thoughts: You've always been your own man, Pem, and in the past I've had a sneaking admiration for the freedom you've found within church discipline. We all have. And in a sense you've paid for it, we both know that. In terms of talent and brains, the way you burned up Yale, you probably should have been my bishop. But in another sense it is harder to do what I do, be the authority that your kind is always testing.

My kind?

Please think about this. The file is getting awfully thick. You are headed for an examination, a Presentment. Is that what you want?

His blue eyes look disarmingly into mine. Boyish shock of hair, now gray, falling over the forehead. Then his famous smile flashes over his face and instantly fades, having been the grimace of distraction of an administrative mind.

What I know of such things, Pem, I know well. Self-destruction is not one act, or even one kind of act. It is the whole man coming apart in every direction, all three hundred and sixty degrees.

Amen to that, Charley. You don't suppose there's time for a double espresso?

ALL RIGHT, THAT WISE old dog Tillich—Paulus Tillichus—how does he construe the sermon? Picks a text and worries the hell out of it. Sniffs at the words, paws them: What, when you get right down to it, is a *demon*? You say you want to be *saved*? But what does that mean? When you pray for *eternal life*, what do you think you're asking for? Paulus, God's philologist, this Merriam-Webster of the DDs, this German . . . shepherd. I loved him. The suspense he held us in—teetering on the edge of secularism, arms waving wildly. Of course, he saved us every time, pulled back from the abyss, and we were okay after all, back with Jesus. Until the next sermon, the next lesson. Because if God is to live, the words of faith must be renewed. The words must be reborn.

Oh, did we flock to him. Enrollments soared.

But that was then and this is now.

We're back in Christendom, Paulus. People are born again, not words. You can see it on television.

—

FRIDAY MORNING. Following his intuition, Divinity Detective wandered over to the restaurant-supply district on the Bowery, below Houston, where the trade is brisk in used steam tables, walk-in freezers, grills, sinks, pots, woks, and bins of cutlery. Back behind the Taipei Trading Company was the antique gas-operated fridge too recently acquired to have a sales tag, with the mark of my shoe sole still on the door where I kicked it when it wouldn't stay closed. And in one of the bins of the used-dish department the tea things from our pantry, white with a green trim, gift from the dear departed Ladies' Auxiliary. Practically named my own price, Lord. With free delivery. A steal.

Evening. I walk over to Tompkins Square, find my friend on his bench.

This has got to stop, I say to him.

My, you riled up.

Wouldn't you be?

Not like the Pops I know.

I thought we had an understanding. I thought there was mutual respect.

They is. Have a seat.

Sparrows working the benches in the dusk.

Told you wastin' your time, but I ast aroun like I said I would. No one here hittin' on Tim's.

Not from here?

Thasit.

How can you be sure?

This regulated territory.

Regulated! That's funny.

Now who's not showin' respeck. This my parish we talkin' bout. Church of the Sweet Vision. They lean on me, see what I'm sayin'? I am known for my compassion. You dealin' with foreigners or some such, thas my word to you.

Ah, hell. I suppose you're right.

No problem. Unsnaps attaché case: Here, my very own personal blend. No charge. Relax yoursel.

Thanks.

Toke of my affection.

MONDAY NIGHT, a new tack. I waited in the balcony with my BearScare six-volt Superbeam. If something stirred, I'd just press the button and my Superbeam would hit the altar at a hundred and eighty-six thousand miles per second—same cruising speed as the finger of God.

The amber crime-preventing lights on the block make a perfect indoor crime site of my church. Intimations of a kind of tarnished air in the vaulted spaces. The stained-glass figures yellowed into lurid obsolescence. How many years has this church been home to me? But all I had to do was sit up in the back for a few hours to understand the truth of its stolid indifference. How an oak pew creaks. How a passing police siren in its two Doppler pitches is like a crisis being filed away in the stone walls.

And then, Lord, I confess, I dozed. Father Brown would never have done that. But there was this crash, as if a waiter had dropped a whole load of dishes. That brought me up smartly. Wait a minute, I thought, churches don't have waiters—they're hitting the pantry again! I had figured them for the altar. I raced my bulk down the stairs, my Superbeam held aloft like a club. "Cry God for Tommy, England, and St. Tim!" How long had I been asleep? I stood in the doorway, found the light switch, and, when you do that, for an instant the only working sense is the sense of smell: hashish in that empty pantry. Male body odor. But also the pungent sanguinary scent of female hormone. And something else, something else. Like lipstick, or lollipop.

The dish cabinets—some of the panes shattered, broken cups and saucers on the floor, a cup still rocking.

A whiff of cool air. They'd gone out the alley door. An ungainly something moving out there. A deep metallic bong sounds up through my heels. Someone curses. It is me, fumbling with the damn searchlight. I swing the beam out and see a shadow rising with distinction, something with right angles in the vanished instant of the turned corner.

I ran back into the church and let my little light shine. Behind the altar where the big brass cross should have been was a shadow of Your crucifix, Lord, in the unfaded paint of my predecessor's poor taste.

WHAT THE REAL DETECTIVE said: Take my word for it, Padre. I been in this precinct ten years. They'll hit a synagogue for the whatchamacallit, the Torah. Because it's handwritten, not a mass-produced item. It'll bring, a minimum, five K. Whereas the book value for your cross has got to be zilch. Nada. No disrespect, we're practically related, I'm Catholic, go to Mass, but on the street there is no way it is anything but scrap metal. Jesus! Whata buncha sickos.

Mistake talking to the *Times*. Such a sympathetic young man. I didn't understand anything till they took the cross, I told him. I thought they were just crackheads looking for a few dollars. Maybe they didn't understand it themselves. Am I angry? No. I'm used to this, I am used to being robbed. When the diocese took away my food-for-the-homeless program and merged it with one across town, I lost most of my parishioners. That was a big-time heist. So even before this happened I was tapped out. These people, whoever they are, have lifted our cross. It bothered me at first. But on further reflection maybe Christ goes where He is needed.

Phone ringing off the hook. I'm getting my very own Presentment. But also pledges of support, checks rolling in. Including some of the old crowd, pals now of my dear wife, who had thought my vocabulary quaint, like a performance of Mozart on period instruments. Tommy Pemberton will scrape a few pieties for us on his viola da gamba. I count nine hundred and change here. Have I stumbled on a new scam? I tell you, Lord, these people just don't get it. What am I supposed to do, put up a fence? Electrify it?

The TV newspeople swarming all over. Banging on my door. Mayday, Mayday! I will raise the sash behind this desk, drop nimbly to the rubbled lot, pass under the window of Ecstatic Reps, where the lady with the big hocks is doing the treadmill, and I'm gone. Thanks heaps, Metro section.

TRISH GIVING A DINNER when I got here. The caterer's man who let me in thought I was a latecomer. Now that I think about it, I was looking straight ahead as I passed the dining room, a millisecond, right? Yet I saw everything: which silver, the floral centerpiece. She's doing the veal-paillard dinner. Château Latour in the Steuben decanters. Oh, what a waste. Two of the hopefuls present, the French UN diplomat, the boy-genius mutual-fund manager. Odds on the Frenchman. The others all extras. Amazing the noise ten people can make around a table. And, in this same millisecond of candlelight, Trish's glance over the rim of the wineglass raised to her lips, those cheekbones, the blue amused eyes, the frosted coif. That fraction of an instant of my passage in the doorway was all she needed from the far end of the table to see what she had to see of me, to understand, to know why I'd slunk home. But isn't it terrible that after it's over between us the synapses continue firing coordinately? What do You have to say about that, Lord? All the problems we have with You, we haven't even gotten around to your small-time perversities. I mean when an instant is still the capacious, hoppingly alive carrier of all our intelligence. And it's the same damn dumb biology when, however moved I am by another woman, the tips of my fingers are recording that she isn't Trish.

But the dining room was the least of it. It's a long walk down the hall to the guest room when the girls are home for the weekend.

We are on battery pack, Lord, I forgot the AC gizmo. And I am exhausted—forgive me.

DEAR FATHER if u want to now where yor cross luk in 7531 w 168 street apt 2A where the santeria oombalah father casts the sea shels an scarifises chickns.

Sure.

Dear Mr. Pemberton, We are two missionaries of the Church of Jesus Christ of Latter-day Saints (Mormon) assigned to the Lower East Side of New York . . . Nuffuvthat.

Dear Father, We have read of your troubles with those aliens who presume to desecrate the Christian church and smirch the Living God. Lest you despair, I am one of a group in nearby New Jersey who have dedicated ourselves to defending the Republic and the Sacred name of Jesus from interlopers wherever they may arise, even if from the federal government. And I mean defend— with skill, and organizational knowhow and the only thing these people understand, The Gun that is our prerogative to hold as free white Americans . . .

Right on.

—

OKAY, ACTION TO REPORT.

Yesterday, Monday, I get a message on the machine from a Rabbi Joshua Gruen, of the Synagogue of Evolutionary Judaism, on West Ninety-eighth: it is in my interest that we meet as soon as possible. Hmm. Clearly not one of the kooks. I call back. Cordial, but will answer no questions over the phone. So okay, this is what detectives do, Lord, they investigate. Sounded a serious young man, one religioso to another—mufti or collar? I go for the collar.

The synagogue a brownstone between West End and Riverside Drive. A steep flight of granite steps to the front door. I deduce that Evolutionary Judaism includes aerobics. Confirmed when I am admitted. Joshua (my new friend) a trim five-nine in sweat-shirt, jeans, running shoes. Gives me a firm handshake. Maybe thirty-two, thirty-four, good chin, well-curved forehead. A knitted yarmulke riding the top of his wavy black hair.

Shows me his synagogue: a converted parlor–*cum*–living room with an ark at one end, a platform table to read the Torah on, shelves with prayer books, and a few rows of bridge chairs, and that's it.

Second floor, introduces me to his wife, who puts her caller on hold, stands up from her desk to shake hands, she, too, a rabbi, Sarah Blumenthal, in blouse and slacks, pretty smile, high cheek-bones, no cosmetics, needs none, light hair short, au courant cut, granny specs, Lord my heart. She is one of the assistant rabbis at Temple Emanu-El. What if Trish went for her DD, wore the collar, celebrated the Eucharist with me? Okay, laugh, but it's not funny when I think about it, not funny at all.

Third floor, I meet the children, boys two and four, in their native habitat of primary-color wall boxes filled with stuffed animals. They cling to the flanks of their dark Guatemalan nanny, who is also introduced like a member of the family . . .

On the back wall of the third-floor landing is an iron ladder. Joshua Gruen ascends, opens a trapdoor, climbs out.

A moment later his head appears against the blue sky. He beckons me upward, poor winded Pem so stress-tested and entranced . . . so determined to make it look effortless I can think of nothing else.

I stand finally on the flat roof, the old apartment houses of West End Avenue and Riverside Drive looming at either end of this block of chimneyed brownstone roofs, and try to catch my breath while smiling at the same time. The autumn sun behind the apartment houses, the late-afternoon river breeze on my face. I'm feeling the exhilaration and slight vertigo of roof-standing . . . and don't begin to think—until snapped to attention by the rabbi's puzzled, frankly inquiring gaze that asks why do I think he's brought me here—why he's brought me here. His hands in his pockets, he points with his chin to the Ninety-eighth Street frontage, where, lying flat on the black tarred roof, its transverse exactly parallel to the front of the building, its upright pressed against the granite pediment, the eight-foot hollow brass cross of St. Timothy's, Episcopal, lies tarnished and shining in the autumn sun.

I suppose I knew I'd found it from the moment I heard the rabbi's voice on the answering machine. I bend down for a closer look. There are the old nicks and dents. Some new ones, too. It's not all of a piece, which I hadn't known: the arms are bolted to the upright in a kind of mortise-and-tenon idea. I lift it at the foot. It is not that heavy but clearly too much cross to bear on the stations of the IRT.

I'D BEEN JUST about convinced it was, in fact, a new sect of some kind. You do let this happen, Lord, ideas of You bud with the profligacy of viruses. I thought, Well, I'll keep a vigil from across the street, watch them take my church apart brick by brick. Maybe I'll help them. They'll reassemble it somewhere as a folk church of some kind. A bizarre expression of their simple faith. Maybe I'll drop in, listen to the sermon now and then. Learn something . . .

Then my other idea, admittedly paranoid: it would end up as an installation in SoHo. Some crazy artist—let me wait a few months, a year, and I'd look in a gallery window and see it there, duly embellished, a statement. People standing there drinking white wine. So that was the secular version. I thought I had all bases covered. I am shaken.

HOW DID RABBI Joshua Gruen know it was there?

An anonymous phone call. A man's voice. Hello, Rabbi Gruen? Your roof is burning.

The roof was burning?

If the children had been in the house I would have gotten them out and called the fire department. As it was, I grabbed our kitchen extinguisher and up I came. Not the smartest thing. Of course, the roof was not burning. But, modest as it is, this is a synagogue. A place for prayer and study. And, as you see, a Jewish family occupies the upper floors. So was he wrong, the caller?

He bites his lip, dark brown eyes looking me in the eye. It is an execrable symbol to him. Burning its brand on his synagogue. Burning down, floor through floor, like the template of a Christian church. I want to tell him I'm on the Committee for Ecumenical Theology of the Trans-Religious Fellowship. A member of the National Conference of Christians and Jews.

This is deplorable. I am really sorry about this.

It's hardly your fault.

I know, I say. But this city is getting weirder by the minute.

The rabbis offer me a cup of coffee. We sit in the kitchen. I feel quite close to them, both our houses of worship desecrated, the entire Judeo-Christian heritage trashed.

This gang's been preying on me for months. And for what they've gotten for their effort, I mean one hit on a dry cleaner would have done as much. Listen, Rabbi—

Joshua.

Joshua. Do you read detective stories?

He clears his throat, blushes.

Only all the time, Sarah Blumenthal says, smiling at him.

Well, let's put our minds together. We've got two mysteries going here.

Why two?

This gang. I can't believe their intent was, ultimately, to commit an anti-Semitic act. They have no intent. They lack sense. They're like overgrown children. They're not of this world. And all the way from the Lower East Side to the Upper West Side? No, that's asking too much of them.

So this is someone else?

It must be. A good two weeks went by. Somebody took the cross off their hands—if they didn't happen to find it in a dumpster. I mean, the police told me it had no value, but if someone wants it it has value, right? And then this second one or more persons had the intent. But how did they get it onto the roof? And nobody saw them, nobody heard them?

I was on the case now, asking questions, my nostrils flaring. I was enjoying myself. Good Lord, Lord, should I have been a detective? Was that my true calling?

Angelina, whom I think you met with the children: she heard noises from the roof one morning. We were already gone. That was the day I went to see my father, Sarah says, looking to Joshua for confirmation.

And I'd gone running, Joshua says.

But the noise didn't last long and Angelina thought no more of it—thought that it was a repairman of some sort. I assume they came up through one of the houses on the block. The roofs abut.

Did you go down the block? Did you ring bells?

Joshua shook his head.

What about the cops?

They exchange glances. Please, says Joshua. The congregation is new, just getting its legs. We're trying to make something viable for today—theologically, communally. A dozen or so families, just a beginning. A green shoot. The last thing we want is for this to get out. We don't need that kind of publicity. Besides, he says, that's what they want, whoever did this.

We don't accept the I.D. of victim, says Sarah Blumenthal, looking me in the eye.

And now I tell You, Lord, as I sit here back in my own study, in this bare ruined choir, I am exceptionally sorry for myself this evening, lacking as I do a companion like Sarah Blumenthal. This is not lust, and You know I would admit it if it were. No, but I think how quickly I took to her, how comfortable I was made, how naturally welcomed I felt under these difficult circumstances, there is a freshness and honesty about these people, both of them, I mean, they were so present in the moment, so self-possessed, a wonderful young couple with a quietly dedicated life, such a powerful family stronghold they make, and, oh Lord, he is one lucky rabbi, Joshua Gruen, to have such a beautiful devout by his side.

It was Sarah, apparently, who made the connection. He was sitting there trying to figure out how to handle it and she had come in from a conference somewhere and when he told her what was on the roof she wondered if that was the missing crucifix she had read about in the newspaper.

I hadn't read the piece and I was skeptical.

You thought it was just too strange, a news story right in your lap, Sarah says.

That's true. News is somewhere else. And to realize that you know more than the reporter knew? But we found the article.

He won't let me throw out anything, Sarah says.

Fortunately, in this case, says the husband to the wife.

It's like living in the Library of Congress.

So, thanks to Sarah, we now have the rightful owner.

She glances at me, colors a bit. Removes her glasses, the scholar, and pinches the bridge of her nose. I see her eyes in the instant before the specs go back on. Nearsighted, like a little girl I loved in grade school.

I am extremely grateful, I say to my new friends. This is, in addition to everything else, a mitzvah you've performed. Can I use your phone? I'm going to get a van up here. We can take it apart, wrap it up, and carry it right out the front door and no one will be the wiser.

I'm prepared to share the cost.

Thank you, that won't be necessary. I don't need to tell you, but my life has been hell lately. This is good coffee, but you don't happen to have something to drink, do you?

Sarah going to a wall cabinet. Will Scotch do?

Joshua, sighing, leans back in his chair. I could use something myself.

THE SITUATION NOW: my cross dismantled and stacked like building materials behind the altar. It won't be put back together and hung in time for Sunday worship. That's fine, I can make a sermon out of that. The shadow is there, the shadow of the cross on the apse. We will offer our prayers to God in the name of His Indelible Son, Jesus Christ. Not bad, Pem, you can still pull these things out of a hat when you want to.

What am I to make of this strange night culture of stealth sickos, these mindless thieves of the valueless giggling through the streets, carrying what? whatever it was! through the watery precincts of urban nihilism . . . their wit, their glimmering dying recognition of something that once had a significance they laughingly cannot remember. Jesus, there's not even sacrilege there. A dog stealing a bone knows more what he's up to.

A phone call just now from Joshua.

If we're going to be detectives about this, we start with what we know, isn't that what you did? What I know, what I start with, is that no Jewish person would have stolen your crucifix. It would not occur to him. Even in the depths of some drug-induced confusion.

I shouldn't think so, I say, thinking, Why does Joshua feel he has to rule this out?

But as you also said something like this has no street value unless someone wants it. Then it has value.

To an already-in-place, raging anti-Semite, for example.

Yes, that's the likelihood. This is a mixed neighborhood. There may be people who don't like a synagogue on their block. I've not been made aware of this, but it's always possible.

Right.

But it's also possible . . . placing that cross on my roof, well, that is something that could have been arranged by an ultra-orthodox fanatic. That's possible, too.

Good God!

We have our extremists, our fundamentalists, just as you have. There are some for whom what Sarah and I are doing, struggling to redesign, revalidate our faith—well, in their eyes it is tantamount to apostasy. What do you think of that for a theory?

Very generous of you, Joshua. But I don't buy it, I say. I mean, I can't think that it's likely. Why would it be?

The voice that told me my roof was burning? That was a Jewish thing to say. Of course, I don't know for sure, I may be all wrong. But it's something to think about. Tell me, Father—

Tom—

Tom. You're a bit older, you've seen more, given more thought to these things. Wherever you look in the world now, God belongs to the atavists. And they're so fierce, these people, so sure of themselves—as if all human knowledge since Scripture were not also God's revelation! I mean, is time a loop? Do you have the same feeling I have—that everything seems to be running backward? That civilization is in reverse?

Oh, my dear Rabbi . . . where does that leave us? Because maybe that's what faith is. That's what faith does. Whereas I am beginning to think that to hold in abeyance and irresolution any firm conviction of God, or of an afterlife with Him, warrants walking in His Spirit, somehow.

MONDAY. The front doors are padlocked. In the rectory kitchen, leaning back on the two hind legs of his chair and reading *People*, is St. Timothy's newly hired, classically indolent private security guard.

I am comforted, too, by the woman at Ecstatic Reps. She is there, as usual, walking in place, earphones clamped on her head, her large hocks in their black tights shifting up and dropping back down like Sisyphean boulders. As the afternoon darkens, she'll be broken up and splashed in the greens and pale lavenders of the light refractions on the window.

So everything is as it should be, the world's in its place. The wall clock ticks. I have nothing to worry about except what I'm going to say to the bishop's examiners who will determine the course of the rest of my life.

This is what I will say for starters:

"My dear colleagues, what you are here to examine today is not in the nature of a spiritual crisis. Let's get that clear. I have not broken down, cracked up, burned out, or caved in. True, my personal life is a shambles, my church is like a war ruin, and, since I am not one to seek counsel or join support groups, and God, as usual, has ignored my communications (let's be honest, Lord, not a letter, not a card), I do feel somewhat isolated. I will even admit that for the past few years, no, the past several years, I have not known what to do when in despair except walk the streets. Nevertheless, my ideas have substance, and, while you may find some of them alarming, I would entreat—would suggest, would recommend, would advise—I would advise you to confront them on their merits, and not as evidence of the psychological decline of a mind you once had some respect for. I mean, for which you once had some respect."

That's okay so far, isn't it, Lord? Sort of taking it to them? Maybe a bit touchy. After all, what could they have in mind? In order of probability: one, a warning; two, a formal reprimand; three, censure; four, a month or so in therapeutic retreat followed by a brilliantly remote reassignment wherein I'm never to be heard from again; five, early retirement with or without full benefits; six, defrocking; seven, the Big Ex. Whatthahell! By the way, Lord, what are these "ideas of substance" I've promised them in the above? The phrase came trippingly off the tongue. I trust You will enlighten me. What with today's shortened attention span I don't need ninety-five, I can get by with just one or two. The point is, whatever I say will alarm them. Nothing of a church is shakier than its doctrine. That's why they guard it with their lives. I mean, just to lay the "H" word on the table, it, heresy, is a legal concept, that's all. The shock is supposed to be Yours but the affront is to sectarian legality. A heretic can be of no more concern to You than someone kicked out of a building cooperative for playing the piano after ten . . . So I pray, Lord, don't let me come up with something worth only a reprimand. Let me have the good stuff. Speak to me. Send me an e-mail. You were once heard to speak:

You Yourself are a word, though deemed by some to be unutterable,

You are said to be The Word, and I don't doubt You are the Last Word.

You're the Lord our Narrator, who made a text from nothing, at least that is our story of You.

So here is Your servant, the Reverend Dr. Thomas Pemberton, the almost no longer rector of St. Timothy's, Episcopal, addressing You in one of Your own inventions, one of Your intonational systems of clicks and grunts, glottal stops and trills.

Will You show him no mercy, this poor soul tormented in his nostalgia for Your Only Begotten Son? He has failed his training as a detective, having solved nothing.

May he nevertheless pursue You? God? The Mystery?

WALTER JOHN HARMON

—

WHEN BETTY TOLD ME SHE WOULD GO THAT NIGHT TO Walter John Harmon, I didn't think I reacted. But she looked into my eyes and must have seen something—some slight loss of vitality, a moment's dullness of expression. And she understood that for all my study and hard work, the Seventh Attainment was still not mine.

Dearest, she said, don't be discouraged. The men have more difficulty. Walter John Harmon knows that and commends your struggle. You can go see him if you wish, it is the prerogative of husbands.

No, I said, I'm all right.

AFTER SHE HAD GONE I went walking in the evening light across the pastures. It is beautiful country here, a broad undulant valley with brooks and natural ponds and no ground light to dim the stars or the moving lights of the jets up among them. This is where the Holy City will descend. The community has in just two short years assembled the parcels of this valley. I did some real estate law back in Charlotte and I am proud to say I have had no small hand in our accomplishment. It is in the nature of a miracle that Walter John Harmon has in his effortless way drawn so many of us to his prophecy. And that we have given everything we possess—not to him, to the Demand that comes through him. We are not idiots.

We are not cult victims. In many quarters we are laughed at for following as God's prophet a garage mechanic who in his teens was imprisoned for car theft. But this blessed man has revolutionized our lives. From the first moment I was in his presence I felt resolved in my soul. Everything was suddenly right. I was who I was. It is hard to explain. I saw the outside world darkened, as in a film negative. But I was in the light. And that I was blessed seemed to be established in his eyes. Walter's pale blue eyes are set so deep under the ridge of his brow that the irises are occluded at the top, like half-moons. It is almost a chilling gaze you feel on you, as gentle as it may be, something not of this world but ineffable, expressive of God, like the gaze of an animal.

So I knew the failing within me when Betty was this night summoned for Purification. Walter is at a level beyond lust. This is apparent, since all the wives, even the plainest, partake of his communion. His ministry annuls the fornications of a secular society. Betty and I, for example, made love many times before we were married. And the Community's children, the children in white, who have never known carnal sin, are not permitted to look at Walter John Harmon lest he inspire them to their confusion. They are the precious virgins, girls and boys, whose singing brings him such joy. He says nothing to them, of course, but smiles and closes those remarkable eyes, and the tears stream from them like rain down a windowpane.

BETTY AND I LEARNED about Walter John Harmon from the Internet. I found myself reading someone's weblog—how that happened I can't remember. I think of it now as the beginning of His summons, for there is nothing without significance in this world made by God. I called Betty and she came into my study and together we read of this most remarkable event of the tornado that had occurred the year before in the town of Fremont in west Kansas. There were links, too, all from this locality and all telling the same story. I logged in to the archives of the regional newspapers and confirmed that there had been a series of tornadoes all through the state at that time, and a particularly destructive twister that had hit Fremont head-on. But beyond that not one news report had the key thing. Not even in the Fremont *Sun-Ledger* was there an account of this one inexplicable occurrence of the cyclone that came through the middle of town, flinging cars into the air, shattering storefronts, lifting houses off their foundations, and, among other disasters, setting off a gas-and-oil fire that pooled on the floor of the repair shop of the Getty station on the corner of Railroad and Division streets, where Walter John Harmon worked as a mechanic.

I hold in my mind a composite account of what happened, from the weblogs and from what we have since heard recounted by the townspeople who witnessed this or that particular moment and who followed Walter in his ministry and are now the Community Elders. Walter John Harmon himself has not been persuaded to write down a testament, nor has he permitted anything to be written in the way of documentation. "It is not the time for that," he says. And then, "May it never be the time, for the day we falter and lose our way, that will be the time." In fact nothing in the Community is written. The Ideals, the Imperatives, the Assignments and Obligations are all pronounced, and once spoken by the prophet are carried and remembered by means of daily prayer. The miracles of the tornado are held in the imaginations of our minds and we speak of them to one another in our workday or social gatherings, so that as the years pass there will be a Consensus of the inner truth and its authority will be unquestionable.

As he stood by the pool of fire, the garage doors first, and then the roof and then the collapsed walls, were lifted and spun into the black funnel. Only Walter John Harmon stood where he stood, and then was slowly raised in his standing and turned slowly in his turning, calmly and silently, his arms stretched wide in the black shrieking, with the things of our lives whirling in the whirlwind above him—car fenders and machines from the Laundromat, hats and empty coats and trousers, tables, mattresses, plates and knives and forks, TV sets and computers, all malignantly alive in the black howling. And then a child flew into Walter John Harmon's left arm and another fell into his right arm, and he held them steadfast and was lowered to the ground where he had stood. And then the dreaded wind that takes all breath away was gone, having blown itself to bits. And the fields beyond the town were strewn with the several dead and dying among their possessions. But the pool of fire in the Getty garage was nothing but a ring of blackened concrete, and the sun was out as if the tornado had never been, and the mothers of those two children came running and found them bruised and bleeding and crying but alive. Only then did Walter John Harmon begin again to breathe, though he stood where he stood, unable to move as if in a trance, until he collapsed and lost consciousness.

All of this is in the Consensus. Other elements of the miracle are still debated by the Community and I suppose come under the heading of apocrypha. One of the Elders, Ansel Bernes, who had owned a clothing store, claims that seven mercury streetlamps on the walking street in the Fremont business district came on and stayed on when the tornado hit. I can't quite accept this. According to the *Sun-Ledger*, Fremont's power outage was total. It took the local utility two days to get everyone back online.

WHEN WE CAME here Betty and I had been married a dozen years with no children to show for it. One of the appeals of the Community is that we are all parents of all children. While the adults live in distinct quarters of their own, as in the outer world, the children room together in the main house. At present we are a hundred ten in number, with a human treasury of seventy-eight children, ranging in age from two to fifteen.

Except for the main house, which was once a retreat for elderly nuns of the Roman Catholic persuasion and to which we have added a new wing, all the Community buildings were built by members according to the specifications of Walter John Harmon. He called for square, box-like structures with gable roofs for the adult houses, each of which contains two apartments of two rooms each. His own residence is slightly larger, with a gambrel roof, which gives it the appearance of a barn. All buildings in the complex are painted white; no colors are permitted exterior or interior. Metal fixtures are not allowed—window frames are wood, all water is drawn by hand from wells, there is no indoor plumbing, and communal showers, men's and women's, are jerry-rigged in tents. Walter John Harmon has said: "We praise what is temporary, we cherish the impermanent, for there can be no comparison with what is coming that is not an impiety."

But in the business suite in the new wing of the main house we do have computers, faxes, copiers, and so on, powered by a gasoline generator behind the building, though we intend when it is practical to switch to solar cells. There are metal filing cabinets as well. All of this is by dispensation because, regrettably, we do have necessary business with the outside world. We handle legal challenges from state and county officials and must deal also with private suits brought by unthinking or opportunistic relations of our family members. But only the Community lawyers, and Elder Rafael Altman, our financial officer and CPA, and his bookkeepers, and the women who provide clerical help, can enter these premises. Three of us practice law, and after morning prayers we

go to work just like everyone else. By dispensation we own the ha-
biliments of the legal profession—suits, shirts, ties, polished shoes,
which we don for those occasions when we must meet with our
counterparts in the world outside. We are driven by horse and
wagon to the Gate down at the paved road some two miles away.
There we have the choice of the three parked SUVs, though never
the Hummer. The Hummer is reserved for Walter John Harmon.
He does not proselytize, but he does schedule spiritual meetings
on the outside. Or he will attend ecumenical or scholarly confer-
ences on this or that religious or social issue. He is never invited to
participate but is eloquent enough sitting quietly in the audience
in his robe, his head bowed, his face almost hidden in the fall of his
hair and his hands folded under his chin.

BETTY RETURNED early the next morning, the sun coming with
her through the door, and I welcomed her with a hug. I meant it,
too—I love seeing her face in the morning. She is very fair and
rises from her sleep with her cheeks flushed like a child's and her
hazel eyes instantly alert to the day. She is as lithe and fit as she was
when she played field hockey at college. If you look closely some
tiny lines radiate from the corners of her eyes, but this only makes
her more attractive to me. Her hair is still the color of wheat and
she still wears it short, as she did when I met her, and she still has
that spring to her step and her typically energetic way of doing
things.

We prayed together and then we had our bread and tea, chat-
ting all the while. Betty served as a Community teacher, she had
the kindergarten, and she was talking about her day's plan. I was
feeling better. It was a beautiful day dawning with coverlets of
white webbing on the grass. I had a renewed confidence in my own
feelings.

All at once the most hideous carnal images arose in my mind. I wanted to speak but could not catch my breath.

What is it, Jim, what?

Betty held my hand. I closed my eyes until the images disappeared and I could breathe again.

Oh my dear one, she said. Last night was not the first time, after all. And have our lives changed? I'm telling you it is not a normal human experience with any of the normal results.

I don't want to hear about it. It is not necessary for me to hear about it.

It is no more, or no less, than a sacrament. It is no more than when the priest placed the wafer on our tongues.

I held my hand up. Betty looked at me inquiringly, as in the old days, a pretty bird with its head cocked, wondering who I could possibly be.

You know, she said, I had to tell Walter John Harmon. You should go see him. Look how your mouth is set, so hard, so angry.

It was not for you to tell him, I said.

I recognized an Obligation.

Outside in the sun, I breathed the sweet air of the valley and tried to calm myself. Everything around me was the vision of serene life. We are the quietest people. You will never hear a loud argument or see a public display of temperament anywhere in the Community. Our children never fight, or push one another, or band together in hurtful cliques the way children do. The muslin we wear that suggests our common priesthood quiets the heart. The prayers we utter, the food we grow for ourselves in our fields, provide an immense and recurring satisfaction.

Betty followed me. Please, Jim, she said. You should talk to him. He will see you.

Yes? And what if I am excused from my work, if I am remanded, who can argue the case?

What case is that?

You're not entrusted to know. But believe me it's critical.

He will not remand you then.

How can you know that? I may not be an Elder, but I'm approved to go beyond the Gate. And doesn't that presuppose the Seventh?

Why was I having to defend myself? Please, I said, I won't talk about this anymore.

Betty turned from me and I felt her coldness. I had the maniacal thought that the Purifications wouldn't be a problem for me if I no longer loved my wife.

At our supper at the end of the day she asked me to do something, some minor chore that I would have done without her asking, and I thought her tone was officious.

TO WHAT EXTENT was my legal work in the outside world holding me back from the prophetic realization offered by Walter John Harmon? Didn't I have one foot in and one foot out? But wasn't that my Imperative? He himself had said the higher Attainments are elusive, difficult, and, as if they had personalities of their own, they were given to teasing us with simulacra of themselves. So there was no shame in being remanded. Perhaps for my own sake I should have requested it. But then would I not be putting myself before the needs of the Community? And wouldn't that be to relinquish the Sixth Attainment?

The following morning before work I went to the Tabernacle to pray.

Our Tabernacle is no more than a lean-to. It stands at the high end of the lawn bordering the apple orchard. On a wooden table of our own making and without any ornamentation or covering sits a white stone and a common latchkey. I knelt in the grass in the

sun with my head bowed and my hands clasped. But even as I uttered the prayers my mind split in two. As I mouthed the words all
I could think of was this question: Had I come to the Community
from the needs of my own heart, or had I deceived myself by taking for my own the convictions of my wife? That's how badly the
doubts were assailing me.

When I looked up Walter John Harmon was standing in the
Tabernacle. I had not seen him approach. Nor was he looking at
me. He was staring at the ground, seeing nothing but his own
thoughts.

Walter does not deliver sermons because, as he maintains, we
are not a church, we are an Unfolding Revelation. He will appear
at the Tabernacle unannounced, any time of the day, any day of the
week, as the spirit moves him. At such times, the word goes out
and the members who can manage it run to hear him, and those
whose work prevents this will hear his words later as committed to
the memory of those in attendance.

People came running now. Because Walter John Harmon is so
soft-spoken it became apparent to the Elders at one point that a
dispensation had to be made for a wireless microphone and a loud-
speaker. As he stood in the Tabernacle in his characteristic way,
with the fingertips of one hand touching the wooden table, and as
he began to speak as he would have even if there were no one to
listen, someone arrived with the speaker and set up the microphone on a stand in front of him. Even amplified, the prophet's
voice was barely more than a whisper. There was such a diffidence
about him, for as he had told us more than once, his was a reluc-
tant prophecy. He had not sought it, or wanted it. Before God
came to him in that whirlwind, he had not even thought about religion. He had led an unruly life in his youth and had done many
bad things, and felt perhaps that was why he'd been chosen—to
demonstrate the mysterious greatness of God.

—

WHAT WALTER JOHN HARMON said on this morning was along these lines: Everywhere and at all times, numeration is the same for all mankind. This is because, no less than the earth or the stars, numbers are the expression of God. And so as they add and subtract and divide and multiply, as they combine and separate and conclude, they are the same always to the understanding of human beings no matter who we are or what language we speak. God in the form of numerical truth will weigh the fruit on the scale, He will measure your height, He will give you the tolerances of your engine parts and tell you the length of your journey. He will offer you numbers to go on forever without end, and we call this infinity, because our mathematics count up to God. And when Jesus the Son of God died for our sins, He took to Himself the infinity of them because He was of God and could die for the sins of the dead and the living and the unborn for generations to come.

A prophet is not the Son of God, he is one of you, he is an ordinary man of remorse, like you, and so his numbers are no more infinite than the years of his life are infinite. He cannot die for mankind's sins. He may only work to remove the sin of this or that soul, taking it into himself and adding it into himself. Whatever faults you in the eyes of God—your carnal desires, your greed, your attachment to what is unworthy—your mortal prophet lifts from you and takes unto himself. And he does that until the weight of the numbers will bury him and he is welcomed in Hell. For he is an ordinary mortal and if he takes on your sins they become his own and it is to Hell he will go—not to God at His right hand but to the Devil in the depths of Hell's eternal torment. "Only the adults purified by this prophecy will join the virgin children in the Holy City to come," Walter John Harmon said. "And I will not be among them."

—

THERE WAS CONSTERNATION at those words. We knew because the Transference of Sin was the key to his teaching that Walter risked exclusion from the Holy City. We had discussed it at our Meetings. The prophecy was Jesus-like but not Jesus, it was Moses-like but not Moses. Yet to hear it put in mathematical terms was shocking—people stood and cried out, because now Walter John Harmon was speaking of something as incontestable as a sum, as measurable as a weight or a volume, and the reality of such a cut-and-dried formulation seemed almost too much for us to bear.

He did not walk away but looked over us with a faint smile on his lips. Was he suggesting that his doom was imminent? His blond and graying hair was tied this morning into a ponytail, which made him seem younger than his thirty-seven years. And at this moment his pale blue eyes were those of a youth unaware of the tragedy of his life. As he stood and waited, the members were slowly calmed by his silence. We went to him, and knelt, and kissed his robe. Perhaps I was the only one this day to feel that his words were a personal communication. They seemed to be responding to my torments, as if, having intuited my reluctance to seek his counsel, Walter John Harmon had chosen this way to remind me of his truth and to restore the strength of my conviction. But that was the effect always, after all, for the power of his word was in its uncanny precise application to whatever had been in your own mind though you might not have before realized it.

All who heard him this day knew the truth of his prophecy and the resolution and peace of surrendering to it. I felt once again the privilege of the Seven Attainments. I loved Walter John Harmon. How then could I fault my wife's love for him?

—

A WEEK OR SO LATER I dressed for the outer world and drove one of our SUVs to the state courthouse in Granger, a trip of some sixty miles. Whenever I walked into a courthouse now, I felt a great unease, as an alien in a strange land. Yet I had passed the bar exams of three contiguous states and had spent my adult life in the general practice of law and so there was simultaneously a professional sense of belonging to such buildings as this old red stone horror with its corner cupolas, which dominated the square at the city's center. It spoke to me as the native architecture of my own American past, and when I climbed the worn steps and heard my heels clicking on the floor of the entry hall, I had to remind myself that I was an envoy from the future, about to address in their own vocabulary the denizens of the dark ages of secular life.

This was to be a hearing before an administrative judge. The state commissioner of education had moved to suspend the Community's license to school its children. A failure to comply with the statutes requiring mandatory literacy for every child was said to be grounds for a suspension. We were met not in a courtroom but in a room used mostly for jury empaneling in tort cases. It had big windows and dark green shades pulled against the morning sun. The state had a trio of lawyers. The judge sat behind another table. There were chairs around the walls for spectators—all filled. As far as I knew there had been no public announcement of this morning's hearing. A couple of policemen stood by the doors.

The state argued that in using only the Book of Revelation to teach our children to read and write, and further, that in permitting them ever after to read nothing else than the Book of Revelation, or write nothing but from its passages, we were in default of the literacy statutes. The distinction was made as between education and indoctrination and that the latter as practiced by our cult

(I rose to object to that derogatory label) contravened the presumption of literacy as a continuing process, generating ever-widening reading experiences and access to information. Whereas in our closed-ended pedagogy, when one text and one text only was all the child was going to read, or recite, or intone, or chant forever after, the open-ended presumption of literacy was negated. The child would learn the text by heart and by rote repeat it with no further call on linguistic skills.

I argued that literacy had no such open-ended presumption, it merely meant the ability to read—that when the state's own inspectors had sat in on our first- and second-grade classes they were satisfied that the principles of reading and writing were being taught in terms of word recognition and phonetics, spelling and grammar, and that it was only when they had discovered, in the upper grades, that the Book of Revelation was the children's sole reading material that they found the Community at fault. Yet the children as taught by us are in fact able to read anything and are literate. Because we direct their reading and contemplation to the sacred text that is the basis of our beliefs and social organization, the commissioner would impinge on our right of free religious expression as set forth in the First Amendment. Every religion teaches its tenets from one generation to the next, I said. And every parent has the right to raise his child according to his beliefs. That is what the parents of our Community were doing and had every right to do, whereas the claim of failed literacy was on the face of it an attempt to interfere with a minority's religious practice of which the commissioner does not approve.

The judge ordered a suspension of our license but declared at the same time that, the issues being substantive, he would defer his order so as to allow time for a court challenge. It was what I expected. The lawyers and I shook hands and that was it.

But as I was leaving the room one of the spectators stopped me, an older man with gnarled hands and a cane. You are working for the Devil, sir, he said. Shame on you, shame, he called after me. And then in the corridor a reporter I recognized was at my side, walking with me at my pace. Playing the freedom-of-religion card, eh, counselor? You know they'll really be down on you now. Studies, tests, videotapes, school records. Process of discovery.

Nice to see you, I said.

Anyway, you bought yourself six months. Six more months of doing what you do. Except of course if your boy is nailed before then.

Christ was nailed, I said.

Yeah, the reporter said, but not for having a Swiss bank account.

I WAS RELIEVED to get back to the great valley as a soldier is relieved to get back to his own lines. There was a lovely sense of bustling anticipation as the weekend approached: we were to have an Embrace.

This was a once-a-month occasion when we received outsiders who had heard of us, and made inquiries, or had perhaps attended one of Walter John Harmon's outside Meetings and found themselves interested enough to spend the day with us. They parked their cars at the Gate and were brought up by hay wagon. In our early days we didn't think of security. Now we copied down driver's licenses and asked for signatures and names of family members.

On this Saturday morning in May perhaps two dozen people arrived, many with children, and we greeted them with heartfelt smiles and coffee and cake under the two oak trees. I was not on the Hospitality Squad, but Betty was. She knew how to make people feel comfortable. She was pretty and compassionate, and altogether irresistible, as I well knew. She could immediately spot the most needful tender souls and go right to them. Of course, no one who appeared on these days was not needful or they wouldn't have come. But some were skittish or melancholic or so on the edge of despair as to be rudely skeptical.

In the end, no one could withstand the warmth and friendliness of our Embrace. We treated all newcomers like long-lost friends. And there was plenty to keep everyone busy. There was the tour of the residences and the main house, where the children put on a sing. And there was the Enrobing. All the guests were given the muslin robe to wear over their clothes. This had the effect of delighting them as a game would delight them, but it also acclimated them to our appearance. We didn't seem so strange then. Several long refectory tables were brought out from the carpentry shop and the guests helped lay the cloths and carry out the bowls and platters with all the wonderful foodstuffs—the meat pies, the vegetables from our gardens, the breads from our bakery, the pitchers of cool well water and homemade lemonade. All the children sat down together at their tables and all the adults at theirs, there in the warm sun. Every guest was placed between two members with another directly across. And our Elder Sherman Beasley, who had a naturally booming voice, stood and he said grace, and everyone tucked in.

It was such a beautiful day. I was able to sit in my place at the end of one of the long tables and to forget for a while the threats to our existence and to feel blessed to be here under a blue sky and to feel the sun on my face as God's warmth.

The conversation was lively. We were instructed to try to answer every question as diplomatically as possible. We were not to give doctrine or theology—only the Elders were entrusted to do that.

A shy young woman on my right asked me why she had not

seen any dogs in our Community. She was physically unprepossessing, with thick glasses, and she held herself on the bench as if to take up as little space as possible. This is sort of like a big farm, she said in her thin voice, and I've never been on a farm that didn't have a dog or two.

I told her only that dogs were unclean.

She nodded and thought awhile and after a sip of lemonade, she said: Everyone here is so happy.

Do you find that odd?

Yes, sort of.

I couldn't help smiling. We are with Walter John Harmon, I said.

AFTER LUNCH came our big surprise. We took everyone to the West Section, where on a prelaid cement base a house was going up for a recently sworn-in couple. The framing was done and now as everyone sat in the grass and watched, we men arose and, under the guidance of our carpenters, some of us went to work on the board-and-batten siding, others were up on the roof beams, laying out the planking, and the skilled among us were fitting out the doors and the windows. Of course none of the inside finishing would be done that day, but the thrill our guests had was in seeing so many of us making such quick work of building a home. It was a lesson without words. In fact it was a kind of performance because we had built the identical home many times over and each man knew what he had to do and where each nail went. There was a natural music to all the hammering and sawing and hauling and grunting and we could hear our audience laugh and occasionally applaud with delight.

At the end, as we all stood by, Elder Manfred Jackson presented a scroll to the new first-floor occupants, the Donaldsons, a gray-haired couple who held hands and wept. After the Donaldsons were embraced by several members and brought to sit down among them, Elder Jackson turned to the visitors and explained what they had witnessed: they had witnessed the Third Attainment.

Manfred Jackson was our only black Elder. He was an imposing figure, tall, his shoulders as squared as a young man's though he was in his eighties. His hair was white and he wore the muslin robe like a king. With the Third Attainment, he said, these communicants of the Unfolding Revelation have forsworn all their personal property and given their wealth to the prophet. The Third Attainment is a considerable step up, for it is no small matter to abjure the false values of the world and rise from its filth. The prophet teaches us there are seven steps to God-worthiness. Ours will be the kingdom of the chaste and the absolved, because whatever is ours, whatever we possess, whatever we think we cannot do without, we give to the prophet as his burden. He has brought us to live apart from the clamor and lies of the unbelieving. We wear his muslin to declare ourselves in transit. We live in homes to be blown away in the tornado of God. Manfred Jackson pointed out over the valley where the Holy City would descend: We wait upon the glory that needs no sun, he said.

ALL THIS TIME Walter John Harmon had not been seen. As the day went on, heads turned this way and that as our guests wondered where was the man who had drawn them here in the first place. By mid-afternoon all the organized events, the choir recital, the walking tour of the sacred land, and so on, were concluded, and the visitors began to think of leaving. We had collected their muslin robes as if to give them leave to depart. They were indecisive. Some of their children were still playing with ours. The parents were looking for someone to make the first move toward the hay wagons. In the meantime we Elders and members continued to walk with them and express pleasure at their coming, gradually drifting with them back toward the Tabernacle. We knew what to expect, but we let them discover for themselves the prophet sitting quietly there beside the wood table. A child saw him first and called out, and it was the children who ran ahead, their parents following, and a murmur of awe went through them as they slowly gathered in the grass and looked upon Walter John Harmon.

This was always a thrilling moment for me, a culmination of the day's Embrace. See? I wanted to call out, do you see? a great surge of pride filling my breast.

The prophet's custom was to speak to the visitors, but this day he was lost in thought. His eyes were lowered. He sat slightly forward in the chair, one ankle tucked behind the other and his hands folded in his lap. His feet were bare. People settled down in the grass, waiting for him to speak, and even the children grew quiet. More and more members joined us, and there was absolute silence. The ground was cool. The light of the afternoon sun was beginning to throw shadows and a small breeze blew across the grass and played in the hair of the prophet. Betty was suddenly beside me, dropping to her knees, and she took my hand and squeezed it.

Minutes passed. He said nothing. The silence passed the point of our uneasiness or expectation and became significant. A great peace entered me and I listened to the breeze as if it were a language, as if it were the language of the prophet. When a cloud passed over the sun I saw the moving shadow on the ground as his writing. It was as if his silence was transmuted to the language of the pure world of God. It said all would be well. It said suffering would cease. It said our hearts would be healed.

As the silence went on, it became so unendurably beautiful that people began to weep. Someone stepped past me and went to the prophet as he sat there in his impassive loneliness. It was one of the visitors, a chubby blond child who couldn't have been more than fifteen or sixteen. She lay down before Walter John Harmon, and curling herself into a fetal position, she touched her forehead to his feet.

SIX FAMILIES among the visitors that day would pledge to the nonresidential tithing that is the First Attainment. But as our Community continued to grow, in a kind of perverse linkage, the attentions of a vindictive world were growing, too. Unfortunately, one of the registrants at the Embrace was a columnist from a Denver newspaper, who must have gotten in under an assumed identity. She described the events of the day accurately enough—such was her craftiness—but the tone of the piece was condescending, if not contemptuous. I could not understand why a columnist would want to come all the way from Denver to sneer at us. The column was not libelous in the legal sense, but I felt personally betrayed when I recognized from the columnist's photo the unprepossessing young woman with thick glasses who had sat next to me at the midday luncheon and asked me how everyone could be so happy. How underhanded she had been, and with such animosity in her mousy being.

At a steering committee meeting, the Elders Imperatived that the monthly Embraces should thenceforth be limited to families with children. I thought, given the needful of this world, that such a restriction was unfortunate, but the fact was that we were beginning to feel embattled. Allegations that we were all familiar with, having heard them many times over, were regularly communicated to us—by relatives, friends, or professional contacts on the outside—as if we had to be enlightened: *Your prophet is an alcoholic. He abandoned a wife and child. He has grown rich at your expense.* How could any of this have been news to us inasmuch as our prophet was what, in our entirety, we had been? As Walter John Harmon took our evil unto himself, we had emerged newborn, with our addictions, our concupiscence, and our depthless greed lifted from us.

His life was no secret. Every moment of it was a confession. But as the outer world was as darkly inverted as the negative of a photograph, so was its logic.

Each instance of negative publicity seemed to encourage another suit or investigation of one kind or another. Elder Rafael Altman, our CPA, informed us one morning that the IRS had applied for a court order to subpoena the Community books. One of our lawyers was dispatched to apply for an injunction. Those others of us with skills still practiced on the outside met in extraordinary session with the Elders to come up with some overall strategy for dealing with an increasingly impinging world. As to bad publicity, up to this point we had met all of it with a pious silence. Now we decided for the prophet's sake that we must speak out on his behalf, we must give witness. We would not proselytize, but we would respond. Judson Berglund, a high Attainist who before coming to us had run his own public-relations firm in California, had the Imperative to organize this effort. He quickly brought order. When a national newsweekly questioned the miracle of the Fremont, Kansas, tornado, Berglund saw to it that they printed Elders' testimony in their letters to the editor. An attack by a well-known anticultist we boldly duplicated on our website, along with the countervailing responses of dozens of our members. And so on.

It only became us, though, to respond to everything patiently, resolutely, and in the spirit of forgiveness.

Walter John Harmon was typically stoic about all the problems mounting up, but as the summer drew to an end and the leaves of the oak trees began to turn, he seemed more and more withdrawn, as on that day of the Embrace. He seemed irritated that nothing he did went unnoticed, as if our devotedness was pressing on him. Yet he was called by God to have no private life, no private feelings, and so we worried about him. Our joyful life of peace and reconciliation, the exultant knowledge infused in all our beings of an exquisite righteousness in the sight of God, and the prayerful anticipation of the coming to our green earth of God's Holy City, was shadowed now by our concern for the spirit of His prophet. When the children sang, he was inattentive. He took long walks alone in the holy site. I wondered if it were possible that the weight of our sins had already become too burdensome for his mortal soul.

WHAT I REMEMBER now is Walter John Harmon standing with my wife, Betty, in the orchard above the Tabernacle on a chilly gray afternoon in October. Clouds dark with rain sailed through the sky. A wind blew. The orchard trees were only three or four years old, the apple, pear, and peach trees not much higher than a man. Only the apple trees were in fruit now, and on this windy gray day, while Betty's charges ran about picking apples off the ground or reaching for them on the lower branches, I watched Betty hold an apple out to Walter John Harmon. He took her wrist in his hand and leaned forward and bit into the apple she held. Then she took a bite, and they stood looking in each other's eyes as they masticated. Then they embraced and their robes, whipped by the wind, clung to their shapes, and I heard the children laughing and saw them running in circles around my wife and Walter John Harmon in their embrace.

SOME MORNINGS after this, members who had gone to pray noticed a robe lying on the ground beside the Tabernacle table. It was his, the prophet's. We knew that because, for ceremonial occasions, he wore not muslin but linen. Now it lay as if he had dropped it at his feet and walked away. The latchkey was still on the table, but the white stone was on the ground. The Elders were quickly summoned to study the scene. Carpenters placed stanchions around the site so that the gathering members would not disturb anything.

Efforts were made to locate Walter John Harmon. We had never ventured past his front door. This was now found to be open. Inside, the place was a shambles. Empty liquor bottles, broken dishes. His closet was empty. Down at the Gate, someone reported that the Hummer was gone.

At noon, with all work stopped, the Elders announced to the stunned Community that Walter John Harmon was no longer among us. There was absolute silence. Elder Bob Bruce said the Elders would convene shortly to make a determination as to the meaning of the prophet's disappearance. He led us in prayer and then urged everyone to go back to their tasks. The teachers were to take their children back to their classrooms. As everyone dispersed, one group of children stood where they were, there being no teacher to lead them. These were Betty's charges. Her puzzled colleagues took the children in hand. Everyone was distracted, unsettled.

I could have told them all the prophet was gone when, the night before, I heard Betty rise from her bed, dress, and slip out the door. I listened, and in a while, in the darkness, I heard through the clear cold night the distant sound of an engine turning over, revving up.

WHEN IT WAS discovered that the prophet had left with my wife, I was called before the Elders. I was invited to join them in their councils. Perhaps they believed the cuckolded husband was enlightened as they were not. Perhaps they thought he was important in other ways. Surely the challenge to no member's faith could have been greater than the challenge to mine, and if I could forbear and sing the praises of God, who would not sing with me?

Whatever their reasoning, I took solace in their dispensation. My personal grief was subsumed. For the sake of my sanity I wanted to find resolution and strength from this crisis. But I also understood quite clearly and unemotionally that were I to think of Betty's betrayal with a forgiving spirit and concentrate on its larger meaning, I would both ease my heart and put myself forward in the minds of the Elders as an exemplar of our Ideals. In a community such as ours one's moral currency might someday be exchanged for an executive role.

The discussion went on for three days. I spoke with increasing confidence and have to admit I had no small part in the deliberations. We came to the following consensus: Walter John Harmon had done what was both required and foreordained by the nature of his prophecy. Not only had he forsaken us who had loved him and depended upon him, but by running off with one of the purified wives, he had cast doubt upon the central tenet of his teaching. What further proof did we need of the truth of his prophecy than his total immersion in sin and disgrace? It was thrilling. Elder Al Samuels, a tiny, bent-over octogenarian with the piping, scratched voice of the very old, was also the most philosophically inclined. He said we were confronted with the beautiful paradox of a prophecy fulfilling itself by means of its negation. Elder Fred Sanders, known and loved for his ebullience, stood up and shouted, Glory be to God for our blessed prophet! We all stood and shouted, Hallelujah!

But while all of this was being worked out, the Community had languished. There was a good deal of crying and wandering about listlessly on the part of many. People could not do their work.

Extra prayer sessions were called but went sparsely attended. And a few of the members, poor souls, even packed their meager belongings and walked down the road to the Gate, heedless of all pleas. I think that is how word got out about our situation—through our dispirited defectors. It did not help that a TV news broadcast showed a picture of the Community from a helicopter flying over us while an announcer spoke of us as collectively duped, robbed of our estates, and left humiliated and penniless in the middle of nowhere.

It was time to act. On the advice of Judson Berglund, who had so far managed our public relations effectively, a great celebration was prepared, with music from our string musicians and tables of good food and a goodly supply of our ceremonial wine. Work and school were suspended for the people of the Community to gather and be together. Thanks be to God, the weather softened into one of those October days when the sun, low in the sky, casts a golden patina over the land. Yet the sense of irresolution, of bewilderment, did not entirely lift. People wanted to hear the Elders. I noticed that some of the children had sought out their natural parents and now clung to them.

After lunch, the musicians retired and everyone gathered before the Tabernacle. The Seven Elders arranged themselves on wooden chairs facing the assemblage. One by one, they rose to speak. Their pronouncement was along the following lines: The prophet had all but warned us this would come to pass. He said he would not be among the blessed who would reside in the Holy City. That he has gone so soon is a stunning blow to those of us who loved him, as we all loved him, but we must love him more now that he has done this thing. That is our Imperative. We cannot question what he has done, for it is nothing else but his final sacrifice. He has taken into himself all the sins of the world that we had accumulated and returned with them to the world that we might be made righteous in the eyes of God. Nor should we mourn him: if we live as we have lived, and learn as we have learned, wherever he is will he not still be in our midst? For this reason, from this day forward we Elders will speak in his voice. We will say his saying and think his thinking. And the prophecy that was is the prophecy that is. For he has cast the stone down and the key is here on the table that will open up the door to the Kingdom of God. And when the four horsemen come riding over the land and the plagues rise like a miasma from the earth and the sun turns black and the moon blood red, and when firestorms engulf whole cities and the nuclear warriors of the world consume one another, the prophet shall be with us and in the carnage and devastation we will be untouched. For God came to earth one day as a tornado, as a whirlwind that spun around this humble man, whose goodness and moral stature only God could see to be His prophet. And we who are your Elders saw it with our own eyes. And we tell you when God comes down again, He will not be a whirlwind, He will be the resplendent self-illuminating city of His glory and His peace, and we who have lived to the prophecy of Walter John Harmon will walk down these pastures and reside there forever.

The Elders were effective. I could see resolution firming up in the postures and facial expressions of the members. Many glances were sent my way. I found myself basking in the reflected glory of my faithless wife, who had been chosen by Walter John Harmon to join him in the ultimate sin, his betrayal of the Community.

A DAY OR TWO LATER, when one of the women went into the prophet's house to clean it up, she noticed something under a chair that had been overlooked in the excitement: a pencil.

Our prophet had never wanted anything written.

The Elder who was summoned discovered something else: in

the fireplace, half buried in the ashes, were three sheets of paper that had curled and were slightly charred on the edges but were still, miraculously, intact.

On these pages Walter John Harmon had laid out plans for a wall to be built around our Community. He'd provided sketches and measurements. The Gate down by the highway was to be drawn back to just one hundred and ten yards from our buildings. The wall was to be of stone, three cubits thick and four cubits high. The stones were to be gathered from the pasture and from brooks and streams. They were to be bonded with a cement mixture whose proportions he had carefully indicated. And then, a cryptic sentence written at the bottom of the last page of instructions added to the mystery: This wall for when the time comes, is what it said.

Clearly, this was a discovery of unsettling magnitude. It brought forth only questions. A wall of stone did not accord with the Ideal of impermanence that had guided all our previous construction. What did that mean? Did it amount to a new Ideal? And when would what time come? But he had thrown the plans into the fire. Why?

We simply didn't know what to do about these plans. Had they not been discarded, almost certainly they would constitute a Demand.

The pages were preserved in a clear plastic folder and put in the safe of the business office pending further study.

In the meantime, we had to sort out our overall situation. We had been left with very little operating capital. All surrendered estates of members were made liquid through a succession of trusts and routinely placed in the prophet's name in several numbered Swiss bank accounts to protect against legal incursion. He had personally dispensed sums as they were applied for by our financial Elder, Rafael Altman. We grew our own food and clothed ourselves humbly, but we were in arrears for the material costs of our building program, which had gone on more or less continuously as new members arrived. Perhaps we would not have that many more new members for a while. But several of our parcels of valley land for the descent of the Holy City were heavily mortgaged. And were we to lose even one of the standing civil suits against us, we would be terribly vulnerable.

As the weeks went by, it became apparent we faced a long cold winter of untold hardship. Our infirmary, with its one doctor and two nurses, tended to a host of ailing children. There were a number of cases of flu. Elder Al Samuels succumbed to pneumonia and we buried him in the rise behind the orchard. The little bent-over man with the piping voice was well loved and the fact that he was almost ninety when he passed was no consolation to the Community. My own sadness was only slightly appeased when the surviving Elders elevated me to their company. We need younger blood, Elder Sanders said to me as he gripped my arm. Our witness is passed to you by decree.

IT IS NOW JANUARY of the New Year and I write secretly at night in the privacy of my house. Perhaps, as the prophet says, the time for documentation comes only when the world overtakes us. So be it. This has not to do with a loss of faith—mine is strong and does not give way. My belief in Walter John Harmon and the truth of his prophecy does not falter. Yes, I say to the skeptics: It is entirely unlikely that someone as uneducated and hapless and imperfect as this simple garage mechanic can have designed such an inspired worship. And only the sacred touch of God upon his brow can explain it.

The Community as it huddles on these snowy plains is smaller, but by that fact tighter and more resolute, and we gather each morning to thank God for our joyous discovery of Him. But the world is overwhelming, and if we do not survive, at least this testimony, and others that may be written, will guide future generations to our faith.

Given the general age and infirmity of the Elders, I now function as the managing partner functions in a law office. And Walter John Harmon has come to live through me and will speak in my voice. I have studied the three pages of his plans and I have made the decision that in the first days of thaw we will send our people out to the holy pastures to collect the rocks and boulders for our wall. And one of the newer members, a retired army colonel to whom I've given the plans, has gone out and paced the land. He says it is amazing that our prophet has no military experience. For, as designed, these breastworks take every advantage of the terrain and give us positions for a devastating enfilade.

We are assured of a clear and unimpeded field of fire.

A HOUSE ON THE PLAINS

—

MAMA SAID I WAS THENCEFORTH TO BE HER NEPHEW, AND TO call her Aunt Dora. She said our fortune depended on her not having a son as old as eighteen who looked more like twenty. Say Aunt Dora, she said. I said it. She was not satisfied. She made me say it several times. She said I must say it believing she had taken me in since the death of her widowed brother, Horace. I said, I didn't know you had a brother named Horace. Of course I don't, she said with an amused glance at me. But it must be a good story if I could fool his son with it.

I was not offended as I watched her primp in the mirror, touching her hair as women do, although you can never see what afterward is different.

With the life insurance, she had bought us a farm fifty miles west of the city line. Who would be there to care if I was her flesh-and-blood son or not? But she had her plans and was looking ahead. I had no plans. I had never had plans—just the inkling of something, sometimes, I didn't know what. I hunched over and went down the stairs with the second trunk wrapped to my back with a rope. Outside, at the foot of the stoop, the children were waiting with their scraped knees and socks around their ankles. They sang their own dirty words to a nursery rhyme. I shooed them away and they scattered off for a minute hooting and hollering and then of course came back again as I went up the stairs for the rest of the things.

Mama was standing at the empty bay window. While there is your court of inquest on the one hand, she said, on the other is your court of neighbors. Out in the country, she said, there will be no one to jump to conclusions. You can leave the door open, and the window shades up. Everything is clean and pure under the sun.

Well, I could understand that, but Chicago to my mind was the only place to be, with its grand hotels and its restaurants and paved avenues of trees and mansions. Of course not all Chicago was like that. Our third-floor windows didn't look out on much besides the row of boardinghouses across the street. And it is true that in the summer people of refinement could be overcome with the smell of the stockyards, although it didn't bother me. Winter was another complaint that wasn't mine. I never minded the cold. The wind in winter blowing off the lake went whipping the ladies' skirts like a demon dancing around their ankles. And winter or summer you could always ride the electric streetcars if you had nothing else to do. I above all liked the city because it was filled with people all a-bustle, and the clatter of hooves and carriages, and with delivery wagons and drays and the peddlers and the boom and clank of the freight trains. And when those black clouds came sailing in from the west, pouring thunderstorms upon us so that you couldn't hear the cries or curses of humankind, I liked that best of all. Chicago could stand up under the worst God had to offer. I understood why it was built—a place for trade, of course, with railroads and ships and so on, but mostly to give all of us a magnitude of defiance that is not provided by one house on the plains. And the plains is where those storms come from.

Besides, I would miss my friend Winifred Czerwinska, who stood now on her landing as I was going downstairs with the suit-cases. Come in a minute, she said, I want to give you something. I went in and she closed the door behind me. You can put those down, she said of the suitcases.

My heart always beat faster in Winifred's presence. I could feel it and she knew it too and it made her happy. She put her hand on my chest now and she stood on tiptoes to kiss me with her hand under my shirt feeling my heart pump.

Look at him, all turned out in a coat and tie. Oh, she said, with her eyes tearing up, what am I going to do without my Earle? But she was smiling.

Winifred was not a Mama type of woman. She was a slight, skinny thing, and when she went down the stairs it was like a bird hopping. She wore no powder or perfumery except by accident the confectionary sugar which she brought home on her from the bakery where she worked behind the counter. She had sweet, cool lips but one eyelid didn't come up all the way over the blue, which made her not as pretty as she might otherwise be. And of course she had no titties to speak of.

You can write me a letter or two and I will write back, I said.

What will you say in your letter?

I will think of something, I said.

She pulled me into the kitchen, where she spread her feet and put her forearms flat on a chair so that I could raise her frock and fuck into her in the way she preferred. It didn't take that long, but even so, while Winifred wiggled and made her little cat sounds I could hear Mama calling from upstairs as to where I had gotten.

We had ordered a carriage to take us and the luggage at the same time rather than sending it off by the less expensive Railway Express and taking a horsecar to the station. That was not my idea, but exactly the amounts that were left after Mama bought the house only she knew. She came down the steps under her broad-brim hat and widow's veil and held her skirts at her shoe tops as the driver helped her into the carriage.

We were making a grand exit in full daylight. This was pure Mama as she lifted her veil and glanced with contempt at the neighbors looking out from their windows. As for the nasty children, they had gone quite quiet at our display of elegance. I swung up beside her and closed the door and at her instruction threw a handful of pennies on the sidewalk, and I watched the children push and shove one another and dive to their knees as we drove off.

When we had turned the corner, Mama opened the hatbox I had put on the seat. She removed her black hat and replaced it with a blue number trimmed in fake flowers. Over her mourning dress she draped a glittery shawl in striped colors like the rainbow. There, she said. I feel so much better now. Are you all right, Earle?

Yes, Mama, I said.

Aunt Dora.

Yes, Aunt Dora.

I wish you had a better mind, Earle. You could have paid more attention to the Doctor when he was alive. We had our disagreements, but he was smart for a man.

THE TRAIN STOP of La Ville was a concrete platform and a lean-to for a waiting room and no ticket-agent window. When you got off, you were looking down an alley to a glimpse of their Main Street. Main Street had a feed store, a post office, a white wooden church, a granite stone bank, a haberdasher, a town square with a four-story hotel, and in the middle of the square on the grass the statue of a Union soldier. It could all be counted because there was just one of everything. A man with a dray was willing to take us. He drove past a few other streets where first there were some homes of substance and another church or two but then, as you moved further out from the town center, worn-looking one-story shingle houses with dark little porches and garden plots and clotheslines out back with only alleys separating them. I couldn't see how, but Mama said there was a population of over three thousand living here. And then after a couple of miles through farm-land, with a silo here and there off a straight road leading due west through fields of corn, there swung into view what I had not ex-pected, a three-story house of red brick with a flat roof and stone steps up to the front door like something just lifted out of a street of row houses in Chicago. I couldn't believe anyone had built such a thing for a farmhouse. The sun flared in the windowpanes and I had to shade my eyes to make sure I was seeing what I saw. But that was it in truth, our new home.

Not that I had the time to reflect, not with Mama settling in. We went to work. The house was cobwebbed and dusty and it was rank with the droppings of animal life. Blackbirds were roosting in the top floor, where I was to live. Much needed to be done, but be-fore long she had it all organized and a parade of wagons was com-ing from town with the furniture she'd Expressed and no shortage of men willing to hire on for a day with hopes for more from this grand good-looking lady with the rings on several fingers. And so the fence went up for the chicken yard, and the weed fields beyond were being plowed under and the watering hole for stock was dredged and a new privy was dug, and I thought for some days Mama was the biggest employer of La Ville, Illinois.

But who would haul the well water and wash the clothes and bake the bread? A farm was a different life, and days went by when I slept under the roof of the third floor and felt the heat of the day still on my pallet as I looked through the little window at the re-moteness of the stars and I felt unprotected as I never had in the civilization we had retreated from. Yes, I thought, we had moved backward from the world's progress, and for the first time I won-dered about Mama's judgment. In all our travels from state to state and with all the various obstacles to her ambition, I had never thought to question it. But no more than this house was a farmer's house was she a farmer, and neither was I.

One evening we stood on the front steps watching the sun go down behind the low hills miles away.

Aunt Dora, I said, what are we up to here?

I know, Earle. But some things take time.

She saw me looking at her hands, how red they had gotten.

I am bringing an immigrant woman down from Wisconsin. She will sleep in that room behind the kitchen. She's to be here in a week or so.

Why? I said. There's women in La Ville, the wives of all these locals come out here for a day's work who could surely use the money.

I will not have some woman in the house who will only take back to town what she sees and hears. Use what sense God gave you, Earle.

I am trying, Mama.

Aunt Dora, goddamnit.

Aunt Dora.

Yes, she said. Especially here in the middle of nowhere and with nobody else in sight.

She had tied her thick hair behind her neck against the heat and she went about now loose in a smock without her usual women's underpinnings.

But doesn't the air smell sweet, she said. I'm going to have a screen porch built and fit it out with a settee and some rockers so we can watch the grand show of nature in comfort.

She ruffled my hair. And you don't have to pout, she said. You may not appreciate it here this moment with the air so peaceful and the birds singing and nothing much going on in any direction you can see. But we're still in business, Earle. You can trust me on that.

And so I was assured.

—

BY AND BY WE acquired an old-fashioned horse and buggy to take us to La Ville and back when Aunt Dora had to go to the bank or the post office or provisions were needed. I was the driver and horse groom. He—the horse—and I did not get along. I wouldn't give him a name. He was ugly, with a swayback and legs that trotted out splayed. I had butchered and trimmed better-looking plugs than this in Chicago. Once, in the barn, when I was putting him up for the night, he took a chomp in the air just off my shoulder.

Another problem was Bent, the handyman Mama had hired for the steady work. No sooner did she begin taking him upstairs of an afternoon than he was strutting around like he owned the place. This was a problem as I saw it. Sure enough, one day he told me to do something. It was one of his own chores. I thought you was the hired one, I said to him. He was ugly, like a relation of the horse— he was shorter than you thought he ought to be with his long arms and big gnarled hands hanging from them.

Get on with it, I said.

Leering, he grabbed me by the shoulder and put his mouth up to my ear. I seen it all, he said. Oh, yes. I seen everything a man could wish to see.

At this I found myself constructing a fate for Bent the handyman. But he was so drunkly stupid I knew Mama must have her own plan for him or else why would she play up to someone of this ilk, and so I held my ideas in abeyance.

In fact I was by now thinking I could wrest some hope from the wide loneliness of this farm with views of the plains as far as you could see. What had come to mind? A sense of expectancy that I recognized from times past. Yes. I had sensed that whatever was going to happen had begun. There was not only the handyman. There were the orphan children. She had contracted for three from the do-good agency in New York that took orphans off the streets and washed and dressed them and put them on the train to their foster homes in the midland. Ours were comely enough children, though pale, two boys and a girl with papers that gave their ages, six, six, and eight, and as I trotted them to the farm they sat up behind me staring at the countryside without a word. And so now they were installed in the back bedroom on the second floor, and they were not like the miserable street rats from our neighborhood in the city. These were quiet children except for the weeping they were sometimes given to at night, and by and large they did as they were told. Mama had some real feeling for them—Joseph and Calvin and the girl, Sophie, in particular. There were no conditions as to what faith they were to be brought up in nor did we have any in mind. But on Sundays, Mama took to showing them off to the Methodist church in La Ville in the new clothes she had bought for them. It gave her pleasure, and was besides a presentation of her own pride of position in life. Because it turned out, as I was learning, that even in the farthest reaches of the countryside, you lived in society.

And in this great scheme of things my aunt Dora required little Joseph, Calvin, and Sophie to think of her as their mama. Say Mama, she said to them. And they said it.

WELL, SO HERE was this household of us, ready made, as something bought from a department store. Fannie was the imported cook and housekeeper, who by Mama's design spoke no English but understood well enough what had to be done. She was heavyset, like Mama, with the strength to work hard. And besides Bent, who skulked about by the barns and fences in the sly pretense of work, there was a real farmer out beyond, who was sharecropping the acreage in corn. And two mornings a week a retired county

teacher woman came by to tutor the children in reading and arith-
metic.

Mama said one evening: We are an honest-to-goodness enterprise here, a functioning family better off than most in these parts,
but we are running at a deficit, and if we don't have something in
hand before winter the only resources will be the insurance I took
out on the little ones.

She lit the kerosene lamp on the desk in the parlor and wrote
out a Personal and read it to me: "Widow offering partnership in
prime farmland to dependable man. A modest investment is required." What do you think, Earle?

It's okay.

She read it again to herself. No, she said. It's not good enough.
You've got to get them up off their ass and out of the house to the
Credit Union and then on a train to La Ville, Illinois. That's a lot
to do with just a few words. How about this: "Wanted!" That's
good, it bespeaks urgency. And doesn't every male in the world
think he's what is wanted? "Wanted—Recently widowed woman
with bountiful farm in God's own country has need of Nordic man
of sufficient means for partnership in same."

What is Nordic? I said.

Well that's pure cunning right there, Earle, because that's all
they got in the states where we run this—Swedes and Norwegies
just off the boat. But I'm letting them know a lady's preference.

All right, but what's that you say there—"of sufficient means"?
What Norwegie off the boat'll know what that's all about?

This gave her pause. Good for you, Earle, you surprise me sometimes. She licked the pencil point. So we'll just say "with cash."

WE PLACED THE Personal in one paper at a time in towns in Minnesota, and then in South Dakota. The letters of courtship com-

menced, and Mama kept a ledger with the names and dates of arrival, making sure to give each candidate his sufficient time. We always advised the early-morning train when the town was not yet up and about. Beside my regular duties, I had to take part in the family reception. They would be welcomed into the parlor, and Mama would serve coffee from a wheeled tray, and Joseph, Calvin, and Sophie, her children, and I, her nephew, would sit on the sofa and hear our biographies conclude with a happy ending, which was the present moment. Mama was so well spoken at these times I was as apt as the poor foreigners to be caught up in her modesty, so seemingly unconscious was she of the great-heartedness of her. They by and large did not see through to her self-congratulation. And of course she was a large, handsome woman to look at. She wore her simple finery for these first impressions, a plain pleated gray cotton skirt and a starched white shirtwaist and no jewelry but the gold cross on a chain that fell between her bosoms and her hair combed upward and piled atop her head in a state of fetching carelessness.

I am their dream of heaven on earth, Mama said to me along about the third or fourth. Just to see how their eyes light up standing beside me looking out over their new land. Puffing on their pipes, giving me a glance that imagines me as available for marriage—who can say I don't give value in return?

Well that is one way to look at it, I said.

Don't be smug, Earle. You're in no position. Tell me an easier way to God's blessed Heaven than a launch from His Heaven on earth. I don't know of one.

AND SO OUR ACCOUNT in the La Ville Savings Bank began to compound nicely. The late-summer rain did just the right thing for the corn, as even I could see, and it was an added few unantic-

ipated dollars we received from the harvest. If there were any com-
plications to worry about it was that fool Bent. He was so dumb he
was dangerous. At first Mama indulged his jealousy. I could hear
them arguing upstairs—he roaring away and she assuring him so
quietly I could hardly hear what she said. But it didn't do any good.
When one of the Norwegies arrived, Bent just happened to be in
the yard, where he could have a good look. One time there was his
ugly face peering through the porch window. Mama signaled me
with a slight motion of her head and I quickly got up and pulled
the shade.

It was true Mama might lay it on a bit thick. She might co-
quette with this one, yes, just as she might affect a widow's piety
with that one. It all depended on her instinct of the particular
man's character. It was easy enough to make believers of them. If I
had to judge them as a whole I would say they were simple men,
not exactly stupid, but lacking command of our language and with
no wiles of their own. By whatever combination of sentiments and
signatures, she never had anything personal intended but the business at hand, the step-by-step encouragement of the cash into our
bank account.

The fool Bent imagined Mama looking for a husband from
among these men. His pride of possession was offended. When he
came to work each morning, he was often three sheets to the wind
and if she happened not to invite him upstairs for the afternoon
siesta, he would go home in a state, turning at the road to shake his
fist and shout up at the windows before he set out for town in his
crouching stride.

Mama said to me on one occasion, The damn fool has feelings.

Well that had not occurred to me in the way she meant it, and
maybe in that moment my opinion of the handyman was raised to
a degree. Not that he was any less dangerous. Clearly he had never
learned that the purpose of life is to improve your station in it. It

was not an idea available to him. Whatever you were, that's what you would always be. So he saw these foreigners who couldn't even talk right not only as usurpers but as casting a poor light on his existence. Was I in his position, I would learn from the example of these immigrants and think what I could do to put together a few dollars and buy some farmland for myself. Any normal person would think that. Not him. He just got enough of the idea through his thick skull to realize he lacked the hopes of even the lowest foreigner. So I would come back from the station with one of them in the buggy and the fellow would step down, his plaid suit and four-in-hand and his bowler proposing him as a man of sufficient means, and it was like a shadow and sudden chilling as from a black cloud came over poor Bent, who could understand only that it was too late for him—everything, I mean, it was all too late.

And finally, to show how dumb he was, what he didn't realize was that it was all too late for them, too.

THEN EVERYTHING GREEN began to fade off yellow, the summer rains were gone, and the wind off the prairie blew the dried-out topsoil into gusty swirls that rose and fell like waves in a dirt sea. At night the windows rattled. At first frost, the two little boys caught the croup.

Mama pulled the Wanted ad back from the out-of-state papers, saying she needed to catch her breath. I didn't know what was in the ledger, but her saying that meant our financial situation was improved. And now, as with all farm families, winter would be a time for rest.

Not that I was looking forward to it. How could I with nothing to do?

I wrote a letter to my friend Winifred Czerwinska, in Chicago. I had been so busy until now I hardly had the time to be lonely. I said that I missed her and hoped before too long to come back to city life. As I wrote, a rush of pity for myself came over me and I almost sobbed at the picture in my mind of the Elevated trains and the moving lights of the theater marquees and the sounds I imagined of the streetcars and even of the lowings of the abattoir where I had earned my wages. But I only said I hoped she would write me back.

I think the children felt the same way about this cold countryside. They had been displaced from a greater distance away, in a city larger than Chicago. They could not have been colder huddled at some steam grate than they were now with blankets to their chins. From the day they arrived they wouldn't leave one another's side, and though she was not croupy herself, Sophie stayed with the two boys in their bedroom, attending to their hackings and wheezes and sleeping in an armchair in the night. Fannie cooked up oatmeal for their breakfasts and soup for their dinners, and I took it upon myself to bring the tray upstairs in order to get them talking to me, since we were all related in a sense and in their minds I would be an older boy orphan taken in, like them. But they would not talk much, only answering my friendly questions yes or no in their soft voices, looking at me all the while with some dark expectation in their eyes. I didn't like that. I knew they talked among themselves all the time. These were street-wise children who had quickly apprised themselves of the lay of the land. For instance, they knew enough to stay out of Bent's way when he was drinking. But when he was sober they followed him around. And one day I had gone into the stable, to harness the horse, and found them snooping around in there, so they were not without unhealthy curiosity. Then there was the unfortunate matter of one of the boys, Joseph, the shorter darker one—he had found a pocket watch and watch fob in the yard, and when I said it was mine he said it wasn't. Whose is it then, I said. I know it's not yours, he said as he finally handed it over. To make more of an issue of it was not wise, so I didn't, but I hadn't forgotten.

Mama and I were nothing if not prudent, discreet, and in full consideration of the feelings of others in all our ways and means, but I believe children have a sense that enables them to know something even when they can't say what it is. As a child I must have had it, but of course it leaves you as you grow up. It may be a trait children are given so that they will survive long enough to grow up.

But I didn't want to think the worst. I reasoned to myself that were I plunked down so far away from my streets among strangers who I was ordered to live with as their relation, in the middle of this flat land of vast empty fields that would stir in any breast nothing but a recognition of the presiding deafness and dumbness of the natural world, I too would behave as these children were behaving.

AND THEN ONE STINGING cold day in December, I had gone into town to pick up a package from the post office. We had to write away to Chicago for those things it would not do to order from the local merchants. The package was in, but also a letter addressed to me, and it was from my friend Winifred Czerwinska.

Winifred's penmanship made me smile. The letters were thin and scrawny and did not keep to a straight line but went slanting in a downward direction, as if some of her mortal being was transferred to the letter paper. And I knew she had written from the bakery, because there was some powdered sugar in the folds.

She was so glad to hear from me and to know where I was. She thought I had forgotten her. She said she missed me. She said she was bored with her job. She had saved her money and hinted that she would be glad to spend it on something interesting, like a train ticket. My ears got hot reading that. In my mind I saw Winifred squinting up at me. I could almost feel her putting her hand under my shirt to feel my heart the way she liked to do.

But on the second page she said maybe I would be interested in news from the old neighborhood. There was going to be another inquest, or maybe the same one reopened.

It took me a moment to understand she was talking about the Doctor, Mama's husband in Chicago. The Doctor's relatives had asked for his body to be dug up. Winifred found this out from the constable who knocked on her door as he was doing with everyone. The police were trying to find out where we had gone, Mama and I.

I hadn't gotten your letter yet, Winifred said, so I didn't have to lie about not knowing where you were.

I raced home. Why did Winifred think she would otherwise have to lie? Did she believe all the bad gossip about us? Was she like the rest of them? I thought she was different. I was disappointed in her, and then I was suddenly very mad at Winifred.

Mama read the letter differently. Your Miss Czerwinska is our friend, Earle. That's something higher than a lover. If I have worried about her slow eye being passed on to the children, if it shows up we will just have to have it corrected with surgery.

What children, I said.

The children of your blessed union with Miss Czerwinska, Mama said.

Do not think Mama said this merely to keep me from worrying about the Chicago problem. She sees things before other people see them. She has plans going out through all directions of the universe—she is not a one-track mind, my Aunt Dora. I was excited by her intentions for me, as if I had thought of them myself. Perhaps I had thought of them myself as my secret, but she had read my secret and was now giving her approval. Because I certainly did like Winifred Czerwinska, whose lips tasted of baked goods and who loved it so when I fucked into her. And now it was all out in the open, and Mama not only knew my feelings but expressed them for me and it only remained for the young lady to be told that we were engaged.

I thought then her visiting us would be appropriate, especially as she was prepared to pay her own way. But Mama said, Not yet, Earle. Everyone in the house knew you were loving her up, and if she was to quit her job in the bakery and pack a bag and go down to the train station, even the Chicago police, as stupid as they are, they would put two and two together.

Of course I did not argue the point, though I was of the opinion that the police would find out where we were regardless. There were indications all over the place—not anything as difficult as a clue to be discerned only by the smartest of detectives, but bank account transfers, forwarding mail, and such. Why, even the driver who took us to the station might have picked up some remark of ours, and certainly a ticket seller at Union Station might remember us. Mama being such an unusual-looking woman, very decorative and regal to the male eye, she would surely be remembered by a ticket seller, who would not see her like from one year to the next.

Maybe a week went by before Mama expressed an opinion about the problem. You can't trust people, she said. It's that damn sister of his, who didn't even shed a tear at the grave. Why, she even told me how lucky the Doctor was to have found me so late in life.

I remember, I said.

And how I had taken such good care of him.

Which was true, I said.

Relatives are the fly in the ointment, Earle.

—

MAMA'S NOT BEING concerned so much as she was put out meant to me that we had more time than I would have thought. Our quiet lives of winter went on as before, though as I watched and waited she was obviously thinking things through. I was satisfied to wait, even though she was particularly attentive to Bent, inviting him in for dinner as if he was not some hired hand but a neighboring farmer. And I had to sit across the table on the children's side and watch him struggle to hold the silver in his fist and slurp his soup and pity him the way he had pathetically combed his hair down and tucked his shirt in and the way he folded his fingers under when he happened to see the dirt under his nails. This is good eats, he said aloud to no one in particular, and even Fannie, as she served, gave a little hmph as if despite having no English she understood clearly enough how out of place he was here at our table.

Well as it turned out there were things I didn't know, for instance that the little girl, Sophie, had adopted Bent, or maybe made a pet of him as you would any dumb beast, but they had become friends of a sort and she had confided to him remarks she overheard in the household. Maybe if she was making Mama into her mama she thought she was supposed to make the wretched bum of a hired hand into her father, I don't know. Anyway, there was this alliance between them that showed to me that she would never rise above her unsavory life in the street as a vagrant child. She looked like an angel with her little bow mouth and her pale face and gray eyes and her hair in a single long braid, which Mama herself did every morning, but she had the hearing of a bat and could stand on the second-floor landing and listen all the way down the stairs to our private conversations in the front parlor. Of course I only knew that later. It was Mama who learned that Bent was putting it about to his drinking cronies in town that the

Madame Dora they thought was such a lady was his love slave and a woman on the wrong side of the law back in Chicago.

Mama, I said, I have never liked this fool, though I have been holding my ideas in abeyance for the fate I have in mind for him. But here he accepts our wages and eats our food then goes and does this?

Hush, Earle, not yet, not yet, she said. But you are a good son to me, and I can take pride that as a woman alone I have bred in you the highest sense of family honor. She saw how troubled I was. She hugged me. Are you not my very own knight of the round-table? she said. But I was not comforted. It seemed to me that forces were massing slowly but surely against us in a most menacing way. I didn't like it. I didn't like it that we were going along as if everything was hunky-dory, even to giving a grand Christmas Eve party for the several people in La Ville who Mama had come to know—how they all drove out in their carriages under the moon that was so bright on the plains of snow that it was like a black daytime, the local banker, the merchants, the pastor of the First Methodist church, and other such dignitaries and their wives. The spruce tree in the parlor was imported from Minnesota and all alight with candles and the three children were dressed for the occasion and went around with cups of eggnog for the assembled guests. I knew how important it was for Mama to establish her reputation as a person of class who had flattered the community by joining it, but all these people made me nervous. I didn't think it was wise having so many rigs parked in the yard and so many feet tromping about the house or going out to the privy. Of course it was a lack of self-confidence on my part, and how often was it Mama had warned me nothing was more dangerous than that, because it was translated into the face and physique as wrongdoing, or at least defenselessness, which amounted to the same thing. But I couldn't help it. I remembered the pocket watch that the little sniveling Joseph had found and held up to me swinging it from its fob. I sometimes made mistakes, I was human, and who knew what other mistakes lay about for someone to find and hold up to me.

But now Mama looked at me over the heads of her guests. The children's tutor had brought her harmonium and we all gathered around the fireplace for some carol singing. Given Mama's look, I sang the loudest. I have a good tenor voice and I sent it aloft to turn heads and make the La Villers smile. I imagined decking the halls with boughs of holly until there was kindling and brush enough to set the whole place ablaze.

JUST AFTER THE NEW YEAR a man appeared at our door, another Swede, with his Gladstone bag in his hand. We had not run the Wanted ad all winter and Mama was not going to be home to him, but this fellow was the brother of one of them who had responded to it the previous fall. He gave his name, Henry Lundgren, and said his brother Per Lundgren had not been heard from since leaving Wisconsin to look into the prospect here.

Mama invited him in and sat him down and had Fannie bring in some tea. The minute I looked at him, I remembered the brother. Per Lundgren had been all business. He did not blush or go shy in Mama's presence, nor did he ogle. Instead, he asked sound questions. He had also turned the conversation away from his own circumstances, family relations and so on, which Mama put people through in order to learn who was back home and might be waiting. Most of the immigrants, if they had family, it was still in the old country, but you had to make sure. Per Lundgren was closemouthed, but he did admit to being unmarried and so we decided to go ahead.

And here was Henry, the brother he had never mentioned, sitting stiffly in the wing chair with his arms folded and the aggrieved expression on his face. They had the same reddish fair skin, with a long jaw and thinning blond hair, and pale woeful-looking eyes with blond eyelashes. I would say Henry here was the younger by a couple of years, but he turned out to be as smart as Per, or maybe even smarter. He did not seem to be as convinced of the sincerity of Mama's expressions of concern as I would have liked. He said his brother had made the trip to La Ville with other stops planned afterwards to two more business prospects, a farm some twenty miles west of us and another in Indiana. Henry had traveled to these places, which is how he learned that his brother never arrived for his appointments. He said Per had been traveling with something over two thousand dollars in his money belt.

My goodness, that is a lot of money, Mama said.

Our two savings, Henry said. He comes here to see your farm. I have the advertisement, he said, pulling a piece of newspaper from his pocket. This is the first place he comes to see.

I'm not sure he ever arrived, Mama said. We've had many inquiries.

He arrived, Henry Lundgren said. He arrived the night before so he will be on time the next morning. This is my brother. It is important to him, even if it costs money. He sleeps at the hotel in La Ville.

How could you know that? Mama said.

I know from the guest book in the La Ville hotel where I find his signature, Henry Lundgren said.

MAMA SAID, All right, Earle, we've got a lot more work to do before we get out of here.

We're leaving?

What is today, Monday. I want to be on the road Thursday the latest. I thought with the inquest matter back there we were okay at least to the spring. This business of a brother pushes things up a bit.

I am ready to leave.

I know you are. You have not enjoyed the farm life, have you? If that Swede had told us he had a brother, he wouldn't be where he is today. Too smart for his own good, he was. Where is Bent?

She went out to the yard. He was standing at the corner of the barn peeing a hole in the snow. She told him to take the carriage and go to La Ville and pick up half a dozen gallon cans of kerosene at the hardware. They were to be put on our credit.

It occurred to me that we still had a goodly amount of our winter supply of kerosene. I said nothing. Mama had gone into action, and I knew from experience that everything would come clear by and by.

And then late that night, when I was in the basement, she called downstairs to me that Bent was coming down to help.

I don't need help, thank you, Aunt Dora, I said, so astonished that my throat went dry.

At that they both clomped down the stairs and back to the potato bin where I was working. Bent was grinning that toothy grin of his as always, to remind me he had certain privileges.

Show him, Mama said to me. Go ahead, it's all right, she assured me.

So I did, I showed him. I showed him something to hand. I opened the top of the gunnysack and he looked down it.

The fool's grin disappeared, the unshaven face went pale, and he started to breathe through his mouth. He gasped, he couldn't catch his breath, a weak cry came from him, and he looked at me in my rubber apron and his knees buckled and he fainted dead away.

Mama and I stood over him. Now he knows, I said. He will tell them.

Maybe, Mama said, but I don't think so. He's now one of us. We have just made him an accessory.

An accessory?

After the fact. But he'll be more than that by the time I get through with him, she said.

We threw some water on him and lifted him to his feet. Mama took him up to the kitchen and gave him a couple of quick swigs. Bent was thoroughly cowed, and when I came upstairs and told him to follow me, he jumped out of his chair as if shot. I handed him the gunnysack. It was not that heavy for someone like him. He held it in one hand at arm's length as if it would bite. I led him to the old dried-up well behind the house, where he dropped it down into the muck. I poured the quicklime in and then we lowered some rocks down and nailed the well cover back on, and Bent the handyman he never said a word but just stood there shivering and waiting for me to tell him what to do next.

Mama had thought of everything. She had paid cash down for the farm but somewhere or other got the La Ville bank to give her a mortgage and so when the house burned, it was the bank's money. She had been withdrawing from the account all winter, and now that we were closing shop, she mentioned to me the actual sum of our wealth for the first time. I was very moved to be confided in, like her partner.

But really it was the small touches that showed her genius. For instance, she had noted immediately of the inquiring brother Henry that he was in height not much taller than I am. Just as in Fanny the housekeeper she had hired a woman of a girth similar to her own. Meanwhile, at her instruction, I was letting my dark beard grow out. And at the end, before she had Bent go up and down the stairs pouring the kerosene in every room, she made sure he was good and drunk. He would sleep through the whole thing in the stable, and that's where they found him with his arms wrapped like a lover's arms around an empty can of kerosene.

—

THE PLAN WAS for me to stay behind for a few days just to keep
an eye on things. We have pulled off something prodigious that
will go down in the books, Mama said. But that means all sorts of
people will be flocking here and you can never tell when the unex-
pected arises. Of course everything will be fine, but if there's
something more we have to do you will know it.

Yes, Aunt Dora.

Aunt Dora was just for here, Earle.

Yes, Mama.

Of course, even if there was no need to keep an eye out you
would still have to wait for Miss Czerwinska.

This is where I didn't understand her thinking. The one bad
thing in all of this is that Winifred would read the news in the
Chicago papers. There was no safe way I could get in touch with
her now that I was dead. That was it, that was the end of it. But
Mama had said it wasn't necessary to get in touch with Winifred.
This remark made me angry.

You said you liked her, I said.

I do, Mama said.

You called her our friend, I said.

She is.

I know it can't be helped, but I wanted to marry Winifred
Czerwinska. What can she do now but dry her tears and maybe
light a candle for me and go out and find herself another boyfriend.

Oh, Earle, Earle, Mama said, you know nothing about a
woman's heart.

BUT ANYHOW, I followed the plan to stay on a few days and it
wasn't that hard with a dark stubble and a different hat and a long

coat. There were such crowds nobody would notice anything that wasn't what they'd come to see, that's what a fever was in these souls. Everyone was streaming down the road to see the tragedy. They were in their carriages and they were walking and standing up in drays—people were paying for anything with wheels to get them out there from town—and after the newspapers ran the story, they were coming not just from La Ville and the neighboring farms but from out of state in their automobiles and on the train from Indianapolis and Chicago. And with the crowds came the hawkers to sell sandwiches and hot coffee, and peddlers with balloons and little flags and whirligigs for the children. Someone had taken photographs of the laid-out skeletons in their crusts of burlap and printed them up as postcards for mailing, and these were going like hotcakes.

The police had been inspired by the charred remains they found in the basement to look down the well and then to dig up the chicken yard and the floor of the stable. They had brought around a rowboat to dredge the water hole. They were really very thorough. They kept making their discoveries and laying out what they found in neat rows inside the barn. They had called in the county sheriff and his men to help with the crowds and they got some kind of order going, keeping people in lines to pass them by the open barn doors so everyone would have a turn. It was the only choice the police had if they didn't want a riot, but even then the oglers went around back all the way up the road to get into the procession again—it was the two headless remains of Madame Dora and her nephew that drew the most attention, and of course the wrapped bundles of the little ones.

There was such heat from this population that the snow was gone from the ground and on the road and in the yard and behind the house and even into the fields where the trucks and automobiles were parked everything had turned to mud so that it seemed even the season was transformed. I just stood and watched and took it all in, and it was amazing to see so many people with this happy feeling of spring, as if a population of creatures had formed up out of the mud especially for the occasion. That didn't help the smell any, though no one seemed to notice. The house itself made me sad to look at, a smoking ruin that you could see the sky through. I had become fond of that house. A piece of the floor hung down from the third story where I had my room. I disapproved of people pulling off the loose brickwork to take home for a souvenir. There was a lot of laughing and shouting, but of course I did not say anything. In fact I was able to rummage around the ruin without drawing attention to myself, and sure enough I found something—it was the syringe for which I knew Mama would be thankful.

I overheard some conversation about Mama—what a terrible end for such a fine lady who loved children was the gist of it. I thought as time went on, in the history of our life of La Ville, I myself would not be remembered very clearly. Mama would become famous in the papers as a tragic victim mourned for her good works whereas I would only be noted down as a dead nephew. Even if the past caught up with her reputation and she was slandered as the suspect widow of several insured husbands, I would still be in the shadows. This seemed to me an unjust outcome considering the contribution I had made, and I found myself for a moment resentful. Who was I going to be in life now that I was dead and not even Winifred Czerwinska was there to bend over for me.

Back in town at night, I went behind the jail to the cell window where Bent was and I stood on a box and called to him softly, and when his bleary face appeared, I ducked to the side where he couldn't see me and I whispered these words: "Now you've seen it all, Bent. Now you have seen everything."

—

I STAYED IN TOWN to meet every train that came through from Chicago. I could do that without fear—there was such a heavy traffic all around, such swirls of people, all of them too excited and thrilled to take notice of someone standing quietly in a doorway or sitting on the curb in the alley behind the station. And as Mama told me, I knew nothing about the heart of a woman, because all at once there was Winifred Czerwinska stepping down from the coach, her suitcase in her hand. I lost her for a moment through the steam from the locomotive blowing across the platform, but then there she was in her dark coat and a little hat and the most forlorn expression I have ever seen on a human being. I waited till the other people had drifted away before I approached her. Oh my, how grief-stricken she looked standing by herself on the train platform with her suitcase and big tears rolling down her face. Clearly she had no idea what to do next, where to go, who to speak to. So she had not been able to help herself when she heard the terrible news. And what did that mean except that if she was drawn to me in my death she truly loved me in my life. She was so small and ordinary in appearance, how wonderful that I was the only person to know that under her clothes and inside her little rib cage the heart of a great lover was pumping away.

WELL THERE WAS a bad moment or two. I had to help her sit down. I am here, Winifred, it's all right, I told her over and over again and I held my arms around her shaking, sobbing wracked body.

I wanted us to follow Mama to California, you see. I thought, given all the indications, Winifred would accept herself as an accessory after the fact.

JOLENE:

A Life

—

S HE MARRIED MICKEY HOLLER WHEN SHE WAS FIFTEEN.
Married him to get out of her latest foster home where her so-
called dad used to fool with her, get her to hold him, things like
that. Even before her menses started. And her foster mom liked to
slap her up the head for no reason. Or for every reason. So she
married Mickey. And he loved her—that was a plus. She had never
had that experience before. It made her look at herself in the mirror and do things with her hair. He was twenty, Mickey. Real name
Mervin. He was a sweet boy if without very much upstairs, as she
knew even from their first date. He had a heel that didn't touch the
ground and weak eyes but he was not the kind to lay a hand on a
woman. And she could tell him what she wanted, like a movie, or
a grilled-cheese sandwich and a chocolate shake, and it became his
purpose in life. He loved her, he really did, even if he didn't know
much about it.

But anyway she was out of the house now, and wearing a wedding ring to South Sumter High. Some of the boys said smutty
things but the girls looked upon her with a new respect.

Mickey's uncle Phil had come to the justice of the peace with
them to be best man. After the ceremony he grinned and said, Welcome to our family, Jolene honey, and gave her a big hug that
lasted a mite too long. Uncle Phil was like a father to Mickey and
employed him to drive one of the trucks in his home oil delivery
business. Mickey Holler was almost an orphan. His real father was

in the state penitentiary with no parole for the same reason his mother was in the burial ground behind the First Baptist Church. Jolene asked Mickey, as she thought permissible now that she was a relation, what his mother had done to deserve her fate. But he got all flustered when he tried to talk about it. It happened when he was only twelve. She was left to gather for herself that his father was a crazy drunk who had done bad things even before this happened. But anyway that was why Jolene was living now with Mickey under the same roof with his uncle Phil and aunt Kay.

Aunt Kay was real smart. She was an assistant manager in the Southern People's Bank across the square from the courthouse. So between her and Uncle Phil's oil business, they had a nice ranch house with a garden out back and a picnic table and two hammocks between the trees.

Jolene liked the room she and Mickey occupied, though it looked into the driveway, and she had what she could do to keep it nice, with Mickey dropping his greasy coveralls on the floor. But she understood the double obligations of being a wife and an unpaying boarder besides. As she was home from school before anyone finished their jobs for the day, she tried to make herself useful. She would have an hour or so to do some of her homework and then she would go into the kitchen and put up something for everyone's dinner.

Jolene had always liked school—she felt at home there. Her favorite subject was art. She had been drawing from the time she was in third grade, when the class had done a mural of the Battle of Gettysburg and she drew more of it than anyone. She couldn't do much art now at this time in her life as a married woman, not being just for herself anymore. But she still noticed things. She was someone who had an eye for what wants to be drawn. Mickey had a white hairless chest with a collarbone that stood out across from shoulder to shoulder like he was someone's beast of burden.

And a long neck and a backbone that she could use to do sums. He surely did love her—he cried sometimes he loved her so much—but that was all. She had a sixteenth birthday and he bought her a negligee he picked out himself at Berman's department store. It was three sizes too big. Jolene could take it back for exchange, of course, but she had the unsettling thought that as Mickey's wife all that would happen in her life to come was she would grow into something that size. He liked to watch her doing her homework, which made her realize he had no ambition, Mickey Holler. He would never run a business and play golf on the weekend like Uncle Phil. He was a day-to-day person. He did not ever talk about buying his own home, or moving toward anything that would make things different for them than they were now. She could think this of him even though she liked to kiss his pale chest and run her fingers over the humps of his backbone.

Uncle Phil was tall with a good strong jaw and a head of shining black hair he combed in a kind of wave, and he had a deep voice and he joked around with a lot of self-assurance, and dark meaningful eyes—oh, he was a man, of that there was no doubt. At first it made Jolene nervous when he would eye her up and down. Or he would sing a line from a famous love song to her. *You are so beautiful to mee!* And then he would laugh to let her know it was all just the same horsing around as he was accustomed to doing. He was tanned from being out on the county golf course, and even the slight belly he had on him under his knit shirt seemed just right. The main thing about him was that he enjoyed his life, and he was popular—they had their social set, though you could see most of their friends came through him.

Aunt Kay was not exactly the opposite of Phil, but she was one who attended to business. She was a proper sort who never sat back with her shoes off, and though kind and correct as far as Jolene was concerned, clearly would have preferred to have her home to herself now that Mickey had someone to take care of him. Jolene knew this—she didn't have to be told. She could work her fingers to the bone and Aunt Kay would still never love her. Aunt Kay was a Yankee and had come to live in the South because of a job offer. She and Uncle Phil had been married fifteen years. She called him Phillip, which Jolene thought was putting on airs. She wore suits and panty hose, always, and blouses with collars buttoned to the neck. She was no beauty, but you could see what had interested Phil—her very light blue icy eyes, maybe, and naturally blond hair, and she had the generous figure that required a panty girdle, which she was never without.

But now Uncle Phil got in the habit of waking them up in the morning, coming into their room without knocking and saying in his deep voice, "Time for work, Mickey Holler!" but looking at Jolene in the meantime as she pulled the covers up to her chin.

She knew the man was doing something he shouldn't be doing with that wake-up routine and it made her angry but she didn't know what she could do about it. Mickey seemed blind to the fact that his own uncle, his late mother's brother, had an eye for her. At the same time she was excited to have been noticed by this man of the world. She knew that as a handsome smiling fellow with white teeth, Phil would be quite aware of his effect on women, so she made a point of seeming to be oblivious of him as anything but her husband's uncle and employer. But this became more and more difficult, living in the same house with him. She found herself thinking about him. In her mind Jolene made up a story: How gradually, over time, it would become apparent that she and Uncle Phil were meant for each other. How an understanding would arise between them and go on for some years until, possibly, Aunt Kay died, or left him—it wasn't all that clear in Jolene's mind.

But Uncle Phil was not one for dreaming. One afternoon she was scrubbing their kitchen floor for them, down on her knees in her shorts with her rump up in the air, and he had come home early, in that being his own boss he could come and go as he liked. She was humming "I Want to Hold Your Hand" and didn't hear him.

He stood in the door watching how the scrubbing motion was rendered on her behind, and no sooner did she realize she was not alone than he was lifting her from the waist in her same kneeling position and carrying her that way into his bedroom, the scrub brush still in her hand.

That night in her own bed she could still smell Uncle Phil's aftershave lotion and feel the little cotton balls of their chenille bedspread in the grasp of her fingers. She was too sore even for Mickey's fumblings.

And that was the beginning. In all Jolene's young life she had never been to where she couldn't wait to see someone. She tried to contain herself, but her schoolwork began to fall off, though she had always been a conscientious student even if not the smartest brain in her class. But it was that way with Phil, too—it was so intense and constant that he was no longer laughing. It was more like they were equals in their magnetic attraction. They just couldn't get enough. It was every day, always while Aunt Kay was putting up her numbers in the Southern People's Bank and Mickey, poor Mickey was riding his oil route as Uncle Phil devised it to the furthermost reaches of the town line and beyond.

Well, the passion between people can never be anything but drawn to a conclusion by the lawful spouses around them, and after a month or two of this everyone knew it, and the crisis came banging open the bedroom door shouting her name, and all at once Mickey was riding Phil's back like a monkey, beating him about the head and crying all the while, and Phil, in his skivvies, with Mickey pounding him, staggered around the combined living and dining room till he backpedaled the poor boy up against their big TV and smashed him through the screen. Jolene, in her later reflections, when she had nothing in the world to do but pass the time, remembered everything—she remembered the bursting sound of the TV glass, she remembered how surprised she was to see how skinny Phil's legs were, and that the sun through the blinds was so bright because daylight saving had come along unbeknownst to the lovers, which was why the working people had got home before they were supposed to. But at the time there was no leisure for thought. Aunt Kay was dragging her by the hair through the hall over the shag carpet and into the kitchen across the fake-tile flooring and she was out the kitchen door, kicked down the back steps, and thrown out like someone's damn cat and yowling like one, too.

Jolene waited out there by the edge of the property, crouching in the bushes in her shift with her arms folded across her breasts. She waited for Phil to come out and take her away, but he never did. Mickey is the one who opened the door. He stood there looking at her, in the quiet outside, while from the house they listened to the shouting and the sound of things breaking. Mickey's hair was sticking up and his glasses were bent broken across his nose. Jolene called to him. She was crying; she wanted him to forgive her and tell her it was all right. But what he did, her Mickey, he got in his pickup in his bloody shirt and drove away. That was what Jolene came to think of as the end of Chapter 1 in her life story, because where Mickey drove to was the middle of the Catawba River Bridge, and there he stopped and with the engine still running he jumped off into that rocky river and killed himself.

MORE THAN ONE NEIGHBOR must have seen her wandering the streets, and by and by a police cruiser picked her up, and first she was taken to the emergency room, where it was noted that her vital signs were okay, though they showed her where a clump of her red hair had been pulled out. Then she was put into a motel off the interstate while the system figured out what to do with her. She was a home wrecker but also a widow but also a juvenile with no living relatives. The fosters she had left to marry Mickey would take no responsibility for her. Time passed. She watched soaps. She cried. A matron was keeping an eye on her morning and night. Then a psychiatrist who worked for the county came to interview her. A day after that she was driven to a court hearing with testimony by this county psychiatrist she had told her story to in all honesty, and that was something that embittered her as the double-cross of all time, because on his recommendation she was remanded to the juvenile loony bin until such time as she was to become a reasonable adult able to take care of herself.

Well, so there she was moping about on their pills, half asleep for most of the day and night, and of course as she quickly learned this was no place to regain her sanity, if she ever lost it in the first place, which she knew just by looking at who else was there that she hadn't. About two months into the hell there, they one morning took off her usual gray hanging frock and put her in a recognizable dark dress, though a size too big, and fixed her hair with a barrette and drove her in a van to the courthouse once again, though this time it was for her testimony as to her relations with Uncle Phil, who was there at the defense table looking awful. She didn't know what was different about him till she realized his hair was without luster and, in fact, gray. Then she knew that all this time she had been so impressed he had been dyeing it. He was hunched over from the fix he was in and he never looked at her, this man of the world. A little of the old feeling arose in her and she was angry with herself but she couldn't help it. She waited for some acknowledgment, but it never came. What it was, Aunt Kay had kicked him out, he was sleeping in his office, his business had gone down the tube, and none of his buddies would play golf with him anymore.

Jolene was called upon to show the judge that she was, at sixteen, underage for such doings, which made Phil a statutory rapist. There was a nice legal argument for just a minute or two as to how she was a married woman at the time, an adulteress in fact, and certainly not unknowing in the ways of carnal life, but that didn't hold water, apparently. She was excused and taken back to the loony bin and put back in her hanging gray frock and slippers and that was it for the real world. She heard that Phil pulled eighteen months in the state prison. She couldn't sympathize, being in one of her own.

Jolene didn't think much about Mickey, but she drew his face over and over. She drew headstones in a graveyard and then drew his face on the gravestones. This seemed to her a worthy artistic task. The more she drew of Mickey the more she remembered the details of how he looked out at her on the last evening of his life, but it was hard with just crayons—they would only give her crayons to draw with, not the colored pencils she asked for.

Then something good happened. One of the girls in the ward smashed the mirror over the sink in the bathroom and used a sliver of it to cut her wrists. Well, that of course wasn't good, but all the mirrors in the bathroom were removed and nobody could see herself except maybe if they stood on the bed and the sunlight was in the right place in the windows behind the mesh screen. So Jolene began a business in portraits. She drew a girl's face, and soon they were waiting in line to have her draw them. If they didn't have a mirror, they had Jolene. Some of her likenesses were not very good, but since in most cases they were a lot better than the originals, nobody minded. Mrs. Ames, the head nurse, thought that was good therapy for everyone and so Jolene was given a set of watercolors with three brushes, and a big thick sketchpad, and when the rage for portraits had played itself out, she painted everything else—the ward, the game room, the yard where they walked, the flowers in the flower bed, the sunset through the black mesh, everything.

But since she was as sane as anyone, she was more and more desperate to get out of there. After a year or so she made the best deal she could, with one of the night attendants, a sharp-faced woman sallow in coloring but decent and roughly kind to people, name of Cindy. Jolene thought Cindy, with the leathery lines in her face, might be no less than fifty years old. She had an eye for Jolene right from the beginning. She gave her cigarettes to smoke outside behind the garbage bins, and she knew hair and makeup. She said, Red—Jolene had what they call strawberry hair, so that of course was her nickname there—Red, you don't want to cover up those freckles. They are charming in a girl like you, they give your face a sunlight. And, see, if you keep pulling back your hair into ponytails your hairline will recede, so we'll cut it just a bit shorter so that it curls up as it wants to and we let it frame your sweet face and, lo and behold, you are as pretty as a picture.

Cindy liked the freckles on Jolene's breasts, too, and it wasn't too bad being loved up by a woman. It was not her first choice, but Jolene thought, Once you get going it doesn't matter who it is or what they've got—there is the same panic, after all, and we are blind at such moments. But anyway that was the deal, and though in order to get herself out of the loony bin she agreed to live with Cindy in her own home, where she would cuddle secretly like her love child, she did so only until she could escape from there as well. With just a couple of clicks of door locks, and some minutes of hiding in a supply closet, and then with more keys turning and a creak of gate swings, Jolene rode to freedom in the trunk of

Cindy's beat-up Corolla. It was even easier, after one night, walking out Cindy's front door in broad daylight once the woman had gone back to work.

Jolene hit the road. She wanted out of that town and out of that county however she could. She had almost a hundred dollars from her watercolor business. She hitched some and rode some local buses. She had a small suitcase and a lot of attitude to get her safe across state lines. She worked in a five-and-ten in Lexington and an industrial laundry in Memphis. There was always a YWCA, to stay out of trouble. And while she did have to take a deep breath and sell it once or twice across the country, it had the virtue of hardening her up for her own protection. She was just seventeen by then but carrying herself with some new clothes like she was ten years older, so that nobody would know there was just this scared girl-child inside the hip slinger with the platform strap shoes.

Which brought her to Phoenix, Arizona, a hot flat city of the desert, but with a lot of fast-moving people who lived inside their air-conditioning.

SHE APPRECIATED THAT in the West human society was less tight-assed, nobody cared that much what you did or who your parents were and most everyone you met came from somewhere else. Before long she was working at a Dairy Queen and had a best friend, Kendra, who was one of her roommates, a northern girl from Akron, Ohio.

The Dairy Queen was at the edge of city life with a view over warehouses to the flat desert with its straight roads and brownish mountains away in the distance. She had to revert back to her real age to get this job. It involved roller-skating, a skill that she fortunately had not forgotten. You skated out to the customers with their order on a tray that you hooked to the car window. It was only minimum, but some men would give you a good tip, though women never did. And anyway that wasn't to last long, because this cute guy kept coming around every day. He had long hair, a scraggly lip beard, and a ring in his ear—he looked like a rock star. He wore an undershirt with his jeans and boots, so you could see the tattoos that went up and down his arms, across his shoulders, and onto his chest. He even had a guitar in the back of his 1965 plum Caddy convertible. Of course she ignored his entreaties, though he kept coming back, and if another girl waited on him he asked her where Jolene was. All the girls wore name tags, you see. One day he drove up, and when she came back with his order he was sitting on the top of the front seat with a big smile, though a front tooth was missing. He strummed his guitar and he said, Listen to this, Jolene, and he sang this song he had made up, and as he sang he laughed in appreciation, as if someone else was singing.

> *Jolene, Jolene*
> *She is so mean*
> *She won't be seen with me*
> *At the Dairy Queen.*

> *Jolene, Jolene*
> *Please don't be mean*
> *Your name it means to me*
> *My love you'll glean from me*
> *I am so keen to see*
> *How happy we will be*
> *When you are one with me*
> *Jolene, Jolene*
> *My Dairy Queen*

Well, she knew he was a sly one, but he'd gone to the trouble of thinking it up, didn't he? The people in the next car laughed and applauded and she blushed right through her freckles, but she couldn't help laughing along with them. And of course with his voice not very good and his guitar not quite in tune, she knew he was no rock star, but he was loud and didn't mind making a fool of himself and she liked that.

In fact, the guy was by profession a tattoo artist. His name was Coco Leger, pronounced Lerjay. He was originally from New Orleans, and she did go out dancing with him the next Saturday, though her friend Kendra strongly advised against it. The guy is a sleaze, Kendra said. Jolene thought she might be right. On the other hand, Kendra had no boyfriend of her own at the moment. And she was critical about most everything—their jobs, what she ate, the movies they saw, the furniture that came with the rental apartment, and maybe even the city of Phoenix in its entirety.

But Jolene went on the date and Coco was almost a gentleman. He was a good disco dancer, though a bit of a show-off with all his pelvic moves, and what was the harm after all. Coco Leger made her laugh, and she hadn't had a reason to laugh in a long time.

One thing led to another. There was first a small heart to be embossed for free on her behind, and before long she was working as an apprentice at Coco's Institute of Body Art. He showed her how to go about things, and she caught on quick and eventually she got to doing customers who wanted the cheap stock tattoos. It was drawing with a needle, a slow process like using only the tip of your paintbrush one dab at a time. Coco was very impressed with how fast she learned. He said she was a real asset. He fired the woman who worked for him, and after a serious discussion Jolene agreed to move in with him in his two rooms above his store, or studio, as he called it.

Kendra, who was still at the Dairy Queen, sat and watched her pack her things. I can see what he sees in you, Jolene, she said. You've got a trim little figure and everything moves the way it should without your even trying. Thank you, Kendra. Your skin is so fair, Kendra said. And you've got that nose that turns up, and a killer smile. Thank you, Kendra, she said again, and gave her a hug because, though she was happy for herself, she was sad for Kendra, whose really pretty face would not be seen for what it was by most men in that she was a heavyset girl with fat on her shoulders who was not very graceful on skates. But, Kendra continued, I can't see what you see in him. This is a man born to betray.

Still, she didn't want to go back to skating for tips. Coco was teaching her a trade that suited her talents. But when after just a couple of weeks Coco decided they should get married, she admitted to herself she knew nothing about him, his past, his family. She knew nothing, and when she asked, he just laughed and said, Babe, I am an orphan in the storm, just like you. They didn't much like me where I come from, but as I understan', neither of us has a past to write home about, he said holding her and kissing her neck. What counts is this here moment, he whispered, and the future moments to come.

She said the name Jolene Leger, pronounced Lerjay, secretly to herself and thought it had a nice lilt to it. And so after another justice of the peace and a corsage in her hand and a flowered dress to her ankles and a bottle of champagne, she was in fact Jolene Leger, a married woman once again. They went back to the two rooms above the store and smoked dope and made love, with Coco singsonging to her in her rhythm *Jolene Jolene she's a love machine*, and after he fell asleep and began to snore she got up and stood at the window and looked out on the street. It was three in the morning by then, but all the streetlights were on and the traffic signals were going, though not a human being was in sight. It was all busyness on that empty street in its silence, all the store signs blazing away, the neon colors in the windows, the Laundromat, the check-cashing store, the one-hour photo and passport, the newsdealer, the coffee shop, and the dry cleaner's, and the parking meters looking made of gold under the amber light of the streetlamps. It was the world going on as if people were the last thing it needed or wanted.

She found herself thinking that if you shaved off Coco's scraggly lip beard and if his tattoos could be scrubbed away, and you took off his boots with the lifts in them and got him a haircut and maybe set a pair of eyeglasses on his nose, he would look not unlike her first husband, the late Mickey Holler, and she began to cry.

For a while she was sympathetic to Coco's ways and wanted to believe his stories. But it became more and more difficult. He was away in his damn car half the time, leaving her to man the shop as if he didn't care what business they lost. He kept all moneys to himself. She realized she was working without a salary, which only a wife would do—who else would stand for that? It was a kind of slavery, wasn't it? Which is what Kendra said, tactlessly, when she came to visit. Coco was critical of most everything Jolene did or said. And when she needed money for groceries or some such he would only reluctantly peel off a bill or two from his carefully hoarded wad. She began to wonder where he got all his cash— certainly not from the tattooing trade, which was not all that great once the dry, cold Arizona winter set in. And when a reasonable-looking woman did come in, he carried on saying all sorts of suggestive things as if they were the only two people in the room. I really don't like that, Jolene told him. Not at all. You married yourself a good-lookin' stud, Coco said. Get used to it. And when Jolene found herself doing a snake or a whiskered fish for some muscleman, and, as you'd expect working so close-up, he'd come on to her, all Coco could say when she complained was, That's what makes the world go roun'. She became miserable on a daily basis. The drugs he was dealing took up more and more of his time and when she confronted him he didn't deny it. In fact, he said, it was the only way to keep the shop going. You should know without I have to tell you, Jolene, no artist in this USA can make it he don't have somethin' on the side.

One day a taxicab pulled up and a woman carrying a baby and holding a valise came into the store. She was a blonde, very tall, statuesque even, and although the sign was clearly printed on the store window, she said, Is this the Institute of Body Art of which Coco Leger is the proprietor? Jolene nodded. I would like to see him, please, the woman said, putting the valise down and shifting the baby from one arm to the other. She looked about thirty or thirty-five and she was wearing a hat, and had just a linen jacket and a yellow dress with hose and shoes, which was most unusual on this winter day in Phoenix, or in any season of the year for that matter, where you didn't see anyone who wasn't wearing jeans. Jolene had the weirdest feeling come over her. She felt that she was a child again. She was back in childhood—she'd only been a pretend adult and was not Mrs. Coco Leger except in her stupid dreams. It was a premonition. She looked again at the baby and at that moment knew what she didn't have to be told. Its ancestry was written all over its runty face. All it lacked was a little lip beard.

And you are? Jolene asked. I am Marin Leger, the wife of that fucking son of a bitch, the woman said.

As if any confirmation was needed, her large hand coming around from under the baby's bottom had a gold band impressed into the flesh of its fourth finger.

I have spent every cent I had tracking him down and I want to see him now, this very instant, the woman said. A moment later, as if a powerful magic had been invoked, Coco's Caddy rolled to the curb and it may have been worth everything to see the stunned ex-

pression on his face as he got out of the car and both saw Marin
Leger and was seen by her through the shop window. But, being
Coco, he recovered nicely. His face lit up and he waved as if he
couldn't have been more delighted. And came through the door
with a grin. Looka this, he said. Will ya looka this! he said, his
arms spread wide. Because she was the taller of the two, the hug he
gave her mashed his face against the baby in her arms, who com-
menced to cry loudly. And as Coco stepped back he suffered the
free hand of the woman smartly against his cheek.

Now, darlin', just be calm, he told her, stay calm. There is an
esplanation for everthin'. Come with me, we have to talk, he said
to her, as if he'd been waiting for her all along. Believe it or not I
am greatly relieved to see you, he said to her. He took no further
notice of the kid in her arms, and as he picked up her bag and ush-
ered her out the door, he looked back at Jolene and told her out of
the side of his mouth to hold tight, to hold tight, and outside he
gallantly opened the car door for Marin Leger and sat her and
their baby down and went off with them in the plum-colored
Caddy 1965 convertible he had once driven up every day to see Jolene wiggle her ass on skates.

*Jolene, Jolene, of the Dairy Queen, she is so mean, she smashed the
machinery* . . . She had never been so calm in her life as she quietly
and methodically trashed the Leger Institute of Body Art, turning
over the autoclave, pulling down the flash posters, banging the tattoo guns by their cables against the rear exposed-brick wall until
they cracked, scattering the needle bars, pouring the inks on the
floor, pulling the display case of 316L stainless-steel body jewelry
off the wall, tearing the paperback tattoo books in the rotating
stand. She smashed the director's chairs to pieces and threw a
metal footstool through the back-door window. She went upstairs
and, suddenly aware for the first time how their rooms smelled of
his disgusting unwashed body, she busted up everything she could,

tore up the bedding, swept everything out of the medicine cabinet, and pulled down the curtains she had chosen to make the place more homey. She took an armful of her clothes and stuffed them into two paper sacks and when she found in a shoe box on their closet shelf a ziplock plastic bag with another inside it packed with white stuff that felt under the thumb like baking powder, she left it exactly where it was and, downstairs again, cleaned out the few dollars that were in the cash register, picked up the phone, left a precise message for the Phoenix PD, and, putting up the BACK IN FIVE sign, she slammed the door behind her and was gone.

She was still dry-eyed when she went to the pawnshop two blocks away and got fifteen dollars for her wedding band. She waited at the storefront travel agency where the buses stopped and didn't begin to cry till she wondered, for the first time in a long time, who her mom and dad might have been and if they were still alive as she thought they must be if they were too young to do anything but name her Jolene and leave her for the authorities to raise.

IN VEGAS SHE waitressed at a coffee shop till she had enough money to have her hair straightened, which is what the impresario of the Starlet Topless told her she had to do if she wanted a job. So if she shook her head as she leaned back holding on to the brass pole, her hair swished back and forth across her shoulders. Wearing a thong and high heels was not the most comfortable thing in the world, but she got the idea of things quickly enough and became popular as the most petite girl in the place. The other girls liked her, too—they called her Baby and watched out for her. She rented a room in the apartment of a couple of them. Even the bouncer was solicitous after she lied to him that she was involved.

When she met Sal, a distinguished gray-haired man of some

girth, it was at the request of the manager, who took her to a table in the back. That this man Sal chose not to sit at the bar and stare up her ass suggested to her he was not the usual bum who came into Starlet's. He was a gentleman who though not married had several grandchildren. The first thing he did on their first date when she came up to his penthouse suite was show her their pictures. That's the kind of solid citizen Mr. Sal Fontaine was. She stood at the window looking out over all of Vegas. Quiet and soft-spoken Sal was not only a dear man, as she came to know him, but one highly respected as the founder and owner of Sal's Line, with an office and banks of phones with operators taking calls from people all over the country wanting Sal's Line on everything from horses to who would be the next president. Without ceremony, which was his way, he put a diamond choker on her neck and asked her to move in with him. She couldn't believe her luck, living with a man highly regarded in the community in his penthouse suite of six rooms overlooking all of Vegas. It had maid service every morning. From the French restaurant downstairs you could order dinner on a rolling cart that turned into a table. Sal bought her clothes, she signed his name at the beauty parlor, and when they went out, though he was so busy it was not that often, she was treated with respect by the greeters, and by Sal's associates, mostly gentlemen of the same age range as his. She was totally over-whelmed. With all the leggy ass in Las Vegas, imagine, little Jo-lene, treated like a princess! And not only that but with time on her hands to develop a line of her own, of greeting cards she drew, psychedelic in style, sometimes inspired by her experience with tattoo designs but always with the sentiments of loving family re-lationships that she dreamed up, as if she knew all about it.

She never thought she could be so happy. Sal liked her to climb all over him, he liked her to be on top, and they were very tender and caressing of one another, certainly on her part, because always in the back of her mind was the fear of his overexerting himself. And he talked so quietly, and he believed or pretended to believe her life story—the parts that were made up as well as the parts that were true.

As she became used to the life, she reflected that Sal Fontaine did not give of himself easily. It wasn't a matter of his material generosity. He never confided in her. There was a distance in him, or maybe even a gloom, that for all his success he could not change in himself. If she had questions, if she was curious, she met a wall. He moved slowly, as if the air set up a resistance just to him. When he smiled it was a sad smile despite his capped teeth. And he had heavy jowls and hooded sad eyes made darker by the deep blue pouches under them. Maybe he could not forget what he had lost, his old country or his original family, who was she to say?

She would tell him she loved him, and at the moment she said it, she did. The rest of the time she sort of shrugged to herself. The contractual nature of their relationship was all too clear to her, and she began to suspect that the regard Sal's friends held for her was not what they might have expressed among themselves. Her life, once the novelty wore off, was like eating cotton candy all day long. Her long straight red hair now shone with highlights. In the mornings she would swim in the hotel Olympic-size pool with her hair in a single braid, trailing. She was this Jolene person who wore different Vegas-style outfits depending on the time of day or night. She saw herself in an I. Magnin fitting-room mirror one day and the word that came to her mind was *hard*. When had it happened that she'd taken on that set of the mouth and stony gaze of the Las Vegas bimbo? Jesus.

One evening they were sitting watching television and Sal said, out of the blue, that she didn't have to worry, she would be taken care of, he would settle something on her. Thank you, sweetheart, she said, not knowing exactly how or when he would do that but understanding the essential meaning—that she was in a situation designed not to last. The next morning she took all her greeting-card designs to a print shop at the edge of town and spent two hours making decisions about the stock she wanted, the layouts, the typefaces, the amounts to print of each item, and so on. It was real business and it made her feel good, even though she had no idea of who would distribute her cards let alone who would buy them. Step by step, she told herself in the cab back. Step by step.

A week later the phone rang just when they were getting up and Sal told her quickly to get dressed and go have breakfast in the coffee shop because some men were coming for a meeting. She said that was okay, she would stay out of the way in the bedroom with a cup of coffee and the *Sun*. Don't argue, he shouted, and threw a dress at her face. She was speechless—he had never yelled at her before. She was waiting for the elevator when the doors opened and they came out, the men to meet with Sal. She saw them and they saw her, two of them looking, like so many of the men in Vegas, as if they had never felt the sun on their face.

But then in the coffee shop it dawned on her. She all at once turned cold and then sick to her stomach. She ran to the ladies' and sat there in a cold sweat. Such stories as you heard were never supposed to intrude into your own life.

How long did she sit there? When she found the courage to come out, and then out of the coffee shop into the lobby, she saw an ambulance at the front entrance. She stood in the crowd that gathered and saw the elevator doors open and someone with an oxygen mask over his face and hooked up to an intravenous line being wheeled on a gurney through the lobby.

That it was Sal Fontaine was quickly agreed upon by everyone. Exactly what had happened to him was less clear. Finally, a police officer walking by said it was a heart attack. A heart attack.

She did not even have her purse, just the orange print mini she wore and the sandals. She didn't even have any makeup—she had nothing. She saw the name of the hospital on the ambulance as it drove off and decided to go upstairs and put something on and take a cab there. But she couldn't move. She walked up the winding staircase to the mezzanine and sat there in an armchair with her hands between her knees. Finally, she got up the courage to go back to the penthouse floor. If it was a heart attack, what were the police and TV cameras doing there? Everyone in the world was in the corridor, and the door to the apartment was sealed with yellow tape and under guard and everything was out of her reach—Mr. Sal Fontaine, and all her clothes, and her diamond choker, and even the money he had given her over time, despite the fact that he never allowed her to pay for anything.

She had over a thousand dollars in the drawer on her side of the bed. She knew that eventually she could reclaim it if she wanted to be questioned by the police. But whatever was to happen to her now might not be as bad as what would happen if she risked it. Even if she told them nothing, what would Sal's Line be on the chances of her living to her nineteenth birthday, which happened also to be the next day? He was not around to tell her.

Which is how life changes, as lightning strikes, and in an instant what was is not what is and you find yourself sitting on a rock at the edge of the desert, hoping some bus will come by and take pity on you before you're found lying dead there like any other piece of roadkill.

TWO YEARS LATER, Jolene was living alone in Tulsa, Oklahoma. She had heard from a truck driver at a whistle stop in north Texas, where she was waiting tables, that Tulsa was a boomtown with not enough people for all the jobs. She'd taken a room at a women's residential hotel and first found work, part-time, in the public library shelving books and then full-time as a receptionist at a firm that leased oil-drilling equipment. She had not been with anyone in a while, but it was kind of nice actually. She was surprised at how pleasant life could be when you were on your own. She liked the way she felt walking in the street or sitting at a desk. Self-contained. Nothing begging inside her. I have come of age, she told herself. I have come of age.

To make some extra cash, she worked after hours on a call basis for a caterer. She had to invest in the uniform—white blouse, black trousers, and black pumps—but each time she was called it meant sixty dollars, for a minimum three hours. She wore her hair in the single braid down her back and she kept her eyes lowered as instructed but, even so, managed to see a good deal of the upper crust of Tulsa.

She was serving champagne on a tray at a private party one evening when this six-footer with blow-dried hair appeared before her. He was good-looking and he knew it. He grabbed a glass of champagne, drank it off, took another, and followed her into the kitchen. He didn't get anything out of her but her name, but he tracked her down through the caterer and sent her flowers with a note, signed Brad G. Benton, asking her out to dinner. Nobody in all her life had ever done that.

So she bought herself a dress and went out to dinner with Brad G. Benton at the country club, where the table linen was starched and there were crystal wineglasses and padded red leather chairs with brass studs. She wouldn't remember what she ate. She sat and listened with her hands in her lap. She didn't have to say much; he did all the talking. Brad G. Benton was not thirty-five and already a senior VP at this stockbrokerage where they kept on giving him bonuses. He didn't want just to get her in bed. He said since Jesus had come into his heart, the only really good sex remaining to him was connubial sex. He said, Of course you need someone precious and special enough for that, like you, Jolene, and looked deeply into her eyes.

At first, she couldn't believe he was serious. After a couple of more dates she realized he was. She was thinking Brad G. Benton must be crazy. On the other hand, this was the Bible Belt—she had seen these super-sincere people at her receptionist's job. They might be rich and do sophisticated business around the world, but they were true believers in God's written word, with no ifs, ands, or buts. From the looks of things it was a knockout combination, though a little weird, like they had one foot in the boardroom and one in heaven.

You don't know anything about me, Jolene told him in an effort to satisfy herself of her integrity. I expect soon to know everything, he said flashing a big handsome smile that could have been a leer.

He was so damn cocky. She almost resented that there was never any doubt in his mind as to what she would say. He insisted she quit her job and move to a hotel at his expense until the wedding day. Oh, what day is that? she said, teasing, but he was a wild man: The engagement will necessarily be short, he said, slipping a diamond ring on her finger.

A week later they were married in the chapel of the First Methodist church there in Tulsa that looked like Winchester Cathedral. Brad G. Benton brought her to live in his apartment in a new building that had a swimming pool in the basement and a gym on the roof. They were high enough to see out over the whole city, though there wasn't that much to see in Tulsa, Oklahoma.

So once more her fortunes had changed and little Jolene was a young matron of the upper class. She wanted to write to someone about this incredible turn in her life, but who could she write to? Who? There was no one. In that sense nothing had changed, because she was as alone as she had always been, a stranger in a strange land.

Things in the marriage were okay at first, though some of Brad G. Benton's ideas were not to her taste. He was very athletic and no sooner satisfied in one orifice than she was turned over for the other. Also, he seemed not to notice her artwork. She had bought an easel and set up a little studio in what was designed to be the maid's room, because the Indian woman who cooked and cleaned had her own home to go to each evening. Jolene painted there and stretched her canvas, and she took a figure-painting class once a week where there were live models. She did well, her teacher was very encouraging, but Brad took none of this in. He just didn't notice—he was too busy with his work and his workouts and his nights out and his nights in her.

It turned out that Brad G. Benton's family was prominent in Tulsa. Not one of them had come to the wedding, their purpose being to define to her what white trash meant. At first she didn't care that much. But she'd see their pictures in the newspapers being honored at charity events. They had wings of buildings named after them. One day, coming from shopping, she looked out of the cab window as it passed a glass office tower that said BENTON INTERNATIONAL on a giant brass cube balanced on one of its corners in the plaza out front.

She said to Brad, I would think they had more respect for you if not for me. But he only laughed. It was not so much that he was a democrat in his ideals, as she was to realize, it was part of his life's work to do outrageous things and raise hell. It was how he kept everyone's attention. He loved to twist noses out of joint. He was contrary. He hadn't joined the Benton family enterprise as he was supposed to—it was a holding company with many different kinds of business in their hands—but had gone off on his own to show what he was made of.

Jolene knew that if she wanted to prove anything to his family, if she wanted any kind of social acceptance in Tulsa, Oklahoma, she would have to work for it. She would have to start reading books and take a course or two in something intellectual and embrace the style of life, the manners, the ways of doing and talking by being patient and keeping her eyes and ears open. She would attend their church, too. As wild as he was, Brad was like his father, what he called a strong Christian. That was the one place they would have to meet and, she was willing to bet, speak to one another. And how then could the family not speak to her?

Oddly enough, she was looking as good as she ever had, and Brad took her once a week to dinner at the country club to show her off. By then everyone in town knew this so-called Cinderella story. Grist for the mill. He was heedless. He just didn't worry about it, whereas she could hardly raise her head. One evening, his father and mother were sitting at a far table with their guests, who looked as if they were there to serve them no less than the waiters. Brad waved—it was more like a salute—and the father nodded and resumed his conversation.

Through no fault of her own Jolene had stepped into a situation that was making her life miserable. Whatever was going on with these people, what did it have to do with her? Nothing. She was as nothing.

To tell the truth, she had made Brad for a creep that first time he came on to her at that cocktail party. He'd padded into the kitchen, stalking her like some animal, taken the empty champagne tray out of her hands, and told her redheads smelled different. And he stood there sniffing her and going, Hmmm, yes, like warm milk.

AFTER HER BABY WAS BORN, when Brad G. Benton started to bat her around, Jolene could not help but remember that first impression. Every little thing drove him crazy. It got so she couldn't do anything, say anything, without he would go off half-cocked. He took to hitting her, slapping her face, punching her. What are you doing? she screamed. Stop it, stop it! It was his new way of getting off. He would say, You like this? You like it? He'd knock her around, then push her down on the bed. She grew accustomed to living in fear of getting beaten up and forced against her will. She was still to learn what they would teach at the shelter—it happens once, that's it, you leave. But now she just tried to see it through. Brad G. Benton had been to college, he came of money and he wore good clothes, and she was flattered that he would fall for her when she hadn't even a high school diploma. And then of course there were the apologies and the beggings for forgiveness and the praying in church together, and by such means she slowly became a routinely abused wife.

Only when it was all over would she realize it wasn't just having the baby; it was their plans for him, the Bentons' plans for her Mr. Nipplebee. He was an heir, after all. The minute they'd found out she was pregnant, they went to work. And after he was born, they slowly gave it to Brad in bits and pieces, what their investigators had learned about her life before. Never mind that she had tried to tell Brad about her marriages, her life on the road. He never wanted to hear it; he had no curiosity about her—none. She had appeared in Tulsa as a vision, God's chosen sex partner for him, a fresh and wet and shining virgin with red hair. All those beatings were what he was told, and all those apologies were the way his love for her was hanging on. She would feel sorry for him if she could because he was so wired, such a maniac. It was as if his wildness, his independent choice of life, was being driven from him, as if it was the Devil. It was those parents slowly absorbing him back into their righteousness.

One day Brad G. Benton appeared at the door to her little studio room when he ordinarily would be at work. She was ruling off a grid on one of her canvases as she had been taught. Brad! she said, smiling, but there was no recognition in his eyes. He kicked the stool out from under her. He broke the easel over his knee, he bashed her canvases against the wall, tore down the drawings she had pinned up there, and then he squeezed tubes of paint into her face as he held her down on the floor. And he began hitting her as she lay there. He punched her face, he punched her in the throat. When he got off her, she could hear his breathing—it was like crying. He stood over her, kicked her in the side, and as suddenly as he had come he was gone.

She lay there moaning in pain, too frightened and shocked even to get up until she thought of the baby. She dragged herself to the nursery. The Cherokee woman who had heard everything sat beside the crib with her hand over her eyes. But the baby was sleeping peacefully. Jolene washed her face and, wrapping up her Mr. Nipplebee, she took him with her as she dragged herself to a doctor. She was told that she had had her cheek fractured, two broken ribs, contusions of the throat, and a bruised kidney. How did this happen? the doctor asked her. She was afraid to tell him, and, besides, it hurt too much to talk. But the nurse in the office didn't have to be told. She wrote out the name and address of a women's shelter and said, Go there right now. I'll order you a cab. And in that way, with her precious in her arms and only what she wore, Jolene left her marriage.

She could hardly bear staying at the shelter, where there were these wimpy women looking for her friendship, her companionship. Jolene wouldn't even go to the group sessions. She stayed by herself and nursed Mr. Nipplebee.

The shelter gave her the name of a woman lawyer and she put down a retainer. Get me a divorce as fast as you can, she told the lawyer. The money—I don't care, I'll take anything they give. I just want out of here and out of Tulsa, Oklahoma. And then she waited, and waited, and nothing happened. Absolutely nothing. This went on for some time. And the next thing Jolene knew, when she was about strapped of her savings account, the lawyer quit on her. She was an older woman who wore pin-striped suits and big loopy bronze earrings. I may be broke, Jolene said to her, but Brad G. Benton has money to burn and I can pay you afterward out of the alimony or child care.

You didn't tell me you had a past including a stretch in juvenile detention, the lawyer said. To say nothing of a previous as yet unannulled marriage to a convicted drug dealer.

Jolene was so stunned she didn't think to ask how the lawyer knew that if she hadn't told her.

She was up against a scumbag husband on his own turf, so what could she expect but that there was worse to come, as there was, if he knew all along where she was hiding, and if he knew by first names everyone in town, as he probably did the very police officers who came one morning to arrest her for unlawful kidnapping of her own child, who they took from her arms and drove off in one squad car with Jolene in another as she looked back screaming.

I don't want to hear about what is the law in this country and what is not, Jolene told the Legal Aid person who was assigned to her. Do you know what it means to have your child torn from you? Do you have to have that happen to you to know that it is worse than death? Because though you want to kill yourself, you cannot have that relief for thinking of the child's welfare in the hands of a sick father who never smiled at him and was jealous of him from the day he was born.

My baby, she said aloud when she was alone. My baby.

He had her coloring and button nose and carrot-red fuzz for hair. He drank from her with a born knowledge of what was expected of him. He was a whole new life in her arms, and for the very first time she could remember she had something she wanted. She was Jolene, his mother, and could believe in God now, who had never before seemed to her to be much of a fact of life.

And so now there was a hearing for the divorce Brad had filed for. And his whole miserable family was there—they loved him after all now that he was getting rid of her and her past was thrown in her face. They had it all down, including the medical records of her STD from Coco, her living in sin, and even her suspension one term at South Sumter High for smoking pot. It was a no-brainer, her Legal Aid kid was out of his league, and without giving it much thought, the judge ruled she was an unfit mother and granted Brad G. Benton sole custody of her Mr. Nipplebee.

On top of everything, in the fullness of her milk that she had to pump out, she must have done something wrong, because she ended up in the hospital with a staph infection that had to be drained, like the milk had gone bad and turned green. But she had a chance to think. She thought of her choices. She could kill Brad G. Benton—it'd be simple enough to buy some kind of gun and wait on him—but then the baby would be raised by the Benton family. So what was the point? She could find a job and see the baby every second Sunday for one hour, as allowed by the judge, and rely on the passing of time for the moment when nobody would be looking and she could steal him back and run for it. But then on her first visitation what happened was that Brad was up in the gym and a new large Indian woman was with Mr. Nipplebee, and Brad's crone of a mother stood with her back to the door and they wouldn't let Jolene hold him but just sit by the crib and watch him sleep. And she thought, If I stay on in Tulsa for my visitations, he will grow up learning to think of me as an embarrassment, a poor relation, and I can't have that.

—

THESE DAYS, JOLENE has this job in West Hollywood inking for a small comic-book company, except they don't call them comic books—they call them graphic novels. Because most of them aren't funny at all. They are very serious. She likes the people at work, they are all good pals and go out for pizza together. But where she lives is down near the farmers' market, in a studio apartment that is sacred to her. Nobody can come in no matter how good a friend. She has a little stereo for her Keith Jarrett CDs and she lights a candle and drinks a little wine and dreams of plans for herself. She thinks someday, when she has more experience, of writing a graphic novel of her own, *The Life of Jolene*.

She has a pastel sketch she once did of her precious baby. It is so sweet! It's the only likeness she has. Sometimes she looks at this sketch and then at her own face in the mirror, and because he takes after her in his coloring and features, she tries to draw him at what he might look like at his present age, which is four and a half.

Friends tell Jolene she could act in movies because she may be twenty-five but she looks a lot younger. And they like her voice that she has courtesy of her ex-husband, the way it cracks like Janis Joplin's. And her crooked smile, which she doesn't tell them is the result of a busted cheekbone. So she's had some photos taken and is sending them out to professional agents.

I mean, why not? Jolene says to herself. Her son could see her up on the screen one day? And when she took herself back to Tulsa in her Rolls-Royce automobile he would answer the door and there would be his movie-star mother.

THE WRITER
IN THE FAMILY

—

—

IN 1955 MY FATHER DIED WITH HIS ANCIENT MOTHER STILL alive in a nursing home. The old lady was ninety and hadn't even known he was ill. Thinking the shock might kill her, my aunts told her that he had moved to Arizona for his bronchitis. To the immigrant generation of my grandmother, Arizona was the American equivalent of the Alps, it was where you went for your health. More accurately, it was where you went if you had the money. Since my father had failed in all the business enterprises of his life, this was the aspect of the news my grandmother dwelled on, that he had finally had some success. And so it came about that as we mourned him at home in our stocking feet, my grandmother was bragging to her cronies about her son's new life in the dry air of the desert.

My aunts had decided on their course of action without consulting us. It meant neither my mother nor my brother nor I could visit Grandma because we were supposed to have moved west too, a family, after all. My brother Harold and I didn't mind—it was always a nightmare at the old people's home, where they all sat around staring at us while we tried to make conversation with Grandma. She looked terrible, had numbers of ailments, and her mind wandered. Not seeing her was no disappointment either for my mother, who had never gotten along with the old woman and did not visit when she could have. But what was disturbing was that my aunts had acted in the manner of that side of the family of making government on everyone's behalf, the true citizens by blood and the lesser citizens by marriage. It was exactly this attitude that had tormented my mother all her married life. She claimed Jack's family had never accepted her. She had battled them for twenty-five years as an outsider.

A few weeks after the end of our ritual mourning my aunt Frances phoned us from her home in Larchmont. Aunt Frances was the wealthier of my father's sisters. Her husband was a lawyer, and both her sons were at Amherst. She had called to say that Grandma was asking why she didn't hear from Jack. I had answered the phone. "You're the writer in the family," my aunt said. "Your father had so much faith in you. Would you mind making up something? Send it to me and I'll read it to her. She won't know the difference."

That evening, at the kitchen table, I pushed my homework aside and composed a letter. I tried to imagine my father's response to his new life. He had never been west. He had never traveled anywhere. In his generation the great journey was from the working class to the professional class. He hadn't managed that either. But he loved New York, where he had been born and lived his life, and he was always discovering new things about it. He especially loved the old parts of the city below Canal Street, where he would find ships' chandlers or firms that wholesaled in spices and teas. He was a salesman for an appliance jobber with accounts all over the city. He liked to bring home rare cheeses or exotic foreign vegetables that were sold only in certain neighborhoods. Once he brought home a barometer, another time an antique ship's telescope in a wooden case with a brass snap.

"Dear Mama," I wrote. "Arizona is beautiful. The sun shines all day and the air is warm and I feel better than I have in years. The desert is not as barren as you would expect, but filled with wildflowers and cactus plants and peculiar crooked trees that look like men holding their arms out. You can see great distances in whatever direction you turn and to the west is a range of mountains maybe fifty miles from here, but in the morning with the sun on them you can see the snow on their crests."

My aunt called some days later and told me it was when she read this letter aloud to the old lady that the full effect of Jack's death came over her. She had to excuse herself and went out in the parking lot to cry. "I wept so," she said. "I felt such terrible longing for him. You're so right, he loved to go places, he loved life, he loved everything."

WE BEGAN trying to organize our lives. My father had borrowed money against his insurance and there was very little left. Some commissions were still due but it didn't look as if his firm would honor them. There was a couple of thousand dollars in a savings bank that had to be maintained there until the estate was settled. The lawyer involved was Aunt Frances' husband and he was very proper. "The estate!" my mother muttered, gesturing as if to pull out her hair. "The estate!" She applied for a job part-time in the admissions office of the hospital where my father's terminal illness had been diagnosed, and where he had spent some months until they had sent him home to die. She knew a lot of the doctors and staff and she had learned "from bitter experience," as she told them, about the hospital routine. She was hired.

I hated that hospital, it was dark and grim and full of tortured people. I thought it was masochistic of my mother to seek out a job there, but did not tell her so.

We lived in an apartment on the corner of 175th Street and the Grand Concourse, one flight up. Three rooms. I shared the bedroom with my brother. It was jammed with furniture because when my father had required a hospital bed in the last weeks of his illness we had moved some of the living-room pieces into the bedroom and made over the living room for him. We had to navigate bookcases, beds, a gateleg table, bureaus, a record player and radio console, stacks of 78 albums, my brother's trombone and music stand, and so on. My mother continued to sleep on the convertible sofa in the living room that had been their bed before his illness. The two rooms were connected by a narrow hall made even narrower by bookcases along the wall. Off the hall were a small kitchen and dinette and a bathroom. There were lots of appliances in the kitchen—broiler, toaster, pressure cooker, countertop dishwasher, blender—that my father had gotten through his job, at cost. A treasured phrase in our house: *at cost.* But most of these fixtures went unused because my mother did not care for them. Chromium devices with timers or gauges that required the reading of elaborate instructions were not for her. They were in part responsible for the awful clutter of our lives and now she wanted to get rid of them. "We're being buried," she said. "Who needs them!"

So we agreed to throw out or sell anything inessential. While I found boxes for the appliances and my brother tied the boxes with twine, my mother opened my father's closet and took out his clothes. He had several suits because as a salesman he needed to look his best. My mother wanted us to try on his suits to see which of them could be altered and used. My brother refused to try them on. I tried on one jacket, which was too large for me. The lining inside the sleeves chilled my arms and the vaguest scent of my father's being came to me.

"This is way too big," I said.

"Don't worry," my mother said. "I had it cleaned. Would I let you wear it if I hadn't?"

It was the evening, the end of winter, and snow was coming down on the windowsill and melting as it settled. The ceiling bulb glared on a pile of my father's suits and trousers on hangers flung across the bed in the shape of a dead man. We refused to try on anything more, and my mother began to cry.

"What are you crying for?" my brother shouted. "You wanted to get rid of things, didn't you?"

A FEW WEEKS later my aunt phoned again and said she thought it would be necessary to have another letter from Jack. Grandma had fallen out of her chair and bruised herself and was very depressed.

"How long does this go on?" my mother said.

"It's not so terrible," my aunt said, "for the little time left to make things easier for her."

My mother slammed down the phone. "He can't even die when he wants to!" she cried. "Even death comes second to Mama! What are they afraid of, the shock will kill her? Nothing can kill her. She's indestructible! A stake through the heart couldn't kill her!"

When I sat down in the kitchen to write the letter I found it more difficult than the first one. "Don't watch me," I said to my brother. "It's hard enough."

"You don't have to do something just because someone wants you to," Harold said. He was two years older than me and had started at City College; but when my father became ill he had switched to night school and gotten a job in a record store.

"Dear Mama," I wrote. "I hope you're feeling well. We're all fit as a fiddle. The life here is good and the people are very friendly and informal. Nobody wears suits and ties here. Just a pair of slacks and a short-sleeved shirt. Perhaps a sweater in the evening. I have bought into a very successful radio and record business and

I'm doing very well. You remember Jack's Electric, my old place on Forty-third Street? Well, now it's Jack's Arizona Electric and we have a line of television sets as well."

I sent that letter off to my aunt Frances, and as we all knew she would, she phoned soon after. My brother held his hand over the mouthpiece. "It's Frances with her latest review," he said.

"Jonathan? You're a very talented young man. I just wanted to tell you what a blessing your letter was. Her whole face lit up when I read the part about Jack's store. That would be an excellent way to continue."

"Well, I hope I don't have to do this anymore, Aunt Frances. It's not very honest."

Her tone changed. "Is your mother there? Let me talk to her."

"She's not here," I said.

"Tell her not to worry," my aunt said. "A poor old lady who has never wished anything but the best for her will soon die."

I did not repeat this to my mother, for whom it would have been one more in the family anthology of unforgivable remarks. But then I had to suffer it myself for the possible truth it might embody. Each side defended its position with rhetoric, but I, who wanted peace, rationalized the snubs and rebuffs each inflicted on the other, taking no stands, like my father himself.

Years ago his life had fallen into a pattern of business failures and missed opportunities. The great debate between his family on the one side, and my mother Ruth on the other, was this: who was responsible for the fact that he had not lived up to anyone's expectations?

As to the prophecies, when spring came my mother's prevailed. Grandma was still alive.

One balmy Sunday my mother and brother and I took the bus to the Beth El cemetery in New Jersey to visit my father's grave. It was situated on a slight rise. We stood looking over rolling fields embedded with monuments. Here and there processions of black cars wound their way through the lanes, or clusters of people stood at open graves. My father's grave was planted with tiny shoots of evergreen but it lacked a headstone. We had chosen one and paid for it and then the stonecutters had gone on strike. Without a headstone my father did not seem to be honorably dead. He didn't seem to me properly buried.

My mother gazed at the plot beside his, reserved for her coffin. "They were always too fine for other people," she said. "Even in the old days on Stanton Street. They put on airs. Nobody was ever good enough for them. Finally Jack himself was not good enough for them. Except to get them things wholesale. Then he was good enough for them."

"Mom, please," my brother said.

"If I had known. Before I ever met him he was tied to his mama's apron strings. And Essie's apron strings were like chains, let me tell you. We had to live where we could be near them for the Sunday visits. Every Sunday, that was my life, a visit to Mamaleh. Whatever she knew I wanted, a better apartment, a stick of furniture, a summer camp for the boys, she spoke against it. You know your father, every decision had to be considered and reconsidered. And nothing changed. Nothing ever changed."

She began to cry. We sat her down on a nearby bench. My brother walked off and read the names on stones. I looked at my mother, who was crying, and I went off after my brother.

"Mom's still crying," I said. "Shouldn't we do something?"

"It's all right," he said. "It's what she came here for."

"Yes," I said, and then a sob escaped from my throat. "But I feel like crying too."

My brother Harold put his arm around me. "Look at this old

black stone here," he said. "The way it's carved. You can see the changing fashion in monuments—just like everything else."

SOMEWHERE IN THIS TIME I began dreaming of my father. Not the robust father of my childhood, the handsome man with healthy pink skin and brown eyes and a mustache and the thinning hair parted in the middle. My dead father. We were taking him home from the hospital. It was understood that he had come back from death. This was amazing and joyous. On the other hand, he was terribly mysteriously damaged, or, more accurately, spoiled and unclean. He was very yellowed and debilitated by his death, and there were no guarantees that he wouldn't soon die again. He seemed aware of this and his entire personality was changed. He was angry and impatient with all of us. We were trying to help him in some way, struggling to get him home, but something prevented us, something we had to fix, a tattered suitcase that had sprung open, some mechanical thing: he had a car but it wouldn't start; or the car was made of wood; or his clothes, which had become too large for him, had caught in the door. In one version he was all bandaged and as we tried to lift him from his wheelchair into a taxi the bandage began to unroll and catch in the spokes of the wheelchair. This seemed to be some unreasonableness on his part. My mother looked on sadly and tried to get him to cooperate.

That was the dream. I shared it with no one. Once when I woke, crying out, my brother turned on the light. He wanted to know what I'd been dreaming but I pretended I didn't remember. The dream made me feel guilty. I felt guilty *in* the dream too because my enraged father knew we didn't want to live with him. The dream represented us taking him home, or trying to, but it was nevertheless understood by all of us that he was to live alone. He was this derelict back from death, but what we were doing was taking him to some place where he would live by himself without help from anyone until he died again.

At one point I became so fearful of this dream that I tried not to go to sleep. I tried to think of good things about my father and to remember him before his illness. He used to call me "matey." "Hello, matey," he would say when he came home from work. He always wanted us to go someplace—to the store, to the park, to a ball game. He loved to walk. When I went walking with him he would say: "Hold your shoulders back, don't slump. Hold your head up and look at the world. Walk as if you meant it!" As he strode down the street his shoulders moved from side to side, as if he was hearing some kind of cakewalk. He moved with a bounce. He was always eager to see what was around the corner.

THE NEXT REQUEST for a letter coincided with a special occasion in the house: my brother Harold had met a girl he liked and had gone out with her several times. Now she was coming to our house for dinner.

We had prepared for this for days, cleaning everything in sight, giving the house a going-over, washing the dust of disuse from the glasses and good dishes. My mother came home early from work to get the dinner going. We opened the gateleg table in the living room and brought in the kitchen chairs. My mother spread the table with a laundered white cloth and put out her silver. It was the first family occasion since my father's illness.

I liked my brother's girlfriend a lot. She was a thin girl with very straight hair and she had a terrific smile. Her presence seemed to excite the air. It was amazing to have a living breathing girl in our house. She looked around and what she said was: "Oh, I've never seen so many books!" While she and my brother sat at the table my mother was in the kitchen putting the food into serving bowls and I was going from the kitchen to the living room, kidding around like a waiter, with a white cloth over my arm and a high style of service, placing the serving dish of green beans on the table with a flourish. In the kitchen my mother's eyes were sparkling. She looked at me and nodded and mimed the words: "She's adorable!"

My brother suffered himself to be waited on. He was wary of what we might say. He kept glancing at the girl—her name was Susan—to see if we met with her approval. She worked in an insurance office and was taking courses in accounting at City College. Harold was under a terrible strain but he was excited and happy too. He had bought a bottle of Concord-grape wine to go with the roast chicken. He held up his glass and proposed a toast. My mother said: "To good health and happiness," and we all drank, even I. At that moment the phone rang and I went into the bedroom to get it.

"Jonathan? This is your aunt Frances. How is everyone?"

"Fine, thank you."

"I want to ask one last favor of you. I need a letter from Jack. Your grandma's very ill. Do you think you can?"

"Who is it?" my mother called from the living room.

"Okay, Aunt Frances," I said quickly. "I have to go now, we're eating dinner." And I hung up the phone.

"It was my friend Louie," I said, sitting back down. "He didn't know the math pages to review."

The dinner was very fine. Harold and Susan washed the dishes and by the time they were done my mother and I had folded up the gateleg table and put it back against the wall and I had swept the crumbs up with the carpet sweeper. We all sat and talked and listened to records for a while and then my brother took Susan home. The evening had gone very well.

ONCE WHEN MY MOTHER wasn't home my brother had pointed out something: the letters from Jack weren't really necessary. "What is this ritual?" he said, holding his palms up. "Grandma is almost totally blind, she's half deaf and crippled. Does the situation really call for a literary composition? Does it need verisimilitude? Would the old lady know the difference if she was read the phone book?"

"Then why did Aunt Frances ask me?"

"That is the question, Jonathan. Why did she? After all, she could write the letter herself—what difference would it make? And if not Frances, why not Frances' sons, the Amherst students? They should have learned by now to write."

"But they're not Jack's sons," I said.

"That's exactly the point," my brother said. "The idea is *service*. Dad used to bust his balls getting them things wholesale, getting them deals on things. Frances of Westchester really needed things at cost. And Aunt Molly. And Aunt Molly's husband, and Aunt Molly's ex-husband. Grandma, if she needed an errand done. He was always on the hook for something. They never thought his time was important. They never thought every favor he got was one he had to pay back. Appliances, records, watches, china, opera tickets, any goddamn thing. Call Jack."

"It was a matter of pride to him to be able to do things for them," I said. "To have connections."

"Yeah, I wonder why," my brother said. He looked out the window.

Then suddenly it dawned on me that I was being implicated.

"You should use your head more," my brother said.

YET I HAD AGREED once again to write a letter from the desert and so I did. I mailed it off to Aunt Frances. A few days later, when I came home from school, I thought I saw her sitting in her car in front of our house. She drove a black Buick Roadmaster, a very large clean car with whitewall tires. It was Aunt Frances all right. She blew the horn when she saw me. I went over and leaned in at the window.

"Hello, Jonathan," she said. "I haven't long. Can you get in the car?"

"Mom's not home," I said. "She's working."

"I know that. I came to talk to you."

"Would you like to come upstairs?"

"I can't, I have to get back to Larchmont. Can you get in for a moment, please?"

I got in the car. My aunt Frances was a very pretty white-haired woman, very elegant, and she wore tasteful clothes. I had always liked her and from the time I was a child she had enjoyed pointing out to everyone that I looked more like her son than Jack's. She wore white gloves and held the steering wheel and looked straight ahead as she talked, as if the car was in traffic and not sitting at the curb.

"Jonathan," she said, "there is your letter on the seat. Needless to say I didn't read it to Grandma. I'm giving it back to you and I won't ever say a word to anyone. This is just between us. I never expected cruelty from you. I never thought you were capable of doing something so deliberately cruel and perverse."

I said nothing.

"Your mother has very bitter feelings and now I see she has poisoned you with them. She has always resented the family. She is a very strong-willed, selfish person."

"No she isn't," I said.

"I wouldn't expect you to agree. She drove poor Jack crazy with her demands. She always had the highest aspirations and he could never fulfill them to her satisfaction. When he still had his store he kept your mother's brother, who drank, on salary. After the war when he began to make a little money he had to buy Ruth a mink jacket because she was so desperate to have one. He had debts to pay but she wanted a mink. He was a very special person, my brother, he should have accomplished something special, but he loved your mother and devoted his life to her. And all she ever thought about was keeping up with the Joneses."

I watched the traffic going up the Grand Concourse. A bunch of kids were waiting at the bus stop at the corner. They had put their books on the ground and were horsing around.

"I'm sorry I have to descend to this," Aunt Frances said. "I don't like talking about people this way. If I have nothing good to say about someone, I'd rather not say anything. How is Harold?"

"Fine."

"Did he help you write this marvelous letter?"

"No."

After a moment she said more softly: "How are you all getting along?"

"Fine."

"I would invite you up for Passover if I thought your mother would accept."

I didn't answer.

She turned on the engine. "I'll say good-bye now, Jonathan. Take your letter. I hope you give some time to thinking about what you've done."

—

THAT EVENING WHEN my mother came home from work I saw that she wasn't as pretty as my aunt Frances. I usually thought my mother was a good-looking woman, but I saw now that she was too heavy and that her hair was undistinguished.

"Why are you looking at me?" she said.

"I'm not."

"I learned something interesting today," my mother said. "We may be eligible for a VA pension because of the time your father spent in the navy."

That took me by surprise. Nobody had ever told me my father was in the navy.

"In World War I," she said, "he went to Webb's Naval Academy on the Harlem River. He was training to be an ensign. But the war ended and he never got his commission."

After dinner the three of us went through the closets looking for my father's papers, hoping to find some proof that could be filed with the Veterans Administration. We came up with two things, a Victory medal, which my brother said everyone got for being in the service during the Great War, and an astounding sepia photograph of my father and his shipmates on the deck of a ship. They were dressed in bell-bottoms and T-shirts and armed with mops and pails, brooms and brushes.

"I never knew this," I found myself saying. "I never knew this."

"You just don't remember," my brother said.

I was able to pick out my father. He stood at the end of the row, a thin, handsome boy with a full head of hair, a mustache, and an intelligent smiling countenance.

"He had a joke," my mother said. "They called their training ship the SS *Constipation* because it never moved."

Neither the picture nor the medal was proof of anything, but my brother thought a duplicate of my father's service record had to be in Washington somewhere and that it was just a matter of learning how to go about finding it.

"The pension wouldn't amount to much," my mother said. "Twenty or thirty dollars. But it would certainly help."

I took the picture of my father and his shipmates and propped it against the lamp at my bedside. I looked into his youthful face and tried to relate it to the father I knew. I looked at the picture a long time. Only gradually did my eye connect it to the set of Great Sea Novels in the bottom shelf of the bookcase a few feet away. My father had given that set to me: it was uniformly bound in green with gilt lettering and it included works by Melville, Conrad, Victor Hugo, and Captain Marryat. And lying across the top of the books, jammed in under the sagging shelf above, was his old ship's telescope in its wooden case with the brass snap.

I thought how stupid, and imperceptive, and self-centered I had been never to have understood while he was alive what my father's dream for his life had been.

On the other hand, I had written in my last letter from Arizona—the one that had so angered Aunt Frances—something that might allow me, the writer in the family, to soften my judgment of myself. I will conclude by giving the letter here in its entirety.

Dear Mama,

This will be my final letter to you since I have been told by the doctors that I am dying.

I have sold my store at a very fine profit and am sending Frances a check for five thousand dollars to be deposited in your account. My present to you, Mamaleh. Let Frances show you the passbook.

As for the nature of my ailment, the doctors haven't told me what it is, but I know that I am simply dying of the wrong life. I should never have come to the desert. It wasn't the place for me.

I have asked Ruth and the boys to have my body cremated and the ashes scattered in the ocean.

Your loving son,
Jack

WILLI

—

O NE SPRING DAY I WALKED IN THE MEADOW BEHIND THE BARN and felt rising around me the exhalations of the field, the moist sweetness of the grasses, and I imagined the earth's soul lifting to the warmth of the sun and mingling me in some divine embrace. There was such brilliant conviction in the colors of the golden hay meadow, the blue sky, that I could not help laughing. I threw myself down in the grass and spread my arms. I fell at once into a trance and yet remained incredibly aware, so that whatever I opened my eyes to look at I did not merely see but felt as its existence. Such states come naturally to children. I was resonant with the hum of the universe, I was made indistinguishable from the world in a great bonding of natural revelation. I saw the drowse of gnats weaving between the grasses and leaving infinitesimally fine threads of shimmering net, so highly textured that the breath of the soil below lifted it in gentle billows. Minute crawling life on the stalks of hay made colossal odysseys, journeys of a lifetime, before my eyes. Yet there was no thought of miracle, of the miracle of microscopic sentience. The scale of the universe was not pertinent, and the smallest indications of energy were in proportion to the sun, which lay like an Egyptian eye between the stalks, and lit them as it lights the earth, by halves. The hay had fallen under me so that my own body's outline was patterned on the field, the outspread legs and arms, the fingers, and I was aware of my being as the arbitrary shape of an agency that had chosen to make me in

this manner as a means of communicating with me. The very idea
of a head and limbs and a body was substantive only as an act of
communication, and I felt myself in the prickle of the flattened
grass, and the sense of imposition was now enormous, a prodding,
a lifting of this part of the world that was for some reason my momentary responsibility, that was giving me possession of itself. And
I rose and seemed to ride on the planes of the sun, which I felt in
fine striations, alternated with thin lines of the earth's moist
essences. And invisibled by my revelation, I reached the barn and
examined the face of it, standing with my face in the painted
whiteness of its glare as a dog or a cat stands nose to a door until
someone comes and lets it out. And I moved along the white barn
wall, sidestepping until I came to the window that was a simple
square without glass, and could only be felt by the geometrical
coolness of its volume of inner air, for it was black within. And
there I stood, as if in the mouth of a vacuum, and felt the insub-
stantial being of the sun meadow pulled past me into the barn, like
a torrential implosion of light into darkness and life into death,
and I myself too disintegrated in that force and was sucked like the
chaff of the field in that roaring. Yet I stood where I was. And in
quite normal spatial relationship with my surroundings felt the
sun's quiet warmth on my back and the coolness of the cool barn
on my face. And the windy universal roar in my ears had narrowed
and refined itself to a recognizable frequency, that of a woman's
pulsating song in the act of love, the gasp and note and gasp and
note of an ecstatic score. I listened. And pressed upon by the sun,
as if it were a hand on the back of my neck, I moved my face into
the portal of the cool darkness, and no longer blinded by the sunlight, my eyes saw on the straw and in the dung my mother,
denuded, in a pose of utmost degradation, a body, a reddened
headless body, the head enshrouded in her clothing, everything
turned inside out, as if blown out by the wind, all order, truth, and

reason, and this defiled Mama played violently upon and being made to sing her defilement. How can I describe what I felt! I felt I deserved to see this! I felt it was my triumph, but I felt monstrously betrayed. I felt drained suddenly of the strength to stand. I turned my back and slid down the wall to a sitting position under the window. My heart in my chest banged in sickened measure of her cries. I wanted to kill him, this killer of my mother who was killing her. I wanted to leap through the window and drive a pitchfork into his back, but I wanted him to be killing her, I wanted him to be killing her for me. I wanted to be him. I lay on the ground, and with my arms over my head and my hands clasped and my ankles locked, I rolled down the slope behind the barn, through the grass and the crop of hay. I flattened the hay like a mechanical cylinder of irrepressible force rolling fast and faster over rocks, through rivulets, across furrows, and over hummocks of the uneven imperfect flawed irregular earth, the sun flashing in my closed eyes in diurnal emergency, as if time and the planet had gone out of control. As it has. (I am recalling these things now, a man older than my father when he died, and to whom a woman of my mother's age when all this happened is a young woman barely half my age. What an incredible achievement of fantasy is the scientific mind! We posit an empirical world, yet how can I be here at this desk in this room—and not be here? If memory is a matter of the stimulation of so many cells of the brain, the greater the stimulus—remorse, the recognition of fate—the more powerfully complete becomes the sensation of the memory until there is transfer, as in a time machine, and the memory is in the ontological sense another reality.) Papa, I see you now in the universe of your own making. I walk the polished floorboards of your house and seat myself at your dining table. I feel the tassels of the tablecloth on the tops of my bare knees. The light of the candelabra shines on your smiling mouth of big teeth. I notice the bulge of your neck produced by your shirt collar. Your pink scalp is visible through the close-cropped German-style haircut. I see your head raised in conversation and your white plump hand of consummate gesture making its point to your wife at the other end of the table. Mama is so attentive. The candle flame burns in her eyes and I imagine the fever there, but she is quite calm and seriously engrossed by what you say. Her long neck, very white, is hung with a thin chain from which depends on the darkness of her modest dress a cream-colored cameo, the carved profile of another fine lady of another time. In her neck a soft slow pulse beats. Her small hands are folded and the bones of her wrists emerge from the touch of lace at her cuffs. She is smiling at you in your loving proprietorship, proud of you, pleased to be yours, and the mistress of this house, and the mother of this boy. Of my tutor across the table from me who idly twirls the stem of his wineglass and glances at her, she is barely aware. Her eyes are for her husband. I think now Papa her feelings in this moment are sincere. I know now each moment has its belief and what we call treachery is the belief of each moment, the wish for it to be as it seems to be. It is possible in joy to love the person you have betrayed and to be refreshed in your love for him, it is entirely possible. Love renews all faces and customs and ideals and leaves the bars of the prison shining. But how could a boy know that? I ran to my room and waited for someone to follow me. Whoever dared to enter my room, I would attack—would pummel. I wanted it to be her, I wanted her to come to me, to hug me and to hold my head and kiss me on the lips as she liked to do, I wanted her to make those wordless sounds of comfort as she held me to her when I was hurt or unhappy, and when she did that I would beat her with my fists, beat her to the floor, and see her raise her hands helplessly in terror as I beat her and kicked her and jumped upon her and drove the breath from her body. But it was my tutor who, some time later, opened the door, looked in with his hand upon the knob, smiled, said a few words, and wished me good night. He closed the door and I heard him walk up the steps to the next floor, where he had his rooms. Ledig was his name. He was a Christian. I had looked but could not find in his face any sign of smugness or leering pride or cruelty. There was nothing coarse about him, nothing that could possibly give me offense. He was barely twenty. I even thought I saw in his eyes a measure of torment. He was habitually melancholic anyway, and during my lessons his mind often wandered and he would gaze out the window and sigh. He was as much a schoolboy as his pupil. So there was every reason to refrain from judgment, to let time pass, to think, to gain understanding. Nobody knew that I knew. I had that choice. But did I? They had made my position intolerable. I was given double vision, the kind that comes with a terrible blow. I found I could not have anything to do with my kind sweet considerate mother. I found I could not bear the gentle pedagogics of my tutor. How, in that rural isolation, could I be expected to go on? I had no friends, I was not permitted to play with the children of the peasants who worked for us. I had only this trinity of Mother and Tutor and Father, this unholy trinity of deception and ignorance who had excommunicated me from my life at the age of thirteen. This of course in the calendar of traditional Judaism is the year a boy enjoys his initiation into manhood.

Meanwhile my father was going about the triumph of his life, running a farm according to the most modern principles of scientific management, astonishing his peasants and angering the other farmers in the region with his success. The sun brought up his crops, the Galician Agricultural Society gave him an award for the quality of his milk, and he lived in the state of abiding satisfaction given to individuals who are more than a match for the life they have chosen for themselves. I had incorporated him into the universe of giant powers that I, a boy, experienced in the changes of the seasons. I watched bulls bred to cows, watched mares foal, I saw life come from the egg and the multiplicative wonders of mudholes and ponds, the jell and slime of life shimmering in gravid expectation. Everywhere I looked, life sprang from something not life, insects unfolded from sacs on the surface of still waters and were instantly on the prowl for their dinner, everything that came into being knew at once what to do and did it unastonished that it was what it was, unimpressed by where it was, the great earth heaving up its bloodied newborns from every pore, every cell, bearing the variousness of itself from every conceivable substance that it contained in itself, sprouting life that flew or waved in the wind or blew from the mountains or stuck to the damp black underside of rocks, or swam or suckled or bellowed or silently separated in two. I placed my father in all of this as the owner and manager. He lived in the universe of giant powers by understanding it and making it serve him, using the daily sun for his crops and breeding what naturally bred, and so I distinguished him in it as the god-eye in the kingdom, the intelligence that brought order and gave everything its value. He loved me and I can still feel my pleasure in making him laugh, and I might not be deceiving myself when I remember the feel on my infant hand of his unshaved cheek, the winy smell of his breath, the tobacco smoke in his thick wavy hair, or his mock-wondering look of foolish happiness during our play together. He had close-set eyes, the color of dark grapes, that opened wide in our games. He would laugh like a horse and show large white teeth. He was a strong man, stocky and powerful—the constitution I inherited—and he had emerged as an orphan from the alleys of cosmopolitan eastern Europe, like Darwin's amphibians from the sea, and made himself a landowner, a husband and father. He was a Jew who spoke no Yiddish and a farmer raised in the city. I was not allowed to play with village children, or to go to their crude schools. We lived alone, isolated on our estate, neither Jew nor Christian, neither friend nor petitioner of the Austro-Hungarians, but in the pride of the self-constructed self. To this day I don't know how he arranged it or what hungering rage had caused him to deny every classification society imposes and to live as an anomaly, tied to no past in a world that, as it happened, had no future. But I am in awe that he did it. Because he stood up in his life he was exposed to the swords of Mongol horsemen, the scythes of peasants in revolution, the lowered brows of monstrous bankers, and the cruciform gestures of prelates. His arrogance threatened him with the cumulative power of all of European history, which was ready to take his head, nail it to a pole, and turn him into one of the scarecrows in his fields, arms held stiffly out toward life. But when the moment came for this transformation, it was accomplished quite easily, by a word from his son. I was the agency of his downfall. Ancestry and myth, culture, history, and time were ironically composed in the shape of his own boy.

I WATCHED HER for several days. I remembered the rash of passion on her flesh. I was so ashamed of myself that I felt continuously ill, and it was the vaguest, most diffuse nausea, nausea of the blood, nausea of the bone. In bed at night I found it difficult breathing, and terrible waves of fever broke over me and left me parched in my terror. I couldn't purge from my mind the image of her overthrown body, the broad whitenesses, her shoed feet in the air; I made her scream ecstatically every night in my dreams and awoke one dawn in my own sap. That was the crisis that toppled me, for in fear of being found out by the maid and by my mother, for fear of being found out by them all as the archcriminal of my dreams, I ran to him, I went to him for absolution, I confessed and put myself at his mercy. Papa, I said. He was down by the kennels mating a pair of vizslas. He used this breed to hunt. He had rigged some sort of harness for the bitch so that she could not bolt, a kind of pillory, and she was putting up a terrible howl, and though her tail showed her amenable, she moved her rump away from the proddings of the erect male, who mounted and pumped and missed and mounted again and couldn't hold her still. My father was banging the fist of his right hand into the palm of his left. Put it to her, he shouted, come on, get it in there, give it to her. Then the male had success and the mating began, the female standing there quietly now, sweat dripping off her chops, an occasional groan escaping from her. And then the male came, and stood front paws on her back, his tongue lolling as he panted, and they waited as dogs do for the detumescence. My father knelt beside them and soothed them with quiet words. Good dogs, he said, good dogs. You must guard them at this time, he said to me, they try to uncouple too early and hurt themselves. Papa, I said. He turned and looked at me over his shoulder as he knelt beside the dogs, and I saw his happiness, and the glory of him in his work pants tucked into a black pair of riding boots and his shirt open at the collar and the black hair of his chest curled as high as the throat, and I said, Papa, they should be named Mama and Ledig. And then I turned so quickly I do not even remember his face changing, I did not even wait to see if he understood me, I turned and ran, but I am sure of this—he never called after me.

There was a sunroom in our house, a kind of conservatory with a glass outer wall and slanted ceiling of green glass framed in steel. It was a very luxurious appointment in that region, and it was my mother's favorite place to be. She had filled it with plants and books, and she liked to lie on a chaise in this room and read and smoke cigarettes. I found her there, as I knew I would, and I gazed at her with wonder and fascination because I knew her fate. She was incredibly beautiful, with her dark hair parted in the center and tied behind her in a bun, and her small hands, and the lovely fullness of her chin, the indications under her chin of some fattening, like a quality of indolence in her character. But a man would not dwell on this as on her neck, so lovely and slim, or the high modestly dressed bosom. A man would not want to see signs of the future. Since she was my mother it had never occurred to me how many years younger she was than my father. He had married her out of the gymnasium; she was the eldest of four daughters and her parents had been eager to settle her in prosperous welfare, which is what a mature man offers. It is not that the parents are unaware of the erotic component for the man in this sort of marriage. They are fully aware of it. Rectitude, propriety, are always very practical. I gazed at her in wonder and awe. I blushed. What? she said. She put her book down and smiled and held out her arms. What, Willi, what is it? I fell into her arms and began to sob and she held me and my tears wet the dark dress she wore. She held my head and whispered, What, Willi, what did you do to yourself, poor Willi? Then, aware that my sobs had become breathless and hysterical, she held me at arm's length—tears and snot were dribbling from me—and her eyes widened in genuine alarm.

That night I heard from the bedroom the shocking exciting sounds of her undoing. I have heard such terrible sounds of blows upon a body in Berlin after the war, Freikorps hoodlums in the streets attacking whores they had dragged from the brothel and tearing the clothes from their bodies and beating them to the cobblestones. I sat up in bed, hardly able to breathe, terrified, but feeling undeniable arousal. Give it to her, I muttered, banging my fist in my palm. Give it to her. But then I could bear it no longer and ran into their room and stood between them, lifting my screaming mother from the bed, holding her in my arms, shouting at my father to stop, to stop. But he reached around me and grabbed her hair with one hand and punched her face with the other. I was enraged, I pushed her back and jumped at him, pummeling him, shouting that I would kill him. This was in Galicia in the year 1910. All of it was to be destroyed anyway, even without me.

THE HUNTER

—

THE TOWN IS TERRACED IN THE HILL, ALONG THE RIVER, A FAC-
tory town of clapboard houses and public buildings faced in red
stone. There is a one-room library called the Lyceum. There are
several taverns made from porched homes, Miller and Bud signs
hanging in neon in the front windows. Down at water's edge sits
the old brassworks, a long two-story brick building with a tower at
one end and it is behind locked fences and many of its windows are
broken. The river is frozen. The town is dusted in new snow.
Along the sides of the streets the winter's accumulated snow is
banked high as a man's shoulder. Smoke drifts from the chimneys
of the houses and is quickly sucked into the sky. The wind comes
up off the river and sweeps up the hill through the houses.

A school bus makes its way through the narrow hill streets. The
mothers and fathers stand on the porches above to watch the bus
accept their children. It's the only thing moving in the town. The
fathers fill their arms with firewood stacked by the front doors and
go back inside. Trees are black in the woods behind the homes;
they are black against the snow. Sparrow and finch dart from
branch to branch and puff their feathers to keep warm. They flut-
ter to the ground and hop on the snow crust under the trees.

The children enter the school through the big oak doors with
the push bars. It is not a large school but its proportions, square
and high, create hollow rooms and echoing stairwells. The children sit in their rows with their hands folded and watch their

teacher. She is cheery and kind. She has been here just long enough for her immodest wish to transform these children to have turned to awe at what they are. Their small faces have been rubbed raw by the cold; the weakness of their fair skin is brought out in blotches on their cheeks and in the blue pallor of their eyelids. Their eyelids are translucent membranes, so thin and so delicate that she wonders how they sleep, how they keep from seeing through their closed eyes.

She tells them she is happy to see them here in such cold weather, with a hard wind blowing up the valley and another storm coming. She begins the day's work with their exercise, making them squat and bend and jump and swing their arms and somersault so that they can see what the world looks like upside down. How does it look? she cries, trying it herself, somersaulting on the gym mat until she's dizzy.

They are not animated but the exercise alerts them to the mood she's in. They watch her with interest to see what is next. She leads them out of the small, dimly lit gymnasium through the empty halls, up and down the stairs, telling them they are a lost patrol in the caves of a planet somewhere far out in space. They are looking for signs of life. They wander through the unused schoolrooms, where crayon drawings hang from one thumbtack and corkboards have curled away from their frames. Look, she calls, holding up a child's red rubber boot, fished from the depths of a classroom closet. You never can tell!

When they descend to the basement, the janitor dozing in his cubicle is startled awake by a group of children staring at him. He is a large bearish man and wears fatigue pants and a red plaid woolen shirt. The teacher has never seen him wear anything different. His face has a gray stubble. We're a lost patrol, she says to him, have you seen any living creatures hereabouts? The janitor frowns. What? he says. What?

It is warm in the basement. The furnace emits its basso roar. She has him open the furnace door so the children can see the source of heat, the fire in its pit. They are each invited to cast a handful of coal through the door. They do this as a sacrament.

Then she insists that the janitor open the storage rooms and the old lunchroom kitchen, and here she notes unused cases of dried soup mix and canned goods, and then large pots and thick aluminum cauldrons and a stack of metal trays with food compartments. Here, you can't take those, the janitor says. And why not, she answers, this is their school, isn't it? She gives each child a tray or pot, and they march upstairs, banging them with their fists to scare away the creatures of wet flesh and rotating eyes and pulpy horns who may be lying in wait around the corners.

In the afternoon it is already dark, and the school bus receives the children in the parking lot behind the building. The new streetlamps installed by the county radiate an amber light. The yellow school bus in the amber light is the color of a dark egg yolk. As it leaves, the children, their faces indistinct behind the windows, turn to stare out at the young teacher. She waves, her fingers opening and closing like a fluttering wing. The bus windows slide past, breaking her image and re-forming it, and giving her the illusion of the stone building behind her sliding along its foundations in the opposite direction.

The bus has turned into the road. It goes slowly past the school. The children's heads lurch in unison as the driver shifts gears. The bus plunges out of sight in the dip of the hill. At this moment the teacher realizes that she did not recognize the driver. He was not the small, burly man with eyeglasses without rims. He was a young man with long light hair and white eyebrows, and he looked at her in the instant he hunched over the steering wheel, with his arms about to make the effort of putting the bus into a turn.

—

THAT EVENING at home the young woman heats water for a bath and pours it in the tub. She bathes and urinates in the bathwater. She brings her hands out of the water and lets it pour through her fingers. She hums a made-up tune. The bathroom is large, with wainscoting of wood strips painted gray. The tub rests on four cast-iron claws. A small window high on the wall is open just a crack and through it the night air sifts into the room. She lies back and the cold air comes along the water line and draws its finger across her neck.

In the morning she dresses and combs her hair back and ties it behind her head and wears small opal teardrop earrings given to her for her graduation from college. She walks to work, opens up the school, turns up the radiator, cleans the blackboard, and goes to the front door to await the children on the yellow bus.

They do not come.

She goes to her teaching room, rearranges the day's lesson on the desk, distributes a sheet of stiff paper to each child's desk. She goes back to the front door and awaits the children.

They are nowhere in sight.

She looks for the school janitor in the basement. The furnace makes a kind of moaning sound, there is rhythmic intensification of its running pitch, and he's staring at it with a perplexed look on his face. He tells her the time, and it is the time on her watch. She goes back upstairs and stands at the front door with her coat on.

The yellow bus comes into the school driveway and pulls up before the front door. She puts her hand on the shoulder of each child descending the steps from the bus. The young man with the blond hair and eyebrows smiles at her.

There have been sacred rites and legendary events in this town. In a semi-pro football game a player was killed. A presidential candidate once came and spoke. A mass funeral was held here for the victims of a shoe-factory fire. She understands the new bus driver has no knowledge of any of this.

ON SATURDAY MORNING the teacher goes to the old people's home and reads aloud. They sit there and listen to the story. They are the children's faces in another time. She thinks she can even recognize some of the grandmothers and grandfathers by family. When the reading is over those who can walk come up to her and pluck at her sleeves and her collar, interrupting one another to tell her who they are and what they used to be. They shout. They mock one another's words. They waggle their hands in her face to get her to look at them.

She cannot get out of there fast enough. In the street she breaks into a run. She runs until the old people's home is out of sight.

It is very cold, but the sun shines. She decides to walk up to the mansion at the top of the highest hill in town. The hill streets turn abruptly back on themselves like a series of chutes. She wears lace-up boots and jeans. She climbs through snowdrifts in which she sinks up to the thighs.

The old mansion sits in the sun above the tree line. It is said that one of the factory owners built it for his bride, and that shortly after taking possession he killed her with a shotgun. The Greek columns have great chunks missing and she sees chicken wire exposed under the plaster. The portico is hung with icicles, and snow is backed against the house. There is no front door. She goes in. The light of the sun and a fall of snow fill the entrance hall and its grand stairway. She can see the sky through the collapsed ceiling and a crater in the roof. She moves carefully and goes to the door of what must have been the dining room. She opens it. It smells of rot. There is a rustle and a hissing sound and she sees several pairs of eyes constellated in the dark. She opens the door wider. Many cats are backed into a corner of the room. They growl at her and twitch their tails.

She goes out and walks around to the back, an open field white in the sun. There is a pitted aluminum straight ladder leaning against a windowsill in the second floor. She climbs the ladder. The window is punched out and she climbs through the frame and stands in a light and airy bedroom. A hemisphere of ice hangs from the ceiling. It looks like the bottom of the moon. She stands at the window and sees at the edge of the field a man in an orange jacket and red hat. She wonders if he can see her from this distance. He raises a rifle to his shoulder and a moment later she hears an odd smack as if someone has hit the siding of the house with an open palm. She does not move. The hunter lowers his rifle and steps back into the woods at the edge of the field.

THAT EVENING the young teacher calls the town physician to ask for something to take. What seems to be the trouble? the doctor says. She conceives of a self-deprecating answer, sounding confident and assertive, even managing a small laugh. He says he will call the druggist and prescribe Valiums, two-milligram so that she won't be made drowsy by them. She walks down to Main Street, where the druggist opens his door and without turning on the store light leads her to the prescription counter in the rear. The druggist puts his hand into a large jar and comes up with a handful of tablets, and feeds the Valium one by one, from his thumb and forefinger, into a vial.

She goes to the movie theater on Main Street and pays her admission. The theater bears the same name as the town. She sits in the dark and swallows a handful of tabs. She cannot discern the picture. The screen is white. Then what she sees forming on the white screen is the town in its blanket of snow, the clapboard houses on the hill, the frozen river, the wind blowing snow along the streets. She sees the children coming out of their doors with their schoolbooks and walking down their steps to the street. She sees her life exactly as it is outside the movie theater.

Later she walks through the downtown. The only thing open is the State News. Several men stand thumbing the magazines. She turns down Mechanic Street and walks past the tool-and-die company and crosses the railroad tracks to the bridge. She begins to run. In the middle of the bridge the wind is a force and she feels it wants to press her through the railing into the river. She runs bent over, feeling as if she is pushing through something, as if it is only giving way to her by tearing.

Across the bridge the road turns sharply left and at the curve, at the foot of a hill of pine trees, is a brown house with a neon sign in the window: THE RAPIDS. She climbs up the porch steps into the Rapids, and looking neither left nor right, walks to the back, where she finds the ladies' room. When she comes out she sits in one of the varnished plywood booths and stares at the table. After a while a man in an apron comes over and she orders a beer. Only then does she look up. The light is dim. A couple of elderly men are at the bar. But alone down at the end, established with his glass and a pack of cigarettes, is the new bus driver with the long blond hair, and he is smiling at her.

HE HAS JOINED HER. For a while nothing is said. He raises his arm and turns in his seat to look toward the bar. He turns his head to look back at her. You want another, he says. She shakes her head no but doesn't say thank you. She digs in her coat pocket and puts a wrinkled dollar beside her bottle. He holds up one finger.

You from around here? he says.

From the eastern part of the state, she says.

I'm from Valdese, he says. Down on Sixteen.

Oh, yes.

I know you're their teacher, he says. I'm their driver.

He wears a wool shirt and a denim jacket and jeans. It is what he wears in his bus. He would not own a coat. There is something on a chain around his neck but it is hidden under the shirt. Blond beard stubble lies sparsely on his chin and along the line of his jaw. His cheeks are smooth. He is smiling. One of his front teeth is chipped.

What do you do to get to be a teacher?

You go to college. She sighs: What do you do to be a driver?

It's a county job, he says. You need a chauffeur's license and a clean record.

What is a dirty record?

Why, if you been arrested, you know? If you have any kind of record. Or if you got a bad service discharge.

She waits.

I had a teacher once in the third grade, he says. I believe she was the most beautiful woman I have ever seen. I believe now she was no more'n a girl. Like you. But she was very proud and she had a way of tossing her head and walking that made me wish to be a better student.

She laughs.

He picks up her beer bottle and feigns reproach and holds up his arm to the bartender and signals for two.

It is very easy, she says, to make them fall in love with you. Boys or girls, it's very easy.

And to herself she admits that she tries to do it, to make them love her, she takes on a grace she doesn't really have at any other time. She moves like a dancer, she touches them and brushes against them. She is outgoing and shows no terror, and the mystery of her is created in their regard.

Do you have sisters? she says.

Two. How'd you know that?

They're older than you?

One older, one younger.

What do they do?

Work in the office of the lumber mill down there.

She says: I would trust a man who had sisters.

He tilts his head back and takes a long pull at his beer bottle, and she watches his Adam's apple rise and fall, and the sparse blond stubble on his throat move like reeds lying on the water.

Later they come out of the Rapids and he leads her to his pickup. He is rather short. She climbs in and notices his workboots when he comes up into the cab from the other side. They're clean good boots, new yellow leather. He has trouble starting the engine.

What are you doing here at night if you live in Valdese? she says.

Waiting for you. He laughs and the engine turns over.

They drive slowly across the bridge, and across the tracks. Following her instructions, he goes to the end of the main street and turns up into the hills and brings her to her house. He pulls up in the yard by the side door.

It is a small house and it looks dark and cold. He switches off the engine and the headlights and leans across her lap and presses the button of the glove compartment. He says: Happens I got me some party wine right here. He removes a flat bottle in a brown bag and slams the door, and as he moves back, his arm brushes her thigh.

She stares through the windshield. She says: Stupid goddamn

mill hand. Making his play with the teacher. Look at that, with his party wine in a sack. I can't believe it.

She jumps down from the cab, runs around the truck, and up the back steps into her kitchen. She slams the door. There is silence. She waits in the kitchen, not moving, in the dark, standing behind the table, facing the door.

She hears nothing but her own breathing.

All at once the back door is flooded with light, the white curtain on the door glass becomes a white screen, and then the light fades, and she hears the pickup backing out to the street. She is panting and now her rage breaks, and she is crying.

She stands alone in her dark kitchen crying, a bitter scent coming off her body, a smell of burning, which offends her. She heats water on the stove and takes it up to her bath.

ON MONDAY MORNING the teacher waits for her children at the front door of the school. When the bus turns into the drive, she steps back and stands inside the door. She can see the open door of the bus but she cannot see if he is trying to see her.

She is very animated this morning. This is a special day, children, she announces, and she astonishes them by singing them a song while she accompanies herself on the autoharp. She lets them strum the autoharp while she presses the chords. Look, she says to each one, you are making music.

At eleven the photographer arrives. He is a man with a potbelly and a black string tie. I don't get these school calls till spring, he says.

This is a special occasion, the teacher says. We want a picture of ourselves now. Don't we, children?

They watch intently as he sets up his tripod and camera. He has a black valise with brass latches that snap as he opens them. Inside are cables and floodlamps.

Used to be classes of kids, he says. Now look at what's left of you. Heat this whole building for one room.

By the time he is ready, the young teacher has pushed the benches to the blackboard and grouped the children in two rows, the taller ones sitting on the benches, the shorter ones sitting in front of them on the floor, cross-legged. She herself stands at one side. There are fifteen children staring at the camera and their smiling teacher holding her hands in front of her, like an opera singer.

The photographer looks at the scene and frowns. Why, these children ain't fixed up for their picture.

What do you mean?

Why, they ain't got on their ties and their new shoes. You got girls here wearing trousers.

Just take it, she says.

They don't look right. Their hair ain't combed, these boys here.

Take us as we are, the teacher says. She steps suddenly out of line and with a furious motion removes the barrette fastening her hair and shakes her head until her hair falls to her shoulders. The children are startled. She kneels down on the floor in front of them, facing the camera, and pulls two of them into her arms. She brings all of them around her with an urgent opening and closing of her hands, and they gather about her. One girl begins to cry.

She pulls them in around her, feeling their bodies, the thin bones of their arms, their small shoulders, their legs, their behinds.

Take it, she says in a fierce whisper. Take it as we are. We are looking at you. Take it.

ALL THE TIME
IN THE WORLD

—

WHAT I'VE NOTICED: HOW FAST THEY PUT UP THESE BUILD-ings. Cart away the rubble, square off the excavation, lay in the steel, and up she goes. Concrete floor slabs and, at night, work lamps hanging like stars. After a flag tops things off as if they were all sailing somewhere, they load in the elevator, do the wiring, the plumbing, they tack on the granite facing and set in the windows through which you see they've walled in the apartments, and be-fore you know it there's a canopy to the curb, a doorman, and up-stairs just across the street from my window, a fully furnished bedroom and a naked girl dancing.

Another thing: how people in the street are pulled along by lit-tle dogs on the leash. Usually a little short-legged dog keeping the leash taut so you know who's in charge. He sniffs out the place to do what he does, does it, and then he's ready to go on, leaving his two-legged body servant to pick it up. They are royalty, these dogs, they stop to nose one another, they wag their coiffed tails, they're on their outing, with their shiny coats and curled ears and glittering eyes and the leash a band of leather, taut as a spinal cord, as if this is one creature, oddly shaped, with four short legs and a brain in front, and two tall legs and no brain in back.

And when it rains in this city? It might be just a few drops, but out floop the umbrellas. People holding these things that are like hats on pikes. It is funny, the simple cartoon logic of it. But when it really rains, wind and rain together, the umbrellas blow out, and that's even funnier, people lifted off their feet.

You can bet they don't avail themselves of umbrellas on the meadows of Mongolia.

TO AVOID THE BENT old ladies and their carts of groceries and their walkers and canes and black women helpers taking up three-quarters of the sidewalk, I run in the street. I mean cars are less of a problem. In typical traffic they are standing still as I run past the horns blowing their dissonant mass protest, and so I wear my earmuffs and I'm fine.

But I run, really, because I don't know what else to do. I have not believed in where I am for a long time. I mean why, outside of every movie theater I run past, are people standing on line waiting to get in? What or who has persuaded them? And the movie theaters themselves with their filmed stories that I am supposed to worry over? Sitting in the dark and worrying over actors acting out stories? And the need to buy popcorn before you do this? To buy popcorn in movie theaters like you light votive candles in cathedrals? The obligation to eat popcorn that you don't eat at any other time while watching moving pictures that you have to worry over is a peculiar, anthropological custom for which I have no reasonable explanation.

I don't belong here. I am outside this realm. If I were inside this realm, I wouldn't feel this way. I wouldn't remark on these things. Why do girls see an apartment in a new building as the occasion to dance naked? And the people on leashes holding umbrellas over their heads. And the cars that can't move, bleating their mass dissonance as if they were Mongolian sheep?

And how can I help thinking everybody I see on the sidewalk is as friendless and alone as I am, that we are total anonymities, talking importantly on our cell phones as we walk along like actors in movies that everyone has to worry over.

OF COURSE ON A closer look we can be told apart. I am a trim, sinewy fellow, I am that way from running. I run. I don't know what else to do by way of filling my lungs with carcinogenic particulate. I could climb up the stairs of the apartment building across the street and knock on the door of the naked girl dancing, but I don't. I run over to the park and then run with the other runners around the reservoir.

This fellow with the T-shirt that says THE PROGRAM IS RUNNING! sometimes comes up and lopes along beside me. I never know when he'll appear. Sometimes there are two or three of them with that logo on their T-shirts like they can't just run, it has to be a cool team thing so that everyone else can feel left out. You run pretty good, the fellow says with an ungrammatical smirk, and with no effort at all he glides past me and bounds away. At such times I feel that my feet are not hitting the ground, but pedaling air.

And then the female runners who run in pairs with their shoulders back and their chins up: they don't have names printed on them, they are like long-legged birds stepping along in their tights and with their sweaters tied by the sleeves at their waists and rippling like little flags over their backsides.

YOU MAY ASK TO WHOM I think I'm talking. Suppose, for instance, you are one of those thin, undocumented Chinese men on balloon-tire bicycles delivering takeout. You would find me just as I find everything else, which is to say not quite right. I mean I am not yet characteristically impassively sad. I do not ride along on balloon tires delivering Chinese food to apartments where naked girls dance and little dogs with curly coats and glittering eyes will eat the leftovers. So even I, in my incomprehensible talking, can be seen as one more aspect of this weird realm.

In Mongolia the air is clean and cold and you see the stars at night, you actually see them. The shepherds look almost Chinese, with their herds of sheep and goats and with camels and yaks for their regal transportation. No cell phones here. You do not see shepherds walking along with cell phones at their ears past door-men giving them the once-over. They are strong men with sturdy builds and they know the kingdom of earth with its yaks and camels and goats and wild horses is their dominion. They accept the responsibility. They would not run just for the sake of running. If they had a reservoir they would not run around it, they would drop on their knees to see the night sky of stars in the water unless it froze opaque at night like everything does on the steppe. In which case they would see the moonlight inside the ice.

YOU MAY ASK HOW I pass the time when I'm not running. Alone, is my answer—as alone as when I am running. My only company is the grammarian who lives with me in my brain. If you ask me with whom am I talking, I am talking always to him or her. So I say to whom. So I don't say lay down, I say lie down. I say would have and will not have. I don't say you and me aren't getting anywhere, I say you and I aren't getting anywhere. I say you and I aren't get-ting anywhere is an idiom. I say you and I aren't getting anywhere may also be something of a metaphor, but is not a synecdoche or a metonym. When I run, too, I am not getting anywhere since I have no destination other than returning to my window across the street from the naked girl dancing. She and I are not getting any-where either.

—

OTHER THAN TO THE grammarian I am never sure to whom I will be talking. I speed-dial my cell phone. I get you. You may ask to whom do I think I'm talking. I say I'm talking to you. And who may that be, you say. And then I recognize who it is, it is my mother.

You have all the time in the world, she says.

Until what?

Until something happens, Mother says.

What can happen?

If we knew, she says, and breaks the connection. I speed-dial her again and get the same assurance that I have all the time in the world on her answering machine. Now can you appreciate why I run? (To whomever I think I'm talking?)

I AM ALWAYS GLAD to have weather, though it is difficult to run past the construction sites with the cranes in the street, and past the cars with their horns of mass dissonance and their windshield wipers clacking and their headlights lighting up the rain. I am competing for the lanes between the cars with the Chinese take-out men on their balloon-tire bikes. I try the sidewalk, but the old ladies with walkers and shopping carts and their angry black women helpers are everywhere with their umbrellas threatening to poke out my eyes. And the little dogs wearing booties now, jumping around and trying to bite off the booties that keep their paws dry and so twisting up their leashes as to make the old ladies trip and fall and runners like me leap over them as if we are in an obstacle race.

I am wet and cold with rainwater dripping down my neck, but only when I reach the park can I see the rainfall in its entirety. I circle the reservoir with the sky black above me and the rain, in large walloping drops, popping like popcorn in the dark water. The Programmers splash past, not speaking today, and up ahead those long-legged women leave momentary footprints in the water as they lope along with their limp black sweaters contoured now to their newly indicated behinds.

When I leave the park the streets are streaming, and in the black morning lit by the headlights of the cars not moving, plastic bags of garbage roll over in the water and people are hurrying to work with their umbrellas blown out in the wind like suddenly sprouted trees.

Only the children are unconcerned as they slog to school in their yellow slickers with their violin cases strapped to their backs.

A SHAFT OF SUNLIGHT lights up the street from a crack in the black sky. The clouds blow off, the air is all at once warm and humid, and in a matter of minutes I'm trotting along in a brilliant blue morning. Water drips from the apartment house canopies, gurgling rivulets run along the curbstone. I feel as if I've risen from one element into another.

On my block, across from my building, some paper trash has spilled out of a torn plastic bag—business letters, bills, flyers. I pick up a handwritten letter on blue vellum, feeling that it was meant for me. My doorman tends to a wet dog on the leash and the dog shakes himself as I pass through my lobby. The ink of my letter runs like tears as I read, while rising to my floor, the grief of an abandoned lover. She can't understand why he has left her, she needs to see him, come back, she says, come to me, for she still loves him, she always will, and it is all so sad, so sad, so sad, and I don't know who threw the letter away, he after reading it or she after writing it, but I want to speed-dial whomever it is I talk to and express my gratitude, because when I get upstairs, across the street the shade is drawn on the window of the naked dancing girl and all I have ever wanted is specificity.

I just have to think that and my cell phone rings. To whom am I talking, I say. To whom do you think you're talking, you say. I say my father. And so it is.

I have warned you about specificity, my father says. Nothing is possible but that which has happened.

And what is that which has happened?

In this case something of great sadness, my father says. There are limits to what even we can do, he says, and breaks the connection.

Despite my father's warning, I shower and shave and dress nicely and wait for the evening hour to call on her. Downstairs I nod at my doorman, jog directly across the street, and ask her doorman to announce me. I feel my heart beating. I rise in the elevator. I reach her floor. Her door is open.

Come in, a voice says, and I enter a dimly lighted room. A large Seeing Eye German shepherd stands there. From its leather harness a leash angles up into the gloom. Patient, forbearing, the dog moves toward me one careful step at a time. I know it's you, the voice says, and the speaker emerges from the darkness, a large old woman holding a walker to which the leash is tied. She looks familiar. Hair bunched like steel wool. A big bony jaw, a thin nose. Blind eyes bulging to see. It is the kind of ancient ugliness that connotes a past beauty. She wears a loose black knit dress with the sleeves pulled up to the elbows. Loops of pearls hang from her neck and clack against her walker. You dare to come back? she says. You dare?

I look past her to a dimly lighted dining room. In the glimmering light of a candle whose flame flares and fizzles like a star in the sky, I can see lying on the table a specifically dead girl, the contours of her body indicated in the tight wrappings of a white shroud. I can't remember her name, but I know I once loved her. Her closed eyes suggest a mind in intense thought. You're too late, the old woman says, you're too late, she says with enormous satisfaction. Her triumph is affirmed by the smell of Chinese food coming from her kitchen. I go there and several mourners sitting around the kitchen table look up from the open white cardboard containers into which they are dipping their chopsticks. For a moment I think I know exactly that which has happened. But then over the heads of the mourners at their Chinese food and through the kitchen window that looks out across a dark side street I see in a lighted window a naked girl dancing.

AND NOW I AM back home and unaccountably sad. At the same time I feel I have been unfairly judged. This was not the kind of specificity for which I long.

You to whom I think I am talking may ask what I do when I'm not running or longing for specificity: I question my station in life. I believe I am retired, but I feel I am too young to have retired. On the other hand, or alternatively, I don't know of any work that I'm doing that would suggest I'm not retired. As you can imagine, it would make anyone uneasy knowing there are things about himself he does not know.

I am not constantly unhappy, I'm not saying that. But my uneasiness builds until I have to talk to someone. At such times I speed-dial my therapist.

Yes? To whom do you think you're talking?

Dr. Sternlicht?

You got him.

I'm having that feeling again.

That is to be expected.

It's like I'm living in exile. I am lonely. I have no one.

That is to be expected.

Why? Why is it to be expected? That's all you ever say.

No, I say other things. I say you're in a rut. I say change your lifestyle, expand your horizons. A whole city is at your disposal: museums, concerts, the passing parade. I say go out and enjoy yourself. You've got all the time in the world.

Until what?

What?

You said I have all the time in the world. Until what?

Until something happens.

What can happen?

If we knew. But we don't, he says, and breaks the connection.

THE THOUGHT OF expanding my horizons is attractive, so I am on my way to the Museum of Natural History. And to change my lifestyle, I'll take the bus. It dawns on me metaphorically that I have never appreciated the bus stop for the ancient invention it is. Carriages pulled up at inns, oxcarts creaked from one village square to another, pirogues made their landings along the rivers of Mongolia. The cartoon logic of the bus stop makes me smile with a love for all mankind. I wait faithfully at this stop and lightly inhale the city's carcinogenic particulate.

An old woman with a walker is here with her black woman helper, whose expressionless face conceals a great anger. Also, three slim middle-aged men with closely cropped hair and matching sweatsuits. More trusting people arrive at the bus stop, a man in a doorman's uniform, a priest, a pretty girl at whose miniskirted backside I steal a glance. Also a pair of small, self-sufficient children, a boy and a girl, each of them holding a violin case. In their jeans and jackets, to say nothing of their mutual commitment to the violin, they might be twins.

I see our bus in the distance. It has been at that same distance for some time now. I see it over the car roofs. Nothing seems to be moving. The way things are going hundreds of us will be waiting at this stop before the bus ever arrives. Waves of dissonant horn blowing break over my ears. All at once I lose my love of mankind. I resume my old lifestyle and take off at a run between the cars because that is the only way I will get to the Natural History Museum.

THE MOMENT I COME through the doors, I hear that characteristic museum murmur. Maybe it is the murmur of visitors long gone because I look around, but I am the only person here. I find I am in the Mongolian Hall. I am tracking through the *taiga*, which is the name for this wild, snow-filled boreal forest of needle-leaf evergreens, spruce, and pine. I say I'm "tracking through" because I am there—this exhibit is a terrarium that you walk into, and as I move through this lush biome, the earth revolves, and from the frigid boreal forest with its cold stars visible even in dark winter daylight and its skulking hunting lynx hush-hushing through the snow, and its leaping snowshoe rabbit, and its stumbling terrorized blind vole, I find myself rotated to the green steppe where the snow has turned to rain and the rainy wind flattens the nap on the shepherds' coats and the sturdy shepherds and their sons, quietly indifferent to the weather, walk their yaks and goats and sheep over the low rises of natural pasture. But things are changing still, and gradually the earth flattens, grows warm, and I am in Mongolia's Gobi Desert, where the sun is blinding and the snakes coil themselves in the shade of rocks, and tiny tornadoes of sand sting one's legs. Here is a Buddhist monk in a saffron robe dancing away from the sand stings. So I am not alone. I follow him as he dances in circles barefoot over the hot sand and spins right out of the Mongolian Hall of the Museum of Natural History and into a waiting bus. It is occupied solely by Buddhist monks in saffron robes. The bus door closes with a hiss as if it could drive off, but of course it can't, not because it is a Buddhist bus but because it is locked in the unmoving traffic.

I resume my run now, I head downtown. I'm running well, still intent on expanding my horizons. But it suddenly comes over me that I have trudged through the *taiga* and hiked over the steppe and into the desert, going from cold to hot, from snow to sun, many times before. The fact is I know the Natural History Museum as well as my own hand. And so what new horizon? Not only have I been to the museum more times than I can count, I have never seen anything but the Mongolian Hall and never has it been without that Buddhist monk spinning in the sand.

There seems to be a flow of people going my way, runners running between the cars, walkers moving at a good pace on the sidewalks. Closing in on Times Square, I step into a doorway that has glass cases with black-and-white photos of dancing girls, and I flip open my cell phone.

Hello? To whom am I speaking?

To whom do you wish to speak?

My internist.

You've got him.

I feel weak, my legs are shaking. I've just run forty blocks, but I'm in good shape and I shouldn't feel this way. I'm here in Times Square, there are thousands of people standing around and waiting for what I don't know and I have never felt more alone. I think my heartbeat is irregular.

You're not alone.

I'm not?

Irregular heartbeats are quite common.

What's the use of talking to you!

You're just frightened. It's understandable. But it will pass. This is not an urgent situation, you know, you have all the time in the world.

I have?

Yes.

Until what?

Until something happens.

What can happen?

If we knew. But we don't. On the other hand, what choice did we have?

You mean I will continue to feel miserably alone in the middle of crowds with my knees shaking?

That is probably the case, he says. And at other times too.

Why didn't you tell me before this?

We've been telling you forever.

You have?

We inform you periodically. So when and if it happens you'll be prepared.

Prepared for what? You are giving me the willies!

The willies is a slang term. Slang terms are time-sensitive, they are really not useful in the long run.

What?

Please use only the durable words. They're no less important than grammatical relations.

I'm ringing off, I say, I'm hanging up, that's two time-sensitive words right there, I say, and I flip the phone closed.

I STEP OUT OF the doorway and am swept into the crowd that's pressing forward with great excitement. Here I am in despair, grieving for what or whom I don't know, and all of it means nothing to the people around me, who are surging forward with eyes alight and shouts of joy. I let myself be carried along and I gaze upward to the array of signs and ads and giant videos of runners racing and racing cars crashing and movie actors shooting one another and other movie actors kissing one another in scenes from movies that they want you to worry over. Times Square is unnaturally brilliant in a light brighter than daylight with gigantic signs of sulking models, and cantilevered broadcast studios with flashing call signs, and modern glass tower office buildings reflecting the rainbow colors of the flashing signs and videos—it is all enough to make me want to forget my troubles here with the enormous swaying crowd, of which I am a part, basking as if it were in the radiant sunshine of the Great White Way, outshining the sun and turning the blue sky white.

But now the crowd, having packed itself tight and motionless, grows still, as all the buzzing signs shut off one by one and the video screens go blank and in the natural light of day an enormous stage rises into view in the heart of Times Square. I fight my way forward and the crowd parts for me.

Seated on the stage is an ensemble of what must be a thousand children, the boys in white shirts and red ties, the girls in white middies with red neckerchiefs, and the violin sections waiting with violins tucked under their chins and bows raised, and the little cellists hunched over their cellos, and the dozens of bassists half hidden behind their basses, and the rows of horn players with their arrayed horns catching the sun, and timpanists triple the usual number waiting with earnest intrepid faces, and banks of child harpists at either end framing it all in celestial gold. A thousand dutiful faces are raised to the conductress who has taken her place at the podium, in her long white gown. She lifts her arms, her chin rises, down comes the baton, and I have to choke back the tears because this is the famous Children's Orchestra of the Universe and they are playing "Welcome Sweet Springtime" only slightly off key.

I am overwhelmed with emotion and find myself crying with remorse for a life almost too painful to endure.

ELBOWING MY WAY through the rapt crowd into one of the side streets, I run heedlessly, crossing avenues where, as if there were no concert back in Times Square, people are going about their ordinary business, dog walkers walking packs of dogs on leashes, joggers jogging, old women with walkers, cars unmoving, the drivers having gotten out to stand by their open doors.

A block or two farther west, I run up the steps and through the oak doors of a steepled church of black stone. It is cold and damp here and smells of cement. Empty pews. Banks of votive candles in little red glasses. I spy a filigreed door off to the side, open it, and step into a box-like container with a bench, and I know exactly what to say because I desperately mean it.

Bless me Father, for I have sinned.

I'm sorry, that is the one consolation we do not offer.

Well then, what consolations do you offer?

The corporeal illusion. A gender identity.

What is the corporeal illusion?

A euphemism for the disgusting belief that you inhabit a body.

Wait just a minute. Is that a consolation, a priest telling me I am an illusion of myself?

And cultural memory. That's nothing to sneeze at. You should be thankful for that. Keeping you within what you knew. Enswathing you in what was.

Enswathing me? Enswathing me?

The ultimate consolation is forgetfulness, of course. There is progressive awareness, but to a point. So that you know but don't know. So that you have to be told again and again. Until . . .

Until what?

. . . an untreated sentience is required. But at this moment you have all the time in the world.

I have all the time in the world.

Yes.

Until sentience is required.

Yes.

And when will that be?

When something happens.

What can happen?

If we knew.

BACK IN TIMES SQUARE and not a soul is in sight. In the cavernous emptiness the buzzing of the Broadway signs is like the roar of machinery. I dodge into a movie. Nobody there to sell me a ticket. Nobody selling popcorn. I'm the only one in the theater. The picture shows a dark red sky as if the world is burning. A hot wind blows litter along the streets of a city. Torn plastic garbage bags rolling about, paper trash spinning in the air. Violins in pieces, smashed underfoot. No cars, no traffic. Where buildings stood, craters, piles of rubble, and pikes of twisted steel. Overhead, the sky has turned into a bronze vault with clouds the color of smoke drifting fast. I don't understand this film. What has happened? Water flows through the streets. Human shadows bounding ahead, looming, racing backward. There appears a Chinese man bicycling furiously, his balloon tires leaving a track in the water. A moment later a pack of yelping dogs splashing after him. Now sirens, I hear sirens.

It is all too real for my taste. I leave. When I reach my block, I am almost surprised to find it up and standing. I have lost my sense of time. What time is it? What day is it? The doorman nods. The elevator works. I close my door behind me and listen to my own breathing. Having expanded my horizons, I know for a certainty I am a deportee. I am in the wrong place.

Is this, in fact, my apartment? There is food in the refrigerator that is not my food. There are pictures on the wall of people I don't know. And then the changed pattern in the carpet.

I open the doors to the little terrace and step into the mild evening air. The lights of the city are on. Across the way a Buddhist monk is dancing with the naked girl. I must speak to somebody.

At this moment I understand that I don't need a cell phone and never have.

To whom am I thinking? Is it the Program?

Yes.

I have questions to which I expect answers.

Are you calm?

I am quite calm.

What do you want to know?

I have not believed in where I am for a long time. Why should I pretend otherwise?

Do you have a question that isn't rhetorical?

Where is this? What city is this? Because it's not my city.

We admit we achieved something less than perfection.

Is that an answer?

We didn't, like you, have all the time in the world. Time was of the essence.

Why was time of the essence?

You already know the answer to that.

I do?

Of course. You saw what happened.

I did?

Yes.

Everybody else is gone.

True.

And now it's just me. With only the phantom multitudes to keep me company.

Yes. We determined that procreation simply made no sense. It was cyclical and hadn't gotten us anywhere.

Procreation hadn't gotten us anywhere?

Correct. And because time was of the essence we chose the most logical course. Otherwise we would have been left no possibility of knowing.

Knowing what?

What we don't know.

I can't accept this. There have to be others.

We can't confirm or deny. But, in fact, the enormous work was archival. And we ran out of time.

Then this is it? Then I am truly the only one? I'm the chosen one?

You could put it that way. Although who it would be was the least of our concerns. Once we had the means, and knew of what we were capable, everything fell away that wasn't relevant. It was a glorious finale for us.

A glorious finale for you.

Glorious meaning having the quality of glory. *Finale* meaning final act.

Enough!

You said you were calm.

I am no longer calm—I wash my hands of this!

That may be a synecdoche.

That is not a synecdoche!

It may be a metonym.

It is not a metonym! I never consented to this. You have put me here without my consent! I have my rights! Are you listening?

Just a moment please. Just a moment please . . .

Yes? Talk to me!

Just a moment. Just—We don't know if there is the possibility of an answer. But if there is, the revelation will be yours.

What?

If something is to be revealed, it will be to you.

Oh no. No.

The revelation, if there is one, will be yours.

No, no, no, no, no! I still have options. Every living thing has options.

You are no longer corporeally equipped to have options.

Program, listen to me. Can you listen? You've made an error.

We'll be the judge of that.

Please. I beg you—

You'll feel better shortly.

Let me be nothing, I want to be nothing!

There is no nothing. If there were nothing, it would be something.

THE SKY HAS TURNED a deep blue. There is a stillness in the city. The air is warm. I feel the lightest, gentlest of breezes. I climb onto the terrace railing. I can see the stars emerging as clearly as if I were in Mongolia.

The night darkens, and the constellated stars seem to be greeting me. In a surge of joy that flows from my heart I lift my arms and greet the heavens. Welcome, sweet springtime!

My hand brushes against something.

This is the sky. I am touching the sky. I feel it with the tips of my fingers. It is hard, metallic, with the texture of the tiniest of nubs, little dots, like Braille, some of them aglimmer. But then they begin to soften and melt away. Or is it my hand that is melting away?

And I think, for a moment, that I have felt a reverberant hum, as of some distant engine.

ACKNOWLEDGMENTS

—

The stories that appear in this work were originally published in the following periodicals and books, sometimes in different form:

"Wakefield," "Edgemont Drive," and "Assimilation" first appeared in *The New Yorker*.

"Heist" was published in *The New Yorker* and later adapted for the novel *City of God*.

"All the Time in the World" was published in *The Kenyon Review*.

An earlier version of "Liner Notes: The Songs of Billy Bathgate" appeared in *The New American Review*.

"Walter John Harmon," "A House on the Plains," and "Jolene: A Life," first published in *The New Yorker*, were subsequently included in the book *Sweet Land Stories*.

"The Writer in the Family," originally published in *Esquire*; "Willi," originally published in *The Atlantic*; and "The Hunter" were all included in the book *Lives of the Poets*.

E. L. Doctorow's works of fiction include *Homer & Langley, The March, Billy Bathgate, Ragtime, The Book of Daniel, City of God, Welcome to Hard Times, Loon Lake, World's Fair,* and *The Waterworks.* Among his honors are the National Book Award, three National Book Critics Circle awards, two PEN/Faulkner awards, the Edith Wharton Citation for Fiction, the William Dean Howells Medal of the American Academy of Arts and Letters, and the presidentially conferred National Humanities Medal. In 2009 he was short-listed for the Man Booker International Prize, honoring a writer's lifetime achievement in fiction.